The Wines of Australia

The Wines of Australia

Oliver Mayo

faber and faber

LONDON · BOSTON

First published in 1986
by Faber and Faber Limited
3 Queen Square London WC1N 3AU

Photoset by Parker Typesetting Service
Leicester
Printed in Great Britain by
Butler and Tanner
Frome Somerset
All rights reserved

*British Library Cataloguing in Publication
Data*

Mayo, Oliver
The wines of Australia.
1. Wine and wine making – Australia
I. Title
641.2'22'0994 TP559.A8

ISBN 0-571-13868-3
ISBN 0-571-13869-1 (pbk)

*Library of Congress Cataloging-in-Publication
Data*

Mayo, Oliver.
The wines of Australia.

1. Wine and wine making—Australia. I. Title.
TP559.A8M39   1986   641.2'2'0994   86-13406
ISBN 0-571-13868-3
ISBN 0-571-13869-1 (pbk.)

Contents

CONTENTS

Maps

Diagrams

Acknowledgements

Writing a book about an industry which spans a continent, even the smallest continent, is not easy. It is a pleasure to thank all of the following for advice, information, criticism and encouragement: J. Baldwin, A. Berry, G. Boboc, B. B. Carrodus, B. G. Coombe, C. L. Cowan, B. Croser, D.Davidson, M. J. Detmold, J. Gladstones, J. Greenshields, R. J. Hague, S. Hamilton, T. W. Hancock, J. R. Hawker, J. Jeffs, C. Kay, C. H. Kay, M. Lake, M. C. Lamey, A. L. C. Ligertwood, E. J. A. Mayo, J. Mayo, M. G. Mayo, J. Middleton, B. C. Rankine, M. Robson, M. Schubert, A. A. Simpson, K. Smith, J. D. Sobey, T. C. Somers, J. Thomson, G. Wiltshire and A. Wynn. I thank A. D. Powell for permission to quote the passage from *To Keep the Ball Rolling* reproduced on p.35 and J. K. Galbraith, Houghton Mifflin Company and André Deutsch Ltd for permission to quote that from *A Life in Our Times* reproduced on p.53. I am most grateful to K. Kain and S. Suter for expertly typing the book. Finally, I thank my wife for putting up with endless discussion of presumption, nervosité and other important properties of wine.

1

Introduction

When the Commonwealth of Australia was established in 1900, by the agreement of the people of New South Wales, Victoria, South Australia, Queensland and Tasmania (Western Australians later), it was determined in the Constitution that the Constitution of each state should continue as before, as would the powers of their parliaments. The founding fathers further recognized the distinctness of the states in section 113 of the Constitution: 'All fermented, distilled, or other intoxicating liquids passing into any state or remaining therein for use, consumption, sale or storage, shall be subject to the laws of the state as if such liquids had been produced in the state.' The manufacture and consumption of intoxicating liquids had had such different histories in the different colonies that it would not have been possible to form a united Commonwealth without this special provision. The Australian wine industry today reflects these differences.

Australia is a very small nation, no more than about 16 million people, spread thinly around the western, southern and eastern margins of an island continent 7,687,900 square kilometres in extent. It is one of the most highly urbanized nations on earth, some 88 per cent of the population living in less than a dozen cities. Virtually all of these cities lie close to land suitable for vineyards. In every one of the colonies which combined to form the Commonwealth, therefore, a wine industry grew up almost as soon as the first settlers arrived. Only in the Northern Territory, once part of South Australia and soon to become a state in its own right, where the climate is mostly unsuitable for wine production, and where beer

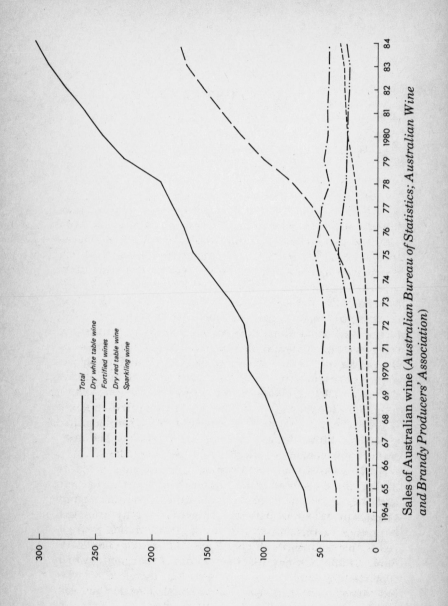

Sales of Australian wine (*Australian Bureau of Statistics; Australian Wine and Brandy Producers' Association*)

consumption is prodigious, has no wine industry been developed.

Each state's wine industry was different, those with more generous climates producing wine more readily and coming to dominate the markets in the middle of the nineteenth century, so that customs duties were levied on wines moving between states, a problem the Commonwealth Constitution set out to solve by making 'trade commerce and intercourse between the states absolutely free'. There were, however, natural barriers to trade in wine, in a country of huge distances and very high transport and labour costs. Thus, until very recently, a small wine industry could persist in any region, having its own regional character and customers, only the largest wine-makers requiring national markets or export markets to flourish.

All this has made Australian wine consumers very parochial. Australians tell each other that their best wines are now as good as the best in the world, that their *vins ordinaires* are of the highest quality in the world, that their wine represents the best value for money in the world. The truth or otherwise of these propositions is only beyond debate in the narrow sense that there is no accounting for tastes, in this case tastes which I tend to share, but I shall attempt to assess their validity by wider standards. I shall try in particular to show how the Australian wine industry differs from other wine industries, and why this is of interest. To do this I shall examine in some detail the history of the industry, as well as its present structure and what it makes but, before doing so, I want to scrutinize closely some of the factors which shaped it.

One of the most important factors is that this wine industry was not established by people with long traditions of wine-making; rather, they were Englishmen with long traditions of wine drinking. Thus, they brought ideas of what wines should be like, but not necessarily much knowledge of how they got that way. This still shows particularly in nomenclature.

The Australian wine industry was well established before Mr Gladstone repealed the discriminatory duties on French wines coming into Britain. In consequence, except among the most discerning wine consumers in Britain, there was a determined preference for heavy, fortified wines. The Methuen Treaty had secured the preference for the relatively cheap Portuguese wines in Britain, and these wines were all fortified for the long sea trip. And only very heavy wines survived the trip from the interior of France. Hence, Britons brought to Australia odd views about what the wines of France were like. 'Claret' described wines which were almost undrinkable when young, on account of their acid and tannin content, and 'Burgundy' described wines that were softer, richer in flavour, lower in acid, and much higher in alcohol. These ideas determined the development of the two Australian Claret and Burgundy styles, which have disappeared only in very recent years, makers and consumers alike recognizing that the Bordeaux and Burgundy styles relate to climate and vine variety, rather than to strength and softness.

It was natural that the English should also use German names, Hock and Moselle, for white wines that were predominantly dry and firm or floral and softer. Similarly, French white wine names, such as Chablis and Sauternes, were used where deemed appropriate. These names have persisted to some extent, though Hock is rarely seen on a bottle today, and White Burgundy has only become popular in the last forty years, largely led by one white wine from Western Australia, Houghton's White Burgundy. In a new departure, 'White Bordeaux' was the remarkable appellation used by a wine-maker from the upper Hunter Valley in New South Wales for a wine made largely from Sauvignon Blanc in the early 1980s. Under protest from consumer organizations, the company withdrew this label and reissued the wine as 'Hunter River White Bordeaux', which was acceptable to the advertising standards authorities of New South Wales. The Clare wine-maker, the Stanley Wine Company, similarly introduced the term 'Beaujolais', for a light red wine which could be kept in the refrigerator, in the mid-1970s, but soon took it off the market.

At the moment, wine descriptions are a shambles. In general, for a wine to be described by the name of a particular variety or as having come from a particular region, it should contain 80 per cent of grapes of that variety or 80 per cent of grapes from that region. These requirements are not policed, however, as are the *Appellation Contrôlée* and *VDQS* descriptions in France.

In this book, except where the European terms are necessary in a historical context or because they are brand names, I shall try to use the names of varieties, whether by themselves or in blends, or otherwise describe the wines in relatively objective terms. But of course copying of styles has been, indeed remains, an important influence on what is made.

The Australian wine industry is very small, about the sixteenth largest in the world. At the moment, the inhabitants of the Commonwealth drink no more than twenty litres per head per year, rather less than one-fifth of the amount consumed per head in France or Italy, and of course the population is less than one-third as large. Furthermore, as in most other countries, the wine industry that is perceived by the wine-writing and wine-reading public is quite different from that perceived by the wine-drinking public. Most of what is written relates to a tiny fraction of the production.

Few people want to read about the problems of growers or cooperatives in the Midi when they can be reading about the Dukes of Burgundy or the châteaux of Bordeaux. I want to give a comprehensive picture of the Australian industry, but shall inevitably dwell on its more interesting and attractive aspects, rather than simply on its power to intoxicate.

It is not an industry which has always had a good press overseas, partly because of the merchants in whose hands it put its wine. Many years ago, when I was living in Edinburgh, far from the red dust under the purple grapes, my brother went into the Chesser Cellar, one of the more enterprising wine merchants in Adelaide, to send me some wines to brighten the grey Christmas we were about to endure. He had read an advertisement which said that wine parcels could readily be dispatched anywhere in Britain, and paid for in Australia. He wandered about for a while, making a list, then sought out the proprietor. 'These are what I want to send to my brother in Edinburgh,' he said.

'A very good choice too, if I may say so,' said the proprietor. 'Now *these* are the wines held in London which you can actually get to him.'

There were no wines common to the two lists.

In recent years, with firms like Berry Bros. & Rudd Ltd beginning to put Australian wines on their lists, there has been some improvement, though not comparable to that extended to the resolutely parochial expatriate Australian beer drinker, who can find Foster's lager everywhere. However, the Australian reputation for only exporting its worst wines dies hard. It is not hard to see why if we look back to the origins of this reputation. In a report on the wine trade to the Victorian Minister of Agriculture in the 1890s, Hans Irvine of Great Western wrote:

> I was introduced by a member of the Australian press, in England, to an historical hotel, 'Ye Cheshire Cheese'. I was unacquainted with the proprietor, and he, upon learning that I was an Australian and identified with the wine trade, at once volunteered to let me taste one of, what he called, the best Australian wines in England, and which he had had laid down in his cellar to improve for some time. I thanked him, and the cellarman was straightway despatched to bring up a bottle. In the meantime another gentleman entered the apartment, to whom I was promptly introduced. I was told that he was the friend of Mr —, a leading light in the wine trade. While conversing with him, the wine sent for had been brought and poured out. Judge then of my astonishment, when, before I had taken my glass in hand, to hear the friend of Mr — exclaim – 'I say, Charlie, this is vinegar!' and I was able to fully endorse the statement without having tasted it, the aroma being quite sufficient to condemn it, and proclaim it 'acetic'. The look of disgust on the countenance of our host was comical to witness, and his air of wounded vanity I shall long remember as he remarked – 'I prided myself that you would be able to taste a glass of wine that would please you, and that would do Australia credit. That wine has been in my possession for years. I thought I would lay it down to improve with age, and it turns out like this! We get no encouragement to buy Australian wines – they will not keep.' I looked at the brand, and to my amazement found it was one of the most expensive and best-advertised samples of Australian wines sold in England, and if any wine ought to have been good and have given good results this certainly should have done so.

By 1906, at least twelve different merchants were selling Australian wine in London, from P. B. Burgoyne & Company through Emu Wines and the Army & Navy Stores Own Brand to de Castella & Rowan and Penfold. Their wines' main advantage was higher strength without fortification: E. Burney Young, who had managed the South Australian Wine Depot in London, was asked about the growing demand for Australian wines in Great Britain and said, 'One reason for this is that Australian wines are kept well advertised, and another is that they are largely used by anaemic persons, who are relatively more numerous in England than in Australia. The full-bodied and generous character of the wines is more palatable in a climate like that of England than the thin acid wines of the continent.'

Only in Victoria, after phylloxera had destroyed most of its wine industry at the turn of the century, and competition with the lower-cost South Australian vineyards had ruined much of the rest, did wine merchants in the English sense have much influence, buying, blending and bottling for the relatively large and affluent Melbourne market.

This lack of informed intermediaries meant that wine-makers in South Australia in particular, and to a lesser extent elsewhere, could not afford to specialize, to search for what they could do best, since customers would ask for a range of wines, so that one of the major differences between the practice in the traditional high-quality areas of wine-making in Europe and that in Australia is that almost no Australian wine-maker, however small, makes only one wine. Indeed, Virgin Hills at Kyneton and Prince Albert at Geelong, in Victoria, are the only such of which I am aware, though there are a number making just two or three, such as Redman at Coonawarra, in South Australia, who makes a Cabernet Sauvignon and a Shiraz. Some of the newest growers in the Margaret River area of Western Australia have planted only one variety, for example Riesling, but it is not clear to what extent they are yet influencing the wine industry in any real sense.

The annual cycle of wine-making at Roseworthy Agricultural College in South Australia illustrates the extraordinary diversity in products and resulting activities of a relatively small producer. Roseworthy is different in that it is Australia's main centre for oenological education, so that much of its wine-making is for teaching purposes, but it is still remarkable how many different wines are made from a total crush of less than 100 tonnes.

Start in March: sultana juice is bought and sterilized for use as the yeast propagation medium during vintage. Pinot Noir and Sauvignon Blanc juice is bought from Lindeman at Padthaway, in the south-east of South Australia. The Pinot Noir will be used by students to make bottle-fermented sparkling wine. Frontignan fruit from Nuriootpa, in the Barossa Valley, is obtained and crushed, Cabernet Sauvignon from Upper Hermitage, in the Adelaide Hills, Pedro and Gordo from the College itself, and Colombard from Berri, on the River Murray.

In April, Grenache is obtained from Lyndoch, in the Barossa, for 'port', and Pinot Noir from the Eden Valley to be crushed for a private grape grower. Also a large quantity of Chardonnay, Riesling and Cabernet from the Eden Valley is crushed for commercial production, as is Shiraz from Upper Hermitage.

During these two months there is a range of activities: racking the previous year's Adelaide Hills Cabernet into wood, and cold-stabilizing a Shiraz to prepare a 'tasting pack' useful for demonstrating particular faults or characteristics in red wines; making ready Sauvignon Blanc and Chardonnay for wood maturing; racking tanks of various wines and fining with bentonite where sufficient clarity has not been obtained; cleaning Colombard and Frontignan for settling; filtering the base wine for a dry 'sherry' ready for introduction into the solera; and other minor works.

In June and July, red wines are racked to wood storage, possibly with filtration on the way, the Pinot Noir sparkling wine base is cold-stabilized ready for transfer to bottles. The Colombard is cleaned up and bottled. The previous year's Cabernet Sauvignon and current Sauvignon Blanc are transferred for cold-stabilization, the current Chardonnay and Riesling, which have fermented very slowly, being fined. Some fortified wines are bottled at Roseworthy, and some dispatched for bottling.

Over the next two months, some bottling will be done at the College, other wines dispatched for contract bottling. The Chardonnay will be moved from stainless steel to new wood, and a Sémillon Riesling blend prepared for stabilization. Some fortified wine, such as a bulk tawny port style, is prepared, drawing various stocks from wood storage, and other fortified wines are bottled. Cleaning continues till Christmas.

Everything is made ready for vintage, at the the start of February, with a crushing of Frontignan from Lyndoch for a sweet white table wine, and Pedro Ximenez from the College for the base for a *flor* sherry.

The cycle is complete: perhaps thirty different varieties have been received and vintaged, for I have not mentioned the small lots used by students for projects, nor some of the minor varieties crushed for experimental purposes. Perhaps fifty different products have been released on to the market, with very varying degrees of success, and the wine-maker, who is also the cellar manager, has to consider pricing, storage and stock management. It is not surprising that he has no teaching duties.

With this diversity of products goes a diversity and a flux among producers.

It is impossible to ensure the inclusion of all Australian wineries in this book. While new ones are opening their doors, others are closing. It is alleged that Charles Babbage, the inventor of the stored-program computer, read Tennyson's lines in 'The vision of Sin': 'Every minute dies a man,/ Every minute one is born,' and wrote to Tennyson correcting them: 'Every moment dies a man/ And one and a sixteenth is born.' Thus it is with Australian wineries.

Altogether, however, there are not many wineries compared to, say, the tiny Rhône appellation Côte Rôtie, where on 100 hectares there are over eighty-five individual growers, of whom thirty make and sell their own wine. Licensing laws in Australia are such that a man can make 1,000 litres or so for his family, provided they drink it, not sell it, yet if he wishes to sell it, he must apply for a licence and then pay a tax which varies from state to state and which in Victoria is as high as 20 per cent of the retail price. Furthermore, he must meet all manner of regulations about opening hours, lavatories and the like. Thus, despite the flowering of vineyards in Australia, there are not many licensed – only 400, and they open and close like a humming-bird's wings.

Driving to the Barossa some time ago, to refresh my memory of the extraordinary stonework of Château Yaldara and the Browning-Hamelin facade of Bernkastel, I noticed a sign saying 'New Winery'. The little winery, in old stone buildings built by Germans more than a century ago, had been open for two weeks. Other than from the clean new gravel of the driveway and from the sign, one could hardly have told that Barossa Settlers had not been in business for a century. Its

Shiraz comes from vines planted in the 1880s, and its Riesling from well-established vines.

On the other hand, comparing at dinner the 1980 Pinot Noir-Shiraz and the 1981 Pinot Noir from Akeringa, I was saddened by the thought that Akeringa, which was in production for a number of years near Willunga, in the Southern Vales region of South Australia, no longer exists. It is a pity, for the wines are showing both that Pinot Noir can stand on its own in McLaren Vale and that in a blend with Shiraz it produces wines cleaner and fresher than the traditional Shiraz, yet full of fruit and likely to gain elegance with time. Akeringa was one of many small wineries started in the 1960s and 1970s by medical practitioners.

The strong links between the medical profession and the wine industry in Australia have long been remarked, and of course the health-giving properties of wine were identified much earlier, by St Paul among others. Perhaps Rabelais was the first medical practitioner of note to cultivate his vineyard, but one remembers him for other reasons. More recently, it was reported in the *Lancet* that there was 'a strong and specific negative association between ischaemic heart disease deaths and alcohol consumption wholly attributable to wine consumption'. This was based on a comparison of heart disease rates and various dietary factors across a large number of countries, and aroused a great deal of controversy. A colleague and I attempted to make a contribution to the controversy in the *Lancet*, but in the event, this appeared in the *Medical Journal of Australia*, perhaps more appropriately, given the relative size of the wine industries in the two countries. Most of the *Lancet* discussion had been about whether the association was a real one, but we wanted to suggest a hypothesis for the origin of association. We pointed out that the potassium-to-sodium ratio in grape berries, and consequently in 'undoctored' wine, is far higher than in any other beverage, natural or synthetic, and thus far more healthy, having regard to the diet of our remote and probably arboreal ancestors.

As I shall discuss elsewhere, modern technology, at least as applied to cheap wines, has removed some of this potassium, replacing it with sodium, so that the best wines are healthier than the cheapest wines.

However, the many medical practitioners who have contributed successfully to the Australian wine industry, from Drs Kelly, Penfold and Lindeman to Drs Middleton, Lake and Cullen, have not been doing so to ensure that the potassium intake of the wine-consuming class is maintained at a proper level. They have mostly done so to make good wine.

In a survey of ninety small wineries, Robin Bradley, a prolific Australian wine writer, noted that eighteen had been established by medical practitioners. The connection between wine and medicine is indeed close. But then so is the connection between ocean-going yachts and medicine, between futures speculation and medicine, between investment in films and medicine, at least in Australia. Until very recently, there were substantial taxation advantages accruing to the public-spirited person who was willing to undertake the development of a vineyard, and therefore many people with a high cash-flow took this opportunity to convert income into capital. When universal medical insurance was introduced in 1972, one of its effects was to add fuel to the vineyard development boom. Whatever the other effects of Medibank, this one seems to have been almost completely beneficial, except for its contribution to the wine glut of the 1980s.

Australian agriculture has historically proved itself highly successful at producing a surplus of whatever commodity was in short supply a decade earlier. Wine is no exception, though of course many of its problems relate to the ending of Imperial Preference when Britain joined the European Economic Community in the early 1970s. As Australia is a high-cost producer, it is not competitive on price and, as the total production is only of the order of that of Bordeaux and is mostly bulk wine for swigging or quaffing, it cannot compete significantly in the high-quality markets. Australia's high costs relate partly to the small size of its home market, which makes protection of its manufacturers almost universal, hence increasing the cost of goods needed by primary producers. More important is the price of labour in a country where only 2 per cent of the workforce is engaged in agriculture, so that agriculture does not affect the demand for labour, and hence wage rates, and where there has never been a peasantry, as in southern Europe.

Since the industry has these difficulties, and since in the end it will be growers who are bankrupted, not marketers, and since many of the growers are soldier-settlers or descendants of soldier-settlers, who grow grapes because the government settled them on smallholdings in irrigation areas after the two world wars, governments have been reluctant to tax wines as heavily as beer and spirits.

Even before John Gorton, one of Australia's most erratic and interesting prime ministers, introduced a tax on table wines, the problem of such a tax haunted the wine industry. It was introduced in 1969, abolished with a change of government in 1972, and has remained an annual worry ever since. Between March and June each year, wine-makers lobby politicians hectically and the premier of South Australia, of whatever party, reminds the prime minister, party again irrelevant, of the damage a wine tax would do to South Australia's chronically depressed economy. Each July, wine-makers remind their mail-order customers of the impending disaster. Each August, for more than a decade, panic buying has occurred, causing a small increase in annual consumption, for most wine is not a consumer durable, and what is bought in a panic is soon consumed.

In 1982, the large wine companies made their forward plans on the basis of a 12½–15 per cent tax, in 1983 on 15–17½ per cent: in neither case were they quite right. However, an excise on fortifying spirit was introduced in 1983. The 1970 tax was 50 cents a gallon, the 1983 excise $2.61 a litre when first introduced, and of significance in the areas where fortified wines are of real importance – north-eastern Victoria and the irrigated areas.

The tax on fortified wine stayed at $2.61 a litre for a month, after which it was lowered to $1.50. Four months later, it was increased to $1.56, and four months later still, in June 1984, it was removed entirely. From August 1984, a sales tax of 10 per cent was imposed, levied at the point of wholesale disposal or at the cellar door for wine-makers' own retail sales. This kind of tinkering confirms the growers' worst suspicions of the motives and competence of the Federal Treasury; like all farmers, they were never in doubt about the politicians themselves. In addition to this Federal tax, sales and licensing taxes of various kinds are levied by all the states. In South Australia, for example, the tax in 1984 was at the rate of 11 per cent of declared stocks at wholesale price. Many small growers absorbed the 10 per cent Federal tax, lowering their profits to ensure that they cleared their stocks. Large companies increased their advertising budgets. The consumer therefore did not feel the full effects of the tax immediately. It may well be permanent, since the government which imposed it was handsomely returned to power in December 1984, owes little to rural interests, and may have motives of public health as well as revenue-raising in mind.

When there was previously an excise related to fortified wines, imposed over 15° Baumé, i.e. sugar corresponding to 15 per cent alcohol by volume in the wine, many big wineries concentrated the must, and made their wines differently. They had a concentrator, useful for fortified wines only, of course, because it cooked the must as the water was extracted. The first run of concentrate might be taken up to 30° Baumé, then the vat would be filled with later runs of only 15°. The excise man would follow the hoses and scratch his head: 'I know you're diddling me, but how?' Then he would climb up and lower his sampling bottle into the less dense concentrate sitting on the top of the more dense concentrate, and it would test out at 15°.

This is not practicable when the tax is on spirit purchased by wineries for fortification. The 1983 tax was therefore very hard to avoid, and was paid years before the product would be sold. An easy tax to collect, it had no other merits.

Consumption of fortified wines has hardly changed over a twenty-year period, and that of white table wine has risen remarkably, as the graph shows. Red wine sales rose steadily for a decade and have been static for another decade; the earlier decade was the red wine boom. This change in consumer tastes has been accompanied by a proliferation of wineries, as I have already emphasized, and of styles of wines. Consumer guidance has mainly come from advertising and from wine writers closely involved with the industry. The other source of information is performance in shows.

Each capital city has a wine show, with a bewildering range of prizes and trophies and basic bronze, silver and gold medals, scored on a points basis, for an extraordinary range of classes. In addition, the Hunter, Griffith, Lilydale, and other areas have shows, and at the McLaren Vale and other festivals prizes are also awarded. As always, wines are scored out of 20 – 3 for appearance, 7 for smell, and 10 for taste. Problems occur in the laboratory when these scores are used to try to determine the relative merits of different trellises or soils: in the shows, the problem is compounded by the sheer stamina needed by the judges.

In the tenth Hunter Valley wine show, in 1983, less than ten judges had to assess over 800 wines in two days. When one considers that many of the red wines showed excessive volatility or hydrogen sulphide, one can only stand back and admire judges as a breed apart.

The results are important in business terms. The Jimmy Watson Trophy is presented for the best young red wine each year at the Melbourne Wine Show. A then-young European wine-maker, Wolf Blass, who makes wine in the Barossa with good fruit from everywhere, made a reputation in the early 1970s by winning the trophy three years running. Then interest turned to wondering when a Victorian wine would first win the trophy: one did in 1980. Mildara, masterly blender from the River Murray in northern Victoria, won it in 1982 with a mixture of Coonawarra Cabernet Sauvignon and Eden Valley Shiraz. Then, in 1983, it was the turn of a new Western Australia area: a Cabernet from Cape Mentelle took out the trophy. Yet Mildara could advertise in the *Australian Financial Review* that its entry had won more points (56½ to 55). Confusion reigns.

The shows serve a useful purpose; in the words of Bryce Rankine, a show judge for more than twenty-five years, 'Wine-makers write all manners of things on labels extolling the virtues of the product, but the quality assessment by a panel of judges in a show gives an independent evaluation of the product, however imperfect.' As Rankine is Dean of the Faculty of Oenology and Viticulture at Roseworthy, Australia's oldest agricultural college, this is not a partisan view, but it is better reinforced by reading what actually appears on labels. For example, on a 1982 Sémillon-Chardonnay from Richmond Grove, in the Upper Hunter, one finds: 'This limited release wine is a blend of 64 per cent Sémillon and 36 per cent Chardonnay. Cold temperature skin-juice contact has resulted in optimal flavour extractiveness and development: Alcohol 12.9 per cent v/v, pH 3.31, Acid 7.1 g/l. Mark Cashmore Wine-maker.' Or take Penfold, one of Australia's oldest and largest wine-makers. It has been advising the members of a long-established club for which it has been making a fine Cabernet-Shiraz blend since 1970 that 'the wine should be stored on its side in a cool cellar, where it should improve in the bottle for many years'. Finally, Ursula Pridham of Marienberg informs readers of her 1978 Cabernet Sauvignon that 'this is the classic Australian style – full-bodied, deep crimson in colour, rich in flavour with a superb tannin/acid balance. A wine which will live for many, many years.'

Thus, the shows are important, the prizes important: the single bottle buyer, bewildered by the offerings of 350 wineries, has to start somewhere, and a trophy-winner offers something identifiable yet intangible.

A wine may say on the label

Silver Medal	1979 Brisbane	Class 5
Silver	1979 Melbourne	15
Bronze	1979 Melbourne	6
Bronze	1980 Sydney	10

One wishes to compare it with another which says

Gold	1981 Melbourne	Class 40
Gold	1981 Brisbane	52
Silver	1980 Perth	18
Silver	1980 Adelaide	18
Silver	1981 Perth	33
Bronze	1981 Adelaide	18
Bronze	1981 Adelaide	17
Bronze	1981 Sydney	15
Bronze	1981 Melbourne	17

The two wines are predominantly Cabernet Sauvignon, one from Clare, one from Central Victoria, both from 1969. There is no overlap in their awards, but the second should be better. All one can do is draw the corks and try the wines.

To show how all this arose, I shall go back to the beginning of the industry. I shall then discuss, non-technically, the technology of wine-making and viticulture in Australia to draw out its distinctive attributes. This I shall follow with a state-by-state review of the wine-growing areas, because, even where climate and soils are very similar, political and social differences between the states have influenced the development of the industry. Distance, too, has been just as important.

In each area, I shall give an indication of the size of each distinct winery by the size of its crush. A tonne of grapes makes between 500 and 750 litres of table wine, depending on variety, ripeness, whether or not the fruit was grown under irrigation, and how hard the grapes were pressed, in the case of black varieties. Thus, a tonne of fruit will make between forty and ninety cases of 12×75 centilitre bottles, the standard size in Australia. If a small grower makes fortified wine, he will buy in his fortifying spirit, so that his case sales will not represent entirely his own production. Where information is available on fruit bought in, I shall try to provide an indication of this. The figures for tonnes crushed will be the most recent available, and will be the maker's desired stable production level where this has been established. However, the figures given are only indicative of the present relative sizes of the different producers, given the industry's permanent state of flux.

I shall also try to indicate the range of wines produced, namely, red and white table wines, sparkling wines, and fortified wines. Since almost all the vignerons of Australia grow or make or sell Cabernet Sauvignon and Riesling, I shall not list varieties for each winery, but it can be assumed that in almost all cases a Cabernet of sorts and a Riesling of sorts are sold; I shall indicate where this is not the case.

Finally, I shall also try to indicate, where appropriate, vineyards of outstanding merit. Failure to include a particular vineyard in this category may be taken to reflect bias or ignorance on my part, but I am not attempting a classification of Australian wines along Bordeaux lines. This was tried in about 1970 by the wine merchant and writer Dan Murphy, just before the very fine wines of the old southern Victorian areas and the new south-western Western Australian areas began to appear on the market. For those seeking such a classification, Robin Bradley's *Australian Wine Vintages* provides one, together with the opportunity to argue indefinitely. I do not think that there is sufficient stability in the industry for such a classification to be more than a current market guide.

I have tried to avoid bias. When I was discussing this book with one Australian wine-writer, he asked, fairly abruptly,

'Don't the publishers want to sell the book in Australia?'

'Of course it's a market. Why?'

'No connection with the trade.'

'Perhaps they want someone disinterested.'

'Hm.'

2

Early History

As can be seen on the map, only in the far south of Victoria
and in the west of Tasmania is rainfall not very variable, the
range of observed values being much smaller than the average. The lower the average, the greater the variation, but the
early settlers did not know this.

Wine was in demand in the earliest days of the first colony,
since we see from the first issues of Australia's first news-
paper, the *Sydney Gazette and New South Wales Almanac*,
that some dozens of casks, of 120 or 150 gallons, of Madeira
and Constantia were sold at between 7s. and 9s. a gallon. In
the same issues, a 'Method of preparing a piece of land for the
purpose of farming a vineyard' was published, 'translated
from the French'. However, this was before the days of scientific agriculture, and in the issue of 12 March 1803 the reader
was told that 'pruning is to be performed in January and
February', which had not been translated from the French.
Furthermore, liming was recommended for orchards, without
qualification; Australia's old, dry, unworked soils are rarely
excessively acid.

Rum, however, was even more in demand, and it was many
years before the labour-intensive luxury of a wine industry
was properly established. Even in the 1860s, an English
writer, T. G. Shaw, could say:

So far as I can learn, Australia is not well adapted,
either by soil or climate, for growing wine, and this
opinion seems confirmed by the unsuccessful efforts of
many years.

Key for all maps

Regions	
Barossa Valley	

Towns
- Adelaide ■

Vineyards & Wineries
- Oliverhill ◆

Approximate boundary
of grape-growing area

Roads ———

Highways ═══

Rainfall Variability Index
= 90th percentile — 10th percentile
              50th percentile
0.5 low — 1.75 extreme

— · — · · Lines of equal rainfall variability

Wine-growing regions of Australia

Regions labelled: Granite Belt, Upper Hunter, Lower Hunter, Mudgee, Murrumbidgee Irrigation Area, North-eastern Victoria, Central Victoria, Northern Tasmania, Riverland, Geelong, South-western Victoria, North-western Victoria, Coonawarra, Southern Vales, Barossa Valley, Clare, Lower Great Southern, Margaret River, Swan Valley

Towns: Darwin, Cairns, Brisbane, Sydney, Canberra, Melbourne, Hobart, Adelaide, Alice Springs, Perth

0   800
         km

So long ago as 1835 [*sic*: obviously wrong] I sent many hundreds of vines to Adelaide, by desire of a very intelligent wine merchant; but no good came of it. Even if soil and climate were favourable, the fact of its being a thinly peopled land must prevent the cultivation and making of fine qualities. It is almost literally true that the vine requires daily manual labour from the 1st of January to the 31st of December, and this can be done only in old countries, with a large population and low wages.

Australia must wait many years before she is in such a position; and she will, in the meantime, be more profitably employed in cultivating her great natural resources, and exchanging these for the wines of Europe. Being one of our colonies, her produce was charged the same as that of the Cape; but, even with such assistance, the importations of wine never rose above two or three hundred pipes a year.

The first vines planted in Australia were probably trodden into the soil in February 1788, soon after the eleven ships under the command of Captain Arthur Phillip established Port Jackson, now Sydney, as a convict settlement, on 26 January 1788. The vines were planted at Farm Cove, in light soil, at the location which is now the Botanical Gardens. So close to the water, the vines grew in very high humidity, allowing the ancient European disease anthracnose to grow luxuriantly on the vines. Today, control over disease is such that a drinkable wine can be made from Chardonnay only a kilometre inland from the sea, but at that time, hot winds, rather than a fungus, were blamed for the vines' failure.

Because of this view of the effects of climate, a government farm was established further inland, on the Parramatta River, which by 1791 had a three-acre vineyard under development, together with a private vineyard of one acre. It is not known whether wine was ever made from these vineyards.

Captain John Macarthur, who pioneered the Merino sheep industry in Australia, was the major identifiable early figure in the development of the wine industry in Australia. Macarthur was given a large grant of land, totalling approximately 8,500 acres, in 1805, and allowed thirty-four convicts to work the land. He was an extraordinarily contentious man, fighting with several successive governors of the struggling colony, and, after the removal of Governor Bligh, he was forced to return to England for a time. He put this time to good use, from the point of view of the wine industry. In 1815 and 1816, with his sons William and James, both born in Australia, he went to France to investigate the vineyards and wine industries. They returned to Australia with a large number of vines and a host of information about vineyards. Meanwhile, Macarthur's nephew Hannibal had bought a Captain Waterhouse's farm, 'The Vineyard', on the river near Parramatta for £160 in 1813. Thus the whole family was involved in wine growing to some extent, but it was William Macarthur who mainly worked on the vine, bringing out German grape growers as colonists, and winning prizes for Australian wine and brandy in London in the 1840s.

There were two other major pioneers of wine in Australia. Gregory Blaxland had been an explorer with William Lawson and W. C. Wentworth, carrying out the first long inland trip, crossing the Blue Mountains in May 1813, and identifying the rich farmlands of the higher country beyond the mountains. Blaxland took up land at Brush Farm, near Eastwood, and brought vines from the Cape of Good Hope, in the hope that they would be resistant to anthracnose. From this vineyard near Parramatta, he shipped a red wine to London in 1822, and was awarded a silver medal by the Royal Society of Arts in 1823. As noted by Laffer (1949), the Society recorded that the wine was 'by no means of superior quality', but nevertheless awarded the medal by way of encouragement. When he was awarded a gold medal in 1828 for another shipment of wine, one may take it that the wine was much better. Blaxland was a thoughtful and purposeful vigneron, noticing that 'as the vines become more matured by age, the wine in every situation is of a much better quality'. The makers of Carruades de Lafite would agree. Furthermore, he found that the best wine was made from the poorest soil, another well-established experience.

Despite Blaxland's persistence and success in wine growing, he suffered setbacks in other business activities, and became morose and embittered; by the time he committed suicide on New Year's Day, 1853, he had long since ceased to be a major influence on the wine industry, or indeed of much interest to anyone.

James Busby is normally regarded as the father of the Australian wine industry. He arrived in Australia in 1824 with his father, John Busby, who had come out as waterworks engineer to the new colony. The son had studied viticulture in France, and within a year had published in Sydney *A Treatise on the Culture of the Vine and the Art of Making Wine*. Initially, he worked at the male orphan school near Liverpool, outside Sydney, in charge of the school farm and teaching of viticulture. The school had been established by Thomas Bowden, a Methodist lay preacher who was sacked for drinking in 1825, at which time the school was moved. Busby found working conditions unsatisfactory at the orphan school and, having been granted 2,000 acres in the Hunter River district, probably began to grow grapes there; certainly he did so later, in 1832. From the vines which he had planted at the orphan school, quite good wine had already been made, wine which he later took to London, where it was well received.

In 1831, Busby travelled to Spain and to France, studying techniques and collecting varieties. According to Laffer, Busby collected 678 vine varieties on his travels, of which seventy-four were collected personally by him from France. From the quality point of view, perhaps the most interesting are Pineau Chardonay [*sic*] and Pineau Noir [*sic*], from Clos Vougeot. It would be of great interest to know whether the very fine Chardonnay clone which has spread from Mudgee in recent years came from that Clos Vougeot material, and whether the old Pinot Noir of the Hunter has all come from Busby's stock. Busby's collection was maintained on land at Farm Cove, but destroyed after his departure for New Zealand, so that it is impossible to trace his vines further. This is particularly unfortunate because Busby's vines were the most important in establishing the Australian industry, the bulk of Macarthur's having been unsatisfactory, for as Kelly (1861) said: 'By the carelessness or knavery of the parties through whom they were transmitted to the colony, these wretched kinds were substituted for a collection of the best varieties grown in France.'

In March 1832, Busby was appointed British resident in New Zealand. He was not successful there, mainly because he had very little to do, and very little power. He was involved in the rather ludicrous attempt to establish the 'United Tribes of New Zealand' in 1835, and stayed in New Zealand after he had been superseded. The Treaty of Waitangi, from which modern New Zealand may be taken to date, was in fact largely of his drafting, but though he remained in Auckland until his death in 1871, his influence was much the same in his second colony as in his first: he imported vines and within a few years was making enough wine to sell to the troops.

James Busby's property, Kirkton, was taken over by his father, then inherited by his brother-in-law, William Kelman, and later by Kelman's son-in-law, C. F. Lindeman, son of Dr H. J. Lindeman. Kirkton, like many other early vineyards, is no longer a vineyard, but it is still the name of a wine. Busby's attitude to Kirkton was ambivalent. William Kelman had been a fellow-passenger on the *Triton* when it brought the Busby family to New South Wales, and Busby took a keen interest in what Kelman was doing. Yet he was not certain that Kirkton should be a vineyard. He wrote to another member of the family in 1837: 'I am sorry Kelman is disappointed with his wine this year, but not surprised. I always told him he had little or no chance of having a wine fit for anything but his own use. I was a little grieved that . . . he should have gone to the expense of planting eight acres.' And Kelman had had 365 varieties among which to choose from Busby's planting of 1832.

Of this collection, like the other at Farm Cove, little notice was taken until it was lost, soon after the First World War. The last wines were made from Busby's or Kelman's plantings in 1924 by Lindeman Ltd, which had owned Kirkton since 1914.

It may be that some of South Australia's earliest vines came from Kirkton, as Busby, although by then in New Zealand, arranged for some to be sent to Adelaide in 1839. Of these too, however, no trace remains. The establishment of South Australian and Victorian wine growing, which dates from 1838 in both cases, will be discussed in later chapters. Today, when Australia is drifting towards being a Japanese quarry, it is salutary to recall Dr Kelly's words in 1861:

> Amidst the overturns and changes in our internal industry caused by the gold discovery, perhaps no interest has suffered more directly than vine growing. After many years' struggle through unwarranted difficulties, vine culture had begun to take its place as one of the per-

manent resources, when the attractions of the precious metal, in 1852, drew away from their industrial pursuits nearly the whole of the working population of these colonies. For a time it appeared as if the plough itself were to be abandoned, and our fertile agricultural lands were again to revert to their primitive state of pasture lands. There was for a time, a suspension of all ordinary industrial pursuits, and the eight years that have elapsed since the gold discovery have brought little change for the better in the habits of our working classes.

In New South Wales, between 1848 and 1852, about 1,000 acres of vines yielded an average of about 100,000 gallons of wine and 1,500 gallons of brandy, but in 1853 and 1854 vineyards were actually taken out of production, while the acreage of vines in South Australia rose from 280 to 750 between 1850 and 1856. In New South Wales vineyards were parts of large estates, profitable with no contribution from wine, whereas around Adelaide they were the small proprietor's livelihood: when his labourers walked to Maryborough or Stawell or Bendigo or Ballarat in search of gold, as did one of my great-great-grandfathers, the proprietor was obliged to work himself harder. (My ancestor found enough gold to buy a pair of boots to replace those which he had worn out on the 400-mile walk, and walked back to Adelaide to sell his last two ounces and try something less uncertain.)

In Victoria, during this period, acreage and production also continued to grow, despite the proximity of the goldfields; the extra population and the higher prices obtainable for the local wines offset the lure of gold for the growers, most of whom, as in South Australia, were wine growers only.

By 1870, when Anthony Trollope visited Australia, the wine industry was an accomplished fact:

In all the Australian colonies, except Tasmania, wine is made plentifully, – and if it were the popular drink of the country, would be made so plentifully that it could suffice for the purpose. All fruits thrive there, but none with such fecundity as the grape. One Victorian wine-grower, who had gone into the business on a great scale, told me that if he could get 2s. a gallon for all that he made, the business would pay him well. The wine of

which he spoke was certainly superior both in flavour
and body to the ordinary wine drunk by Parisians. It is
wholesome and nutritious, and is the pure juice of the
grape.

Accustomed to French and Spanish wines, – or perhaps to wines passed off upon me as such, – I did not like
the Australian 'fine' wines. The best that I drank were in
South Australia but I did not much relish them. I
thought them to be heady, having a taste of earth, and
an after-flavour which was disagreeable. This may have
been prejudice on my part.

Thus, the first half-century of wine growing saw considerable success, in terms of quality of table wines, a success that
was not built on, as we shall see in later chapters, because of
changes in export markets and the failure to develop an
indigenous love of good wine and food. Only when extensive
immigration after the Second World War changed the community's awareness of civilized living did the true potential of
the land begin to be realized. Naturally there were wine-
makers producing fine wines during this long interval, but
few wanted to know about them. Coonawarra, the Hunter
Valley and the Yarra Valley were the most notable sufferers,
and have since been among the greatest beneficiaries, of these
wild swings in consumer preferences.

3

A Few Technical Details

Geography and geology have shaped Australia's wine industry as much as recent history. Lying between latitude 20°S
and 43°S, with cold currents sweeping from the great southern
ocean, Australia could be covered with vines, most of them
producing fruit fit merely for eating. Only small areas have
the right combination of rainfall, seasonal change and soil to
grow good fruit for wine. Wine-making has had to be adapted
to the fruit from this hot, old continent, with its extremes of
temperature and eroded, impoverished soils; Europe's soils
are more recently formed and therefore richer.

Climate

By trial and error, over about 150 years, de Candolle and
others developed methods to predict the success of viticulture
in climatic terms. De Candolle enunciated a rule, which I
quote from the translation of James Prescott, pioneering Australian soil scientist and climatologist:

> The cultivation of the vine, for the manufacture of wine,
> can be undertaken in Europe, on slopes with a favour-
> able exposure, up to those localities which provide a sum
> of 2,900 day-degrees (centigrade) from the day when the
> mean temperature first reaches 10°C until the day when
> the temperature falls below 10°C in the shade, provided
> that at the approach of maturity, the number of days
> with rain does not exceed a dozen per month.

The figure of 2,900 was the sum of the daily mean temperatures over the period he described. This has been modified to sum the excess over 10°C (or 50°F), which would give for Geisenheim, where mainly white wines are grown, 2,900 on de Candolle's scale or 1,000 on the modified scale. A limit of about 890 on the modified scale is the minimum for reliable annual grape ripening. This rules out a little of south-eastern Australia and much of Tasmania.

In Europe grapes are grown on the warm fringes of a cold continent, and in Australia they are grown on the cold margins of a hot continent, so a maximum is also needed. Prescott (1969) showed, on the basis of comparisons between Australia and the Mediterranean region, that the mean temperature for the warmest month should lie between 18°C and 27°C. The table below shows a comparison of most Australian viticultural regions with some French and Mediterranean regions. It has been modified from the work of Prescott.

European and Mediterranean localities	°C	Australian localities
Champagne (France), Rheingau (Germany)	18	Piper's Brook (Tasmania)
	19	Geelong (Vic.) Coonawarra (S. Aust.) Mt Barker (W. Aust.)
Burgundy, Bordeaux (France)	20	Margaret River (W. Aust.)
	21	Stawell (Vic.)
	22	Clare (S. Aust.) Mudgee (NSW)
Montpellier (France)	23	Rutherglen (Vic.) Berri (S. Aust.)
	24	Griffith (NSW) Cessnock (NSW)
	25	Mildura (Vic.)
Tunis (Tunisia)	26	
Izmir (Turkey)	27	
	28	Roma (Qld)
El Fayum (Egypt)	29	Alice Springs (NT)
Jordan Valley (Israel)	32	

Vines are grown in quite unsuitable places, such as Roma and Alice Springs, just as they are in Britain, for some of the same reasons as people keep Rhodesian Ridgebacks in small city flats. Nevertheless, as the table illustrates (compare the map on p.18), for the most part the viticultural areas are where they would be expected to be on the basis of temperature requirements for growing European vines suitable for making wine.

The other main requirements are soil and water. Water has always been a critical determinant of agricultural activity in Australia: in the 1870s, farmers spread north in South Australia, believing that 'rain followed the plough'. Houses were built, crops sown, towns planned and, when the good years ended, they withered away. Farina is a name on a map which symbolizes this failure: the crops which the name suggests never grew, and the town was never built. Even today, in dryland vineyards, one old 'gardener' will say to another over a chilled glass of ruby port that four rootlings were planted for every bearing vine in his garden, and the second will nod wisely and agree that drip irrigation is a risk. They feel that when the mechanism fails, the vines will have insufficiently deep roots, and will wither in the heat.

John Gladstones, of the Western Australian Department of Agriculture, pointed out that experience had shown that good wines could be made at latitudes as high as 32°S or 33°S, despite temperature summations of considerably more than 1,200 degree days. Thus, the European optima might need modification. Hence, without the effects of time and loss of memory, one can see in the development of the south-western Western Australian vineyards what actually contributes to an outstanding vineyard area.

First, consider climate: the requirements are lack of strong winds at flowering, lack of frosts after budburst, low, uniform temperatures, lack of variability in temperature, and reasonable relative humidity so that there is not excessive transpiration followed by excessive uptake of potassium by the developing berry, leading to raised pH (lowered acidity) and all the consequent problems of flat flavour and poor staying power.

Next, consider soils. There are salt and drainage problems in Western Australia, so good drainage is critical. Vines do not like wet feet in spring, and Western Australia has most of

its rain in winter, a climatic pattern usually called mediterranean, and found also in parts of Chile, California and South
Africa. Growers are advised to seek out gravel or stone or clay
over limestone.

Harold Olmo, from California, identified the Mount Barker
area, and made Maurice O'Shea, the legendary Hunter wine-
maker, enthusiastic about the south-west just before he died,
according to Gladstones, who himself suggested Margaret
River, slightly warmer but safer. In the event, both Olmo and
Gladstones have been proved correct.

Soils

Vines are grown on an extremely wide range of soils. This is
because the decision to plant grapes can be based on at least
four criteria: where the grower wants to live, suitability of
climate, suitability of soil type and availability of irrigation.
Soil types on which vines have been grown in Australia
include everything from red-brown earths through the highly
desirable terra rosa soils to heavy alluvial soils and deep
sands. Almost any level of soil fertility is therefore found
somewhere in Australian soils used for growing grapes. In
addition to the very pervasive phosphorus deficiency, particular problems may arise with trace elements and, in the
highest rainfall areas, potassium deficiency.

Thus, the most suitable soils for growing vines are generally
regarded, following French experience, as those such as terra
rosa, as found at Coonawarra, and red-brown earths or sandy
loams with underlying limestone, found in many areas.

Terra rosa is a red soil overlying hard limestone, which in
turn overlies deep clay with a high calcium content. It is well
drained, which is vital for vines, and relatively easily worked.
The water table is usually about three metres below the surface, but the extreme use of irrigation in the Coonawarra area
in particular can be expected to lower it over the years now
that more than 2,000 hectares have been planted. The terra
rosa area is no more than fifteen kilometres long and less than
two kilometres wide throughout its length. Eighty kilometres
north is Keppoch, where there is also considerable usable
terra rosa soil. Driving past the Hardy Vineyards at Keppoch
in the early evening in November, after a fairly wet spring,
one can see the setting sun glinting on the irrigation flood

between the vines. At this time of year the worry is frost, for the vines are flowering. However, putting so much water into the soil makes for high yields, perhaps ten to twelve tonnes per hectare for Shiraz, for example.

These very high yields seem hardly compatible with the very highest quality wines, and many commentators have noted that the oenologists of Petaluma, one of Australia's most scientific wine-makers, have carefully tested the effects of reducing yield by severe pruning and the elimination of irrigation. The results suggest that the unirrigated fruit makes far better wine.

Australian soils, as has been discovered by agricultural practice and research, are quite extraordinarily variable, and large vineyards planted in one season generally show very erratic performance for a number of years, until cultivation, nutrition and pruning render them relatively uniform. Even after this, production is very patchy. Few of the viticultural areas are sufficiently long established for the very best land for a particular variety to be determined, as has been the case in such areas as Burgundy, Bordeaux and the Rhineland.

The grower, then, seeks well-drained soil, preferably on a slight slope because of the problem of frost, and perhaps, except in very hot areas, a north-easterly aspect. If the area has a phylloxera, or salt, or nematode problem, so that he must plant vines on hybrid rootstocks, he will have to take account of the special problems of the rootstocks themselves: some, for example, do not grow well on calcareous soils, unlike *Vitis vinifera*. Nematodes, minute worms which attack and gall roots, flourish in irrigated vineyards on sandy soil along the Murray, and it has been fortunate that some rootstocks possess both salt tolerance and nematode tolerance and resistance.

What the grower would like to know, in assessing likely country which has never grown grapes, is how soil variations affect wine quality. This is an unsolved problem.

Trace elements, the minute quantities of gold, silver, zinc, molybdenum and so on in the soil, are carried into the grape berries. The relative proportions of these elements vary between soils, and so do the proportions in the grape berries. Thus, for any given season and variety, the source of the fruit may be determined with some accuracy. This may aid prosecutions under laws such as the Unfair Advertising Act (1970) or the Trade Standards Act (1979) but not in planning how to make better wine.

In the late 1960s, the Australian Wine Research Institute and the Commonwealth Scientific and Industrial Research Organization (CSIRO) spent a great deal of money and rather more time trying to associate wine quality with soil type. They concluded that differences in composition could indeed be reliably detected and associated with soil or district, but not differences in quality. The reason was twofold: small lot wine-making, to compare carefully controlled batches of fruit, was unreliable; and the assessment of wine quality was not as precise as the assessment of differences in composition. A colleague of mine was moved to develop novel statistical methods so that he could show conclusively what other tasters had suspected, that one of a panel of carefully trained scientific tasters was reliable only for the first part of any trial. This was not because he consumed more alcohol, for he did not; he simply suffered palate fatigue of unknown origin. He therefore had to be excluded from future trials; assessing differences in wine quality between grapes from Sultana vines trellised in different ways, or Crouchen vines pruned long or short, requires reliability above all else.

The relationship of climate and soil to the Vintage Chart (Table 2 in the Appendix) needs some explanation. Every area has special problems, many of which relate to wine quality but not necessarily to fluctuations in wine quality.

The Swan Valley is too hot, which leads to rapid ripening and coarse fruit. It also has nematodes in the more sandy soils, requiring vines to be grown on hybrid rootstocks.

South-western Western Australia suffers from the depredations of birds, occasional severe frost and continual salt-laden wind. The wind can badly affect fruit set, and also means that supplementary watering is essential during the long, dry summer.

Clare, in South Australia, has endemic oidium (powdery mildew, a fungus disease) and a long, hot summer, which necessitates supplementary watering. There is a minor problem of excessive vigour on the deeper, more fertile soils.

The Barossa Valley has the same problems as the Swan. Only in the cooler Eden Valley can wines with any real delicacy be made.

McLaren Vale is similar to the Barossa but the sea is a

moderating influence, so that some finesse can be achieved with white varieties.

The south-east of South Australia has many erratic problems. A hot start to summer can be devastating as the winds sear through the level vineyards and shrivel late-flowering varieties such as Cabernet Sauvignon. Summer rain leads to fungal disease – grey mould rather than noble rot.

South-western Victoria has problems with both high winds and summer humidity. Further south, at Drumborg and Geelong, frosts are particularly bad, though elevated sites with a north aspect, like Anakie, miss many of these problems. Although phylloxera was the main reason for the disappearance of the Geelong vignoble, it is not a problem at the moment. Frost and summer rain should be the main problems in the Yarra Valley; since the area's revival, there have been few really disastrous seasons.

North-central Victoria has both phylloxera and an excessively hot summer. For the few vineyards, as opposed to orchards, planted on the Goulburn Valley clays, there is a particular management problem, as these soils can be quite impervious to water, so that vines suffer moisture stress while being irrigated.

North-eastern Victoria is hot and has phylloxera.

The Hunter Valley has the problem of summer rain and fungal disease, and the converse problem of low spring sub-soil moisture because of the low winter rainfall.

Mudgee is surrounded by agricultural and pastoral land, and so has problems with birds and other pests. Otherwise, supplementary watering meets the usual difficulty of moisture stress.

Tasmania may have an early end to the growing season in some years. Ocean winds are also likely to be a problem quite frequently, as are frosts in many localities.

The Granite Belt in Queensland has the problems of summer rainfall and indigenous pests.

These various difficulties are not all such as to lead to wide fluctuations in vintage quality. Indeed, there is little variation in some of the traditional areas, apart from the occasional exceptionally poor year, like 1969 or 1974 in the warmer South Australian districts. Even these two years were very different, in that some 1969 reds have come good whereas 1974 wines show no sign of ever being other than thin, unbalanced and dirty.

In all the newer areas, there are very few mature vines and no old vines. When one sees the difference in character of fruit from ninety-year-old Shiraz vines as against five- or ten-year-old Shiraz in the Clare area, one feels that many current vintage assessments for areas such as south-western Western Australia or the Yarra Valley will need substantial revision. On the other hand, assessments of vintages more than a decade ago are influenced by the surviving better wines, whereas the recent vintages mainly reflect the quality of the fruit at vintage. The table needs to be used with all this borne in mind.

Varieties

As we have already seen, the Australian wine industry has a unique history, reflected in the varieties grown today. First, there are large areas of grapes suitable for either wine-making, drying or fresh consumption: Sultana (Thompson's Seedless) is the most obvious. Secondly, there are large areas of grapes suitable mainly for fortified wine production: Mataro, Doradillo, the Muscats, Palomino, Pedro Ximenez. Thirdly, there are increasing areas planted to varieties regarded as being suitable for premium table wine production.

The state of flux in which the industry perpetually finds itself is reflected in the areas not yet bearing and planned to be ripped out (Table 1 in the Appendix). One can predict that a number of varieties, to be discussed in more detail below, will disappear from the Australian wine-making scene if the exports of wine continue to be only two or three per cent of production, and if table wine consumption continues to rise at a rate slightly greater than population increase. Some varieties, which are strange relics of what early settlers could collect in the Cape Province in South Africa on their way out to Australia, may survive, others may not.

To see just what a strange collection of varieties is used to make Australian wine, let us look more closely at some of them, beginning with the black grapes, Cabernet Sauvignon, Grenache, Mataro, Pinot Noir, Shiraz (Syrah), Tarrango and Gamay.

As you drive north-east out of Auburn, the little town at the southernmost extremity of the Clare wine-growing area, you are confronted with a large sign which says, among other things, 'The home of the noble Cabernet Sauvignon grape'. Here, in the wine boom of the late 1960s and early 1970s, which was reinforced financially by the nickel boom of the same period, approximately 200 hectares of Cabernet Sauvignon were planted in one year, with every intention of producing the best red wine possible in Australia. The land used had never grown this variety, or for that matter any other, before. All over Australia, Cabernet Sauvignon was planted at about the same time. Extensive plantings were even made in the Hunter Valley, where the experience of a century had suggested that it was not a very satisfactory variety. Perhaps with modern methods of disease control and mechanical pruning and harvesting, it will perform well in some of the previously unsuitable areas, perhaps not. Meanwhile, in southern Australia it is the main grape variety used to produce the best red wines. The character of the wines varies greatly. From the south of Western Australia, the south-east of South Australia and the cooler parts of Victoria, it produces wines of great complexity, character and elegance, recalling the Bordeaux area, whence the variety originally came. From other areas, such as Clare, the Barossa and north-eastern Victoria, it produces wines with enormous berry flavour and aroma, and rather less balance. From the irrigated areas, the wines are somewhat similar, though with less staying power. It is frequently blended with other varieties, especially the ubiquitous Shiraz and, to a lesser extent, Malbec, Cabernet Franc, Merlot or Grenache.

As the major grape for many successful wines of the port type, Grenache has been very widely grown in both irrigated and dryland areas. When markets changed from predominantly fortified wines to predominantly table wines, Grenache was used by itself, with varying degrees of success, for both red wines and rosés, and in blends of various kinds. Because the grapes acquire colour late, relative to their sugar production, they have even been harvested green on quite a large scale for white wine production. Wines made solely from Grenache tend to be unbalanced, with a pronounced nose, showing very little of the rose-petal character which is said to be inherent in the variety, rather full fruit on the palate, and a coarse finish, which may be succeeded by bitterness as the wine ages. As the wine-makers of Châteauneuf-du-Pape have long known, a small proportion of Grenache in a wine is often a very desirable thing but, while Grenache has been very successfully used in this manner in Australia, the more recent Australian fashion for wines made solely from a particular variety has meant that Grenache has been rather left out in the cold. As a grower of Grenache, I have suffered from this problem, having to make wine in the bath with unsold grapes.

Everything that has just been said about Grenache (except that I grow it) could be repeated more strongly for Mataro. Most people who have learnt to detect Mataro character seem not to like it, but in small proportions it can add to the complexity and interest of a wine. Despite this, one expects less and less of it to be used for table wine production. For port, it has continuing prospects, but fortified wines seem unlikely ever to return to their earlier levels of sales, dependent as these were on Imperial Preference.

Both Grenache and Mataro have been used more than was desirable because of their low price and ready availability.

In the 1890s, sound Australian wine could be bought in a cask in London for 1s. 6d.–3s. a gallon, and retailed at great profit for 16s.–40s. a case, that is, 1s. 9d.–4s. 6d. a litre.* In 1983, it was reported in the *Australian Financial Review* that Orlando (part of Reckitt & Colman) had imported Italian Merlot juice for 35¢ a litre in 1982, had blended it with a small quantity of Australian Merlot juice, and had sold the resulting wine as Orlando Cardinale Italian-Australian Merlot. At about $5.00 retail for 750ml, the wine was much cheaper in real terms than provided by the reverse trade a century before, but one feels that a profit was still available for Reckitt & Colman. The managing director of Orlando, Guenter Prass, however, was reported as saying: 'We believe by purchasing in such a fashion we can encourage people to grow Merlot under proper conditions.' One hopes that he is proved right, for little Merlot is grown. Certainly it is not needed for softness, as in Bordeaux, but while there are promising Merlot and Cabernet-Merlot wines about, mainly from Victoria, there is too little to assess whether in any particular area we have a future St Emilion on our hands. In a tasting of 1982, Cabernet Sauvignon-Cabernet Franc from Jeffrey Grosset at Auburn

---

* One gallon equals approximately 4.54 litres. At the time of writing, UK £1 = $A 2.10 = $US 1.50. In pre-decimal currency, £1 = 20s. (twenty shillings) in both UK and Australian currency, and 1s. =12 pence.

and Cabernet Sauvignon-Merlot from Horrocks Wines, but made at Grosset's winery, both showed considerable clean fruit and depth of flavour, but this is the modern style rather than the blending varieties.

Tradition has it that Pinot Noir, which is shy-bearing everywhere, is unsuitable for Australian conditions. However, as Australia is an island continent, one would expect conditions somewhere to be suitable for this grape. Perhaps the inherent conservatism of those who work on the land and the protected Imperial markets were among the reasons which led to so little of this variety being grown for so long. However, this shortcoming has been rectified in the last ten or twenty years and, while the acreages planted of this variety are still very small, they are increasing and, as will be discussed elsewhere, wine-makers such as Carrodus, Middleton, Tyrrell and Robson are showing what can be done, as did O'Shea many years ago. Nonetheless, one expects it to be some time before one can enjoy with an Australian Pinot Noir an experience such as that recounted by Anthony Powell:

> That August [1939] we set off once more for France, this time making for Dijon, with the aim of moving about Burgundy, as the previous year through the Gironde. At Beaune, the Hotel de la Poste (I record, at the risk of being a wine-bore), we drank an Echézeaux '23, about third or fourth on the list of Burgundies, priced at 7s 6d in English money, providing one of the only two occasions when I have experienced the vinous exhalation spoken of in wine manuals, the bursting from the newly opened bottle of the scent of violets.

Shiraz has been used everywhere in Australia, usually with some success. From the earthy (or even dirty), soft, brick-red triumphs of the Hunter to elegant, spicy Coonawarra wines, Shiraz reveals itself in as many forms as Proteus. In Clare, in South Australia, and north-eastern Victoria, the grape produces table wines as long-lasting as any port and with much the same character, yet it can also produce light, clean, austere wines which are at their best in a mere five years. The fruit character, emphatic or restrained, is what remains constant. A. C. Kelly commented in 1867:

The Sirrah, or Scyras, largely cultivated in Europe on account of the very deep colour, astringency and body of its wine, which is used for making up wines deficient in these qualities, is remarkable for the same peculiarities, which it possesses in perhaps a great degree. Our warm sunny climate, where the soil is suitable, produces a wine from the Scyras which is not inappropriately termed inky, from its excess of astringency and colour. M. Cazalis also mentions this grape as an instance of a vine retaining its essential characters, even to the nature of its produce, under all circumstances, so much so, in fact, that the wine of the Scyras, grown under different climates in France, can at once be identified by any one acquainted with it. The same holds good with perhaps every wine which we grow in these colonies: under similar circumstances each will give wine similar in general character to that which it produces in Europe.

Although grown on a minuscule scale as yet, Tarrango is mentioned because it has been bred for certain Australian conditions by the Division of Horticultural Research of the CSIRO. It is one of three named varieties resulting from a plant-breeding programme aimed at producing vines well adapted to the hot, inland irrigation areas. That is, they must mature slowly and hold their acid well. The breeding programme began in 1965, and Tarrango was commercially released in 1979, after several years' testing. It was the result of a cross between the prolific multi-purpose white variety Sultana (Thompson's Seedless) and a Portuguese black variety, Touriga. Wines have been made by Brown Brothers and when very young are bright, light, fruity and fresh. As they age, they lose some of their early charm, rather like an early harvest Cinsault (Blue Imperial). Whether the CSIRO's now defunct breeding programme will have long-term benefits remains obscure, but the attempt was courageous.

The Gamay grape, from which Beaujolais is made, ripens about two weeks before Pinot Noir and yields much more copiously. However, it is not allowed in many *Appellation Contrôlée* Burgundies, only in *Passe-Touts-Grains*, Beaujolais, Mâcon and *Bourgogne Ordinaire*, following the edict issued by Philip the Bold, Duke of Burgundy, on 31 July 1394. Describing the Gamay vine as 'a very bad and very disloyal plant' which makes 'quite foul' wine, the Duke gave growers eight months to grub out their vines, fining them if they did not. He was also against organic fertilizers, which, he claimed, made wines turn 'yellow and coarse'. The introduction of Gamay into Burgundy and the use of dung formed part of the replanting and rehabilitation of vineyards which was necessary at the end of the century because of the lack of labour resulting from the Black Death in 1348. Gamay was a quick and easy way to increase production.

However Gamay does make a light, fresh, fruity wine of a kind ideally suited to summer drinking in Australia and to the 'fast foods' so many family drinkers favour. It is hard to understand why almost no one in Australia has used it successfully. It grows well in various vine-growing regions, and the berries are full of flavour. Philip the Bold's edict seems to linger strangely.

There are other black grapes grown, sometimes with considerable success, like Morris's Durif in north-eastern Victoria, but few apart from Zinfandel are likely to increase in popularity in the near future. Particularly surprising is the almost complete absence of good Italian varieties, such as Nebbiolo. Barbera has been tried on a small scale, making attractive tannic wines in Victoria, but on the whole they have made little impact since they became available out of quarantine in the early 1970s. Zinfandel, the Italian variety which California has made its own, has been grown with some success in both South Australia and Western Australia, but it is too soon to say what its future will be. At Mudgee, in New South Wales, Montrose's Italian wine-maker is trying Sangiovese as well as Barbera and Nebbiolo, already with some success.

White wine is inherently less complex than red. The absence of the flavours associated with the pigments is a problem that has been overcome by the making of magical confections like Sauternes, Tokay and champagne, and by the use of a vast range of varieties. In Australia, this problem has been compounded by the confusion over wine styles. In red wines, as I have mentioned, Australian wine-makers, for the most part from the British Isles, have had the English conceptions of 'Claret' – firm, tannic, complex – and 'Burgundy' – strong and soft – at which to aim, but in whites they have had a plethora of French and German models, elusive moving targets.

The variety to enjoy the greatest vogue after Riesling,

Chardonnay, was to be found in very few areas until recently. There was a fine clone at Mudgee, though not identified as Chardonnay for a long time, and limited plantings in the Hunter. In the last ten years, there has been a dramatic increase in plantings, as every maker who has any claim to producing high-quality wines has sought this fruit.

In good hands, it unquestionably produces white Burgundy-like wines of the very highest quality, whether the fruit has come from northern Tasmania, the Yarra Valley, Mudgee, Cowra, the lower Hunter or the highest part of the Eden Valley.

Until recently almost invariably called Rhine Riesling, to distinguish it from Clare Riesling (Crouchen), Hunter River Riesling (Sémillon), and other misnomers, Riesling was grown extensively when the modern techniques of cold-fermentation came into wide use. For this reason, it enjoyed a great boom from the late 1960s to the late 1970s, when a reaction set in against the very light, floral wines, which were being produced with considerable residual sweetness, but with none of the depth of flavour of German wines. Now, as wine-makers try to use the grapes to make wines with more body, it can be more rationally appraised, and while it may not be the dominant high-quality white grape any longer, it will continue to provide very fine wines from all the southern states.

From the many recent attempts to produce Trockenbeerenauslese wine by artificially inoculating the grapes with *Botrytis cinerea*, noble rot, very small quantities of very high quality wine will be produced, though whether the German description will be appropriate remains to be seen.

As Hunter River Riesling, Sémillon has produced (and continues to produce) some of Australia's finest and most distinctive wines. Often aggressive when young, mature Hunter River Sémillon develops a beautiful soft flavour, a delicate lingering finish and a honeyed bouquet; it can improve for fifteen years or more. At their best, these Sémillons have sometimes been compared with the Montrachets; I shall discuss this further in Chapter 6.

Like Riesling, Sémillon is being treated with botrytis, in order to make wines resembling Sauternes or Barsac.

When one walks into a cellar and finds the proprietor and wine-maker selling his wares while wearing a singlet emblazoned 'Robert Mondavi Fumé Blanc' and finds that a 'Fumé Blanc' is indeed on sale, one sees the closeness of the Australian-Californian wine-making connection. However, a range of styles of wine is made from Sauvignon Blanc in Australia, as is the case in France. The full-bodied, dry kind matured in oak has achieved great popularity as makers such as Enterprise Wines have learnt how to match the oak to the fruit, but very sweet wines have also been made successfully from Sauvignon Blanc. Blends of Sémillon, Sauvignon Blanc and Muscadelle (or Tokay, as it is called in Australia) are as yet very infrequent, but they may also appear in the future.

Although Traminer is a well-established variety in Australia, having long been used for blends with Sémillon in the Hunter, it is only with the advent of low-temperature fermentation that it has been able to reveal its true aromatic character. From the cooler areas, it makes spicy wines, full of the varietal character, especially if the grapes have been picked fairly ripe. However, because it so easily makes a very coarse wine, many makers have picked it early, resulting in a loss of character and interest. To make wines even remotely approaching in character the best Alsatian examples will require exceptional skill.

Crouchen has been grown in the Clare area for more than a century, hence its misnomer, Clare Riesling. It has been much used to provide fullness of flavour in wines aimed at the White Burgundy style, but by itself makes a wine which tends to be flabby and uninteresting. Although it has a place as a blending variety, it is becoming less fashionable, which is a pity, as it has an attractive fruit character when well handled.

Muscat Gordo Blanco, also called Muscat of Alexandria, is responsible for some of Australia's finest wines, the extraordinarily rich, raisiny muscats of north-eastern Victoria, their style generally agreed to be unlike dessert wines from anywhere else in the world. Elsewhere in Australia, it makes good dessert wines, though without the intensity, power and finesse of the Rutherglen examples. It is also used very widely to provide fruit flavour in cheap white wines, both still and sparkling. Enormous quantities are grown in the irrigated areas and some of this wine finds itself misleadingly labelled.

Marsanne is not widely grown at all – a little at Mudgee and a little at Tahbilk and elsewhere in northern Victoria – but produces rich, mouth-filling wines of considerable charm when carefully treated. Château Tahbilk has been growing it continuously for a long time and makes the most reliable wine from it. In a good year it is lively and smells of fresh grass, and some allege that they can detect the character of honeysuckle. Sometimes when one opens a bottle of three- or four-year-old Blanquette, it smells of Turkish delight, and the palate can also be a little cloying, but at its best, from the Hunter, it makes a firm, durable, full-bodied white wine only a little less enjoyable than the Sémillon of the same area.

In addition to the varieties already discussed, large quantities of wine are made from the varieties previously grown very extensively for dry sherry production – Pedro Ximenez, Palomino and Doradillo – but even the best of these tend to lack fruit character and interest. If there is a revival in sherry consumption, they will be returned to their proper use.

Ondenc, under the name Irvine's White, has long been a mainstay of the Great Western area, both for Great Western Sparkling Wines made by Seppelt and for some of Best's wines, both still and sparkling, such as the 'Bin O Hock'. Nearby, other wineries, such as Montara, use Ondenc to make wines such as 'Moselle', a syrupy wine like a still Spumante.

Chasselas is not a variety widely grown in Australia, and from the few examples which have come to my attention, this is not surprising, since it makes clean, boring wines, yellow rather than green, with a dull finish.

Minor white varieties, like White Frontignan, Tokay (Muscadelle) and Trebbiano (White Hermitage) are used for both table and fortified wine production, but seem unlikely to make much of an impact in the market-place, either in quality or quantity. It is very difficult to ensure that the desired varieties are grown. Constantly one is struck by the grower's inherent conservatism, which, until widespread bankruptcy supervenes, can make nonsense of careful econometric predictions of what will be grown in the future. I noticed it at the butcher's.

The grey dusty track led round the front of the new cream-brick triple-fronted bungalow to the butcher's shop at the back. Climbing out of the car, I saw a man with a mattock grubbing out some old vines on one of the steepest parts of the block, where it would be hard to pull a ripper. The ripper had been through a couple of acres on the flat, and beside them was a crop of lucerne, flowering purple in the heat.

'Going to replant down there this winter?' The butcher's wife would know, for they were her vines.

'Mmm.'

'What with? Riesling, Chardonnay, Cabernet?'

'Yes, a bit of Riesling – Clare's. And some Shiraz. And some Pedro.'

'Pedro? But the Co-op isn't taking any this year.'

'No, but there's others that will.' She spoke and smiled equally slowly. 'These new varieties. It's just a fashion. My nephew's got a heap of Sauvignon Blanc, and it's just a heap of trouble.'

'But so are Clare's, and the price hasn't changed for two years.'

'You might get a bit of splitting if you're really tough, but you get tonnes of fruit. Now what did I have for you? Two hoggets? Wife all right? She couldn't get over here?'

Wine-making

Wine-making is an essentially simple and natural process. It was introduced into Australia in the state in which it had remained, subject only to minor modification, for perhaps a millennium or more. Grapes were picked when they tasted right – that is, when they contained sufficient sugar to produce, after fermentation, between 10 and 15 per cent alcohol by volume, this varying with the variety, region, season and desired end product.

The grapes were picked as quickly as possible, taken to the winery and crushed. White fruit had the skins, pips and stalks removed and was then transferred to fermenting vats, which could be wooden barrels, earthenware vessels or stone tanks, normally open to the atmosphere so that the carbon dioxide – which is, with alcohol, the main product of the breakdown of sugar by yeasts – could dissipate harmlessly. When the fermentation had ceased, the wine would be racked, that is, drained into other vessels, leaving a slurry of yeast on the bottom of the fermentation vat.

With black grapes, on the other hand, the skins, which impart the colour and much of the flavour to red wine, were either not removed or returned to the must after the removal of the stalks (*égrappage*). Writing in the 1860s, A. C. Kelly noted that '[i]n these colonies the removal of the stalk from

41

the vat has been the universal practice. How far we have been right in the exclusive adoption of this system is exceedingly questionable; and it is advisable that we submit ourselves to the teaching of those whose experience is of old standing, while the results of their practice, as seen in the very high quality of the wines, ought to command our attention.' It is evident from Kelly's discussion and his quotations from French writers that retention of the stalk in the fermentation made for much harder, slower-maturing wines which would eventually be better than those made without stalks; this applied equally to Burgundy and to Bordeaux. Removal of stalks is modern practice in both Bordeaux and Burgundy, of course, especially Burgundy.

Thus, most Australian makers followed the practice which led to softer, more immediately appealing wines. They did not, however, use *macération carbonique*, the recently revived ancient technique which makes very fresh wines. If grapes are simply put in an enclosed vessel, the berries will begin to ferment, especially towards the bottom, where they have been crushed by the weight of fruit above. As the fermentation becomes more active, so more berries will be broken, and the fermentation will accelerate. Fermented juice run off black grapes will be coloured by the pigments which have been extracted by the activity of the fermentation, and there will be little of the harsher tannin extracted by hard pressing. If, in addition, the pressure in the fermenter is suddenly released, the carbon dioxide dissolved in the fermenting juice will bubble out of solution, bursting the berries and releasing most of the juice.

The length of the fermentation was hard to control before refrigeration became available. Kelly quoted a French writer as saying that '[t]he duration of fermentation is so prolonged in many southern countries that they may well be dismayed by the labour required in beating down the head once a day during fifteen, twenty, thirty days or more. The beating down would no doubt shorten the fermentation but not so much as to compensate for the labour required.' The head or cap was the mass of skins (and stalks, where these were retained) and it was lifted by the gas given off in fermentation to float on the surface of the seething must. It needed to be beaten down or plunged to accelerate the fermentation, to prevent the alcohol in the cap turning to vinegar and of course to extract the pigments from the skins.

In the cooler areas, fires might be lit in the winery at night to prevent fermentation from stopping. In the warmer areas, cold water might be added to the wine or run down the sides of the vats, and when ice became available blocks were thrown in during the day. Roly Birks, wine-maker at Wendouree, at Clare, for sixty years from the end of the First World War, defended the addition of water as mere replacement of what was lost as the must seethed and frothed. After this treatment, his young wines normally contained more than 12½ per cent alcohol, and enough tannin to deprive the unwary taster temporarily of breath, so it was hardly a harmful practice.

After several rackings to improve clarity and brightness, the wines were stored for some time in oak vessels of various sizes, usually large (2,000 litres or more). White wines were generally bottled within a year, red wines after rather longer, up to three or four years.

Fortified wines had the spirit added when the fermentation had reached the desired stage, with several per cent sugar unconverted to alcohol for port or sweet sherry styles, less to none for the drier sherry and madeira styles. These wines were also matured in large wood for considerable periods before blending for bottling.

These, then, were the traditional processes, carried out with skill and knowledge which varied widely. Even in the greatest European wine-producing areas, there is wide divergence in practice, so that what is traditional in one need not be acceptable in others. In Burgundy, for example, the house of Louis Latour ferments its Pinot Noir for six days and pasteurizes the wine, whereas other firms, such as Prosper Maufoux, ferment the wine for 'as long as it takes', which might be eight or 20 days, and do not pasteurize it.

Vintage is a time of controlled panic for the grower. First of all, depending whether he has another job, as many of the smaller growers do, he has to arrange his annual holiday for a period which is slightly indeterminate as to both starting date and duration. Next, depending on region, if his vineyard is part of a mixed farming enterprise, vintage may interfere with other seasonal activities, a very late vintage running into lambing, for example, in parts of southern Australia.

Pickers are another problem. Will the usual reliable team be available, or have some of them died or retired? Will the unemployed young people be as good as their elders? Will vintage last long enough to give them the work which they have been promised? In both Clare and the Yarra, Vietnamese refugees have been among the most reliable recent workers, though they have never seen vines before in their lives. However, it is not practicable to depend on recent immigrants, as immigration policies constantly change.

Most of all, the grower is at the mercy of the winery. He has to deliver fruit during the period which the winery specifies, and in the few weeks up to full ripeness for any particular variety the advice of the winery will often change several times. Told that he must deliver his Riesling between 10.5° and 13° Baumé, the grower watches anxiously as the birds begin to attack in earnest with the Baumé just over 9°, and an enormous amount of acid, perhaps 15 grammes per litre, still present: this fruit should be magnificent if the birds leave any, the grower thinks to himself. Then a cool week, and nothing at all happens except bird damage. The grower may have negotiated a bonus if the fruit is over 13° and still has plenty of acid, and as the last few days of receipt of Riesling at the crusher approach, he has to decide whether to hold off for a very high Baumé for an Auslese wine, should there be noble rot about, or rush them through in these last days of normal Riesling delivery.

At the winery, after jolting several kilometres over the rough metal roads in the hot sun, the grower joins the queue at the weighbridge. Perhaps his load is smaller than the others, for big trucks from the river are delivering ten or twenty tonnes at a time. So the big growers stroll over and eat a few berries from the small dryland grower's modest few tonnes.

The man at the weighbridge tries to guess the weight, to relieve the boredom of his task, and a further delay results. Finally, the grower watches the deep golden-green fruit spill out of the bin into the crusher, and the big archimedean screw drags the fruit out of sight. A few minutes later, there is a roar as the stems and pips are discharged on to an enormous heap, which will be delivered to Tarac in the Barossa for fermentation, distillation and extraction of tartaric acid.

When the final delivery is over, there is a tremendous feeling of relief. I remember one year borrowing a large four-wheeled trailer to tow behind a four-wheel-drive vehicle because there was a threat of rain at vintage. As the last load was being driven to the winery, a wheel fell off the trailer. The entire cast of pickers, both in the four-wheel-drive and the following car, sat at the side of the road and laughed, while a messenger ran the last few hundred metres to the winery and brought back the wine-maker and a cellar-hand with a truck and a fresh bin. They too roared with laughter. Only I remained impassive. Growers of the best fruit are better organized.

Farmers in Australia tend to assume that, having grown their crop and delivered it somewhere, they will see their produce snapped up by a market eager to buy, even feeling it has a duty to buy. Grape-growers are just the same: if the fruit is in reasonable condition, delivered on time and to specification, they expect the winery to buy it and pay the growers. Yet the problems, in the hot areas especially, have only just begun.

When James Busby started drafting his first book on wine-making, in the ship from Scotland to Australia, he very naturally drew on continental writers, mainly French, at both the theoretical and the practical level. Forty years later, A. C. Kelly did the same. Another eighty years on, John Fornachon, first director of the Australian Wine Research Institute, would still quote nearly twice as many writers in French as in other languages in his book on the bacterial spoilage of fortified wines. However, it was Fornachon who first made a distinctively Australian contribution to the science of oenology.

In the late 1920s and the early 1930s, as fortified wine production expanded, bacterial spoilage of wine, which had, of course, been studied intensively in France from the time of Pasteur onward, had been thought to affect only wines weaker than about 15 per cent alcohol by volume. However, from about the time of the First World War, wines of more than 20 per cent alcohol were discovered to have been spoilt by bacteria in all the hotter wine-growing areas, including Australia. This was a serious problem for the substantial exports of fortified wine to the United Kingdom, so in the early 1930s the Australian Wine Board asked the University of Adelaide to investigate the problem.

Extraordinary measures were attempted within cellars to stop bacterial spread. A visitor to a cellar would be amazed, as he walked around, by the hessian curtains hung between the stacks of casks containing the maturing wine, and by the strong smell of formalin. If the formalin killed anything, it was the ubiquitous vinegar flies, *Drosophila melanogaster*, not the bacteria. Later, companies such as Penfold tried pasteurizers. As these had iron heating plates and copper fittings, they caused major metal problems in the wine, even if the bacteria were killed. Ozonizers were also tried, and a wine of the port or sweet sherry style which had been through this treatment had little left to recommend it.

It was in this atmosphere that John Fornachon began his work. He was well aware of most of the European work on bacterial spoilage and also, of course, of the malolactic fermentation which was encouraged in the light, dry European wines from the colder areas, to convert the large amounts of malic acid, which contributes a harsh character to the wine, to lactic acid, which is a softer-tasting acid. However, this had rarely been investigated in Australia, since most of the wine was grown in areas where stopped fermentation was not a problem and where, indeed, little malic acid might be present in the must.

Fornachon was able to show that the bacteria responsible for the spoilage of fortified wine in Australia were indeed the rod-shaped lactic acid bacteria, *Lactobacillus*, which include the species responsible for the valuable malolactic fermentation. In fact, he found that some of the lactobacilli which he isolated from Australian wines could bring about the malolactic fermentation in wines containing malic acid.

Following others, Fornachon found that the bacteria causing the spoilage were very fastidious in their requirements for growth. The more acid the wine, the less they grew, but of the two attributes of acid, that is to say the amount present and the degree to which the acid disassociates into ions in solution, the latter, usually described by pH, which is a measure of hydrogen ion concentration, was by far the more important. pH has a range from 0 to 14, 7 representing neutrality, as with distilled water, and wines have values lying in the range 2.5 to 4.5, with rather few below 3 and rather few above 4. The scale of pH is logarithmic, so that a wine with pH 3 is ten times as acid as a wine with pH 4. Fornachon found that bacteria would grow in wines containing as much as 20 per cent alcohol if the pH was higher than about 3.6. He also found that the bacteria would grow quite rapidly between 15°C and 28°C. In unfortified wines, however, bacterial growth could be most rapid at even higher temperatures.

The most important antiseptic, as it was called, in the winery was – and still is – sulphur dioxide (SO_2). Fornachon was able to show that, under Australian conditions, virtually no lactobacilli were able to grow in wine containing eighty parts per million of sulphur dioxide and all were killed by 100 parts per million. Fornachon therefore recommended that 'When SO_2 is added to fortified wine for the purpose of checking the growth of actively growing bacteria, sufficient should be added to raise the SO_2 content to one hundred and fifty parts per million, and it should be thoroughly mixed throughout the wine. The wine should then be freed from bacteria by filtration or fining and racking.' These very high levels of sulphur contributed to the character of many Australian wines for many years.

It is now recognized in Australia, especially as a result of the more recent work of T. C. Somers, of the Australian Wine Research Institute, that sulphur dioxide has two distinct roles in red wine-making, firstly as an antiseptic before fermentation and then, in red wine conservation, by chemically binding acetaldehyde, a break-down product of alcohol, in young wine. However, excessive levels of sulphur dioxide react with the anthocyanin pigments, producing the smell, so disliked by many, reminiscent of rotten eggs and caused by reduced sulphur compounds, together with some components of the earthy character liked by equally many in even some of the best Hunter River or McLaren Vale reds.

In white wines, a given quantity of sulphur dioxide will produce much higher levels of free sulphur dioxide in the wine, thereby eliminating free acetaldehyde from the bouquet and maintaining freshness.

To get the benefits of sulphur dioxide without the problems, it is therefore added at the crush to the extent of thirty to forty parts per million, sometimes even less, and with careful management of low temperature fermentation this is quite sufficient.

Thus, when one walks into a small winery like Jeffrey Grosset's, and asks the wine-maker how much sulphur dioxide he is using in his wines, he might well say: 'Well, I'd like it to be only twenty-eight [parts per million], but these wines are going to last for years, and I'd like my customers to lay them down, so I play it safe and add thirty-five. But when you think that most of the customers probably drink the stuff within a month, perhaps I should use less.'

Such makers ferment everything in stainless steel, which makes for control and cleanliness but is very expensive, especially for a large, long-established maker with a substantial investment in plant. For the most part, they also obtain from the Wine Research Institute yeasts specially selected for the production of a desired type of wine. This yeast selection arose naturally from the earlier work on faults and diseases of wines. It means that yeasts are available for a range of sugar levels in the fruit, so that a high sugar level can be left at the end of fermentation for a sweet wine, or the wine can be fermented to dryness for any alcohol level. Also, a yeast can be chosen which works best at a given fermentation temperature, or which imparts little character to a wine, or a great deal of character, for example the 'tropical fruit salad' character of acetate esters. A yeast which produces significant quantities of these last components was very widely used with Riesling in the late 1970s and many of these wines are still to be found.

Open fermenters – big open concrete vats paraffin-lined just before vintage – are still used in the colder areas. As a small boy, I can recall watching the cap being plunged at Seppeltsfield, and wondering why it was being done: closed fermentation has brought many improvements, but it makes vintage less interesting. Can you smell the fruit? The winemaker's face shows worry: he is using closed stainless steel tanks to keep all the flavour in, and inside the winery all you should smell is yeast. At the crusher, the grapey smell is such that varieties are better distinguished by their appearance or by chewing them, than by smell, and the bees lurch and stagger away, gorged on sugar, no pollen in their saddle bags.

After the fermentation, or even for the later stages in some cases, oak storage is needed by many wines. In Australia, many – perhaps most – white wines and some red are bottled soon after fermentation. This applies particularly to cheap wines, which can be rapidly cleared and stabilized by filtration and centrifugation.

Oak is a preoccupation of many small wine growers, red wine growers in particular. For many years, storage in large oak was the rule, probably very old oak, partly on account of the cost, partly because this was traditional. In this, Australian wine practice resembled Italian rather than French custom.

When wine-makers, mainly following the lead of Penfold, started to use small oak for about a year to introduce the wood tannins which so enhance the flavour of the best French wines, they immediately began to confront a new range of problems. First, there was the considerable cost. A grower who crushes 70 tonnes will be using about 120 hogsheads to mature his wine. These 65-gallon (300-litre) vessels cost, in 1983, about $400 each. Thus, there is a maturation cost directly attributable to the vessel of about 25 to 50 cents a litre before one considers interest and other opportunity costs. Using small oak is very expensive.

There are other problems: should the grower import the casks fully assembled, as is the case at Mount Mary, in the Yarra Valley, or should they be reassembled in Australia from numbered imported pieces? Or should growers rely on Babidge or Schahinger, or some other Australian cooper? There are very few Australian coopers, and most of them are located in South Australia, where the industry has been largest for longest, but as Australian costs are so high, it may be cheaper to import the barrels. Then, it may be that the oak which reaches Australia, like the cork, is not very good, on the average. The best oak from France is used in Bordeaux, Burgundy or Cognac, the best German oak on the Rhine or Mosel, and the American oak is regarded by most Australian wine-makers as too aggressive, with its strong, vanilla-like phenols. (In fact, the best American oak goes to Spain to the sherry producers, so it, too, is not widely available.)

Small quantities of wine can be given very individual attention with the use of oak. A strange blend of equal quantities of Zinfandel, Pinot Noir and Cabernet Sauvignon, from a high-trellised, drip-irrigated experimental plot on a red-brown earth near Clare, is fermented at a low temperature, 20°C or so, in stainless steel, under a blanket of carbon dioxide, for about two weeks. Pressed in an air-bag press, a hogshead-full is taken off as free-run juice, after a little sulphur treatment. Left to itself, deep purple but quite bright, it loses a little of its acid in the malolactic fermentation. By now, it has been moved to another winery, for bottling 65 gallons is hard in a big winery.

The wine-maker screws a huge corkscrew into the bung and bangs the collar up against the handpiece, lifting the bung out through the screen of paraffin wax. His eyes light up. 'Listen to that!' And one can hear the crackle of the ferment without putting ear to bung hole. 'Let's see, it's November now: we'll bottle it after vintage.'

He centrifuges and filters it first, and bottles the tiny quantity with hand-operated equipment. A light wine, rather unlike most Clare wines, with surprisingly deep fruit on the palate, it needs a year or two in bottle for the small amount of oak tannins it has absorbed to integrate. The labour it has taken makes it impossible to reproduce.

Not all red wines receive or deserve such care, however.

When the consumption of red wines stopped increasing in the early 1970s, many makers who mainly sought to produce red wines tried various tricks to make red wines interchangeable with white. In essence, an Australian equivalent of Beaujolais was sought. It is worth describing one such exercise, called 'April Red', which was successful technically but not in the market-place.

The name was chosen because it was to be a wine which could be sold six to eight weeks after vintage. The aim, in the words of T. C. Somers, was to make light reds with 'bright clarity of colour with an impression of freshness and fruit flavour, and they must be "light in style".' In his work on the effects of time on wine, Somers had noted that newly fermented red wines with very limited extraction showed these desirable characteristics, which are then lost in conservation. Thus, from a hot area, low alcohol and a pH in the range 3.4–3.7 are possible, because malic acid is still present. If the pH is higher, acid may be added at the crusher. To avoid phenolics, the wines could be taken off skins at 10°–11° Baumé, during a cold fermentation with almost no sulphur dioxide. The wines would be promptly racked, and cold-stabilized and fined with bentonite under carbon dioxide or nitrogen blanketing for seven to ten days at $-3°C$. They could then be bottled with sterile filtration or hot bottled at 60°C.

The pigments in the resulting wines are rather different from those produced by traditional fermentation, and the wines were found to be very stable and fresh in character. However, without the market resources of a Philip Morris or a

Reckitt & Colman, these wines have not captured the public imagination; perhaps their merits were insufficient. Perhaps carbonic maceration will produce the right light dry red wines for drinking in copious quantities in hot weather. Perhaps the Gamay will provide them. Perhaps no one wants them, but this is very hard to believe.

Viticulture

The grape vine grows vigorously for half the year, and as a true vine cannot support its own weight. It bears fruit on the canes, or new wood, which have grown since the previous winter's dormancy. For both of these reasons, the vine has always required training and pruning.

Left to itself, each bud on the old wood yields a cane with several bunches, so that an unpruned vine will produce large numbers of very small bunches. As each bunch must be removed with a separate cut of the picker's blade, picking time is roughly proportional to the number of bunches. Pruned hard, a vine will produce small numbers of large bunches. Hard pruning, therefore, is the norm. It is frequently stated that ripening is more certain and more even if there are few bunches, all located close to the main branches of the vine, but this may not be true in regions of superabundant sun.

Because a vine, like water, finds its own level, it needs support. It can be pruned as a bush, into a goblet shape, so that four or five arms rise half a metre above the ground and the new wood grows from a few buds left on a couple of spurs on each arm. This is the simplest, cheapest method; growth is contained, bunches are large, the fruit is kept off the ground. Alternatively, the vine can be trained up a post or along a wire. Because of the type of timber available and the prevalence of termites, wires tend to be used supported by steel spacers at intervals with wooden strainer posts at the ends of the rows. Initially, such trellising raises the canopy of new growth hardly any higher than that on a bush vine, but it allows more buds to be left, and more fruit to be supported, since the trellis takes the weight. With every cane requiring removal by a separate cut, the number of buds left one winter determines how many cuts would be needed the one after.

In the vineyard it is dawn, but the sun is invisible, partly because of the low grey cloud coming in from the east, partly because the patch of brightness in the grey has yet to reach the dry-stone dyke along the skyline. The pruner groans, rubs his eyes and rolls out of bed. He shrugs on an old boiler suit, pulls on an older army greatcoat and a scruffy knitted woollen cap. He makes tea and fries two eggs and, in ten minutes, unshaven, is hunched up at the end of a quarter of a mile of gnarled bushes, fifteen or twenty canes rising a yard from each one's five stumpy arms.

After half an hour, his spare hand is blue with cold, and his nose, acting like a condenser, runs steadily. He has not yet brought out the old Ferguson to weed under the vines, so the Salvation Jane (*Echium*), soursob (*Oxalis pescaprae*) and dock which dominate the weeds along the rows have soaked the skirts of his greatcoat. He has to weed by hand a little at the base of every vine to check that there has been no shooting from the fifteen-year-old wood, and the red-brown earth is slowly transferring itself in larger quantities to his soaked sleeves.

Then the rain begins, and he curses and pulls his cap down closer over his eyes. Rain drips into them, and he cuts the fleshy part of his thumb just a little and curses again.

The rain is still a light drizzle, but coming from the east it will get worse. He raises his eyes momentarily and looks across the valley to the light grey gums above the vines. They merge into the gusting drizzle. He takes a bottle of raisin liqueur muscat from the deep pocket of the greatcoat and swigs, a big mouthful. Then he bends to his task. Another hour and the sodden greatcoat weighs a ton and there is a minor torrent down his spine, where the pleats open as he moves, and there is only one thickness of khaki felt. He sighs and plods on.

At noon, he stops and stomps back to the house, hangs his coat over an electric heater and, as he heats some tomato soup, reflects that electricity prices have risen 50 per cent in a year.

After donning dry clothes and a plastic raincoat with a rip under one arm, he plods out again, but the storm has arrived and he cannot prune where he cannot see a foot. The midweek movie is Ray Milland in *The Lost Weekend*, enlivened by crackles and flashes of lightning.

The storm passes and, as the sun disappears behind the trees on the far slope, the clear, pale-red sky suggests that he may make up time next day. As the moon rises behind the stone wall, he squelches back for a meal of fried lamb chops, potatoes and peas, and the news.

He is not a pioneer: he is a blocker. As J. K. Galbraith wrote:

> A more commonplace consequence of an early exposure to agriculture is a deeply valid appreciation of manual labour. It leaves all of minimal sensitivity with an enduring knowledge of its unpleasantness. A long day following a plodding, increasingly reluctant team behind a harrow endlessly back and forth over the uninspiring Ontario terrain persuaded one that all other work was easy.

Yet pioneering in Australia was much harder. How hard is difficult to appreciate, almost impossible to experience. The first vineyards in Australia were planted on land cleared by convicts hired out to landowners, and few records exist of how they worked, but manual labour, rarely supported by animals, felled the trees, burnt the stumps, cut and sawed the logs, hoed and dug the unworked soil, collected the stones into heaps or built walls with them and planted and tended the vines.

When we think of the pioneers in New South Wales – Blaxland, Busby, Macarthur – we are thinking of the colonial elite; their land was worked by forced labour, nameless and unremarked. In the other colonies, the pioneering vignerons had no alternative but to work their own land or pay free labourers.

The pruner, Australia's nearest equivalent to the peasant farmer, will go on working his own vines in this dismal fashion indefinitely. However, over the last fifteen years, it has become more difficult for larger enterprises to hire satisfactory pruners, and much more expensive to pay them. For this reason, mechanical pruning has become quite widespread. Even in Bordeaux, of course, similar influences are at work, but a shortage of rural labour has been widespread in Australia for many years.

For best results, mechanical pruning requires mechanical harvesting since so many more buds are left that hand harvesting would be hopelessly uneconomic.

As with any innovation in an industry where tradition is vitally important, the merits of mechanical pruning, or more properly machine-assisted pruning, have been fiercely argued. The machines used include hand-held cutter-bars, i.e. with reciprocating blades, circular saws, chain saws and band saws. Those with cutter-bars or band saws are much safer than circular saws, and may be expected to dominate the industry, either imported from France or locally made.

Several different approaches to machine-assisted pruning have been made. In some irrigated areas, it was initially introduced with no follow-up hand pruning, and the result was a dense, tangled hedge of new and old wood, which after three years required extensive hand pruning. Since these early experiences, it has been used more judiciously, the vines being first hedged with machines and then pruned by hand. In the irrigated river areas, where vines have massive trellises to support huge loads of fruit, as much as 90 per cent of the pruning can be done mechanically, whereas in dryland areas mechanical pruning is simply a preliminary to the handwork necessary to keep bud numbers adjusted to water availability, whether supplementary watering is used or not. Used in this way, mechanical pruning can reduce the cost of pruning by between 30 and 50 per cent, including an allowance for depreciation of machinery. Such a major saving in costs means that mechanical pruning will certainly be a permanent feature of the wine-growing industry in Australia but, as it requires mechanical harvesting, it will not be universal. This is partly because of the vexed question of wine quality and partly because the economies of scale in mechanical harvesting are not the same as in mechanical pruning.

Both the CSIRO at Merbein, on the Murray, and some of the major growers, such as Penfold, at Coonawarra, have carried out trials of wines made from fruit from mechanically pruned vines, and could not detect any differences. However, some of this lack of difference may relate to the fact that sensory evaluation of wines is not sufficiently sensitive to detect the small differences which may be occurring, so over a period there may be a consistent small advantage to hand pruned as against mechanically pruned fruit.

Mechanical harvesting is a different question but, as noted, very closely related. If a contractor can be obtained, and the vineyard has been planned for mechanical harvesting, with long rows so that most of the contractor's time is spent harvesting and not manoeuvring, then as small an area as one hectare may be profitably harvested mechanically. More commonly, however, four hectares would be a minimum. Anyone who wishes to buy a machine should have at least forty hectares of producing vines. This is where decisions about mechanical harvesting and mechanical pruning interact. There will also be extraneous factors, such as how easy it is to deliver mechanically harvested fruit, which, having been torn from the bunch by vibration, is even more unstable and likely to oxidize than fruit picked by hand. It is for this reason that most mechanical harvesting is carried out in the cool of the evening, and this too imposes constraints on its use. Crushers must be open at night, or else there must be field crushers available, together with gas blanketing for transport to the winery.

When mechanical harvesting was first introduced, most of the large companies carried out trials, comparing quality of wines made from mechanically harvested fruit and those from the traditional method. There is no general agreement about the effect on the best possible fruit, though most wine-makers seem slightly dubious, but for bulk wines it is unquestionably true that the fruit is of acceptable quality. There are, of course, advantages other than cost. Stems and leaves may be present in the harvested fruit to a much smaller extent, and if suitable arrangements are made to prevent the fruit oxidizing, then it will be received into the fermenters in better condition than fruit which has been picked during the hottest period of the day and trucked in the hot sun to the winery.

Provided that the soil is well drained and rain has not been excessive, so that the machines become bogged, both mechanical harvesting and pruning allow about an acre an hour to be covered. Thus, if yields are very high, the overall saving may be very great, but shy-bearing vines in low-yielding country will not return such savings. Like all moves towards capital intensity, this mechanization carries its own risks, such as inability to use the machines after very heavy rain. The sight of the ungainly machines trapped like blowflies in gravy at Coonawarra in the wet 1983 vintage would put many off mechanical harvesting for ever.

Apart from such exceptional cases, timing of harvest can be much more precise, given control of the equipment, so that this final advantage may be the critical one for a big company with a large area of vines in an area producing high-quality fruit. Not having to coordinate a large team of pickers in a relatively remote location allows a vineyard manager to make more exact decisions under less stress and uncertainty. In Burgundy, the house of Prosper Maufoux now uses mechanical harvesting wherever possible and has after two years' trial identified a further advantage, though not one which is hoped for or expected every year. If early rain has caused bunch rot, but there has been a dry period before vintage, the rotten berries will have dried and shrivelled on to their stalks, so that only the sound berries are shaken off.

Fungal diseases may more generally be controlled by mechanization. It is possible to spray from the air precisely when the weather and vines require it. For some of the more humid regions, frequent spraying with heavy metal or sulphur compounds may cause oenological problems, but these are soluble in principle.

Phylloxera has a different cause, but one which is also preventable. It is the worst insect pest of grapes and vines. A root louse, it used to be called *Phylloxera vastatrix*, a much more descriptive name than its present correct name, *Phylloxera vitifoliae*. As is well known, it is a native of North America, confined to the area east of the Rocky Mountains, where it exists in small numbers on the various North American relations of *Vitis vinifera*, such as *Vitis riparia*, *Vitis rupestris* and *Vitis labrusca*.

Examples were brought to Europe for scientific investigation in about 1860 and, whether from these or as illegal immigrants on American vines brought to Europe, the insect was first noticed just north of Avignon on *Vitis vinifera* in 1865. By 1872, it was found from the west of Montpellier to north of Valence to south-east of Marseilles. By 1880 virtually every important vignoble was affected.

The devastation to this very important industry was such that an extraordinary variety of remedies was tried but, by the late 1870s, various French scientists had suggested grafting *Vitis vinifera* on to North American rootstocks, such as *V. riparia* and *V. rupestris*, which were resistant to the root louse.

It was about the same time that phylloxera was first reported in Australia, near Geelong. Soon afterwards it was found near Melbourne, then in central and north-eastern Victoria, reaching Sydney by 1900, where the Minchinbury champagne vineyards were devastated, as were those around Albury and Corowa, on the Murray.

Grafted vines were very expensive and, since South Australia had already come to dominate wine production, in many areas wine growing was simply abandoned. Around Rutherglen, in north-eastern Victoria, resistant rootstocks were used quite extensively, but half a century after the first discovery of phylloxera there, the area under vines was still not back to what it had been in 1899.

The virtual abandonment of Geelong and Bendigo as wine-growing districts between 1900 and the mid-1920s probably reflects the economic difficulties which growers had as much as the problems of phylloxera. These areas have been re-established on the basis of small production of very high-quality wine, so that they do not compete with the *vins ordinaires* produced on an enormous scale by the national marketing companies.

None of this means that the problem of phylloxera has been solved. It still lurks near Sydney, and in the Goulburn Valley and, further east, in Victoria. Where the wine industry was kept going with resistant rootstocks, phylloxera was able to survive on the roots, and not be a problem. It is thus waiting to devastate large plantings of vines on their own roots. It is a particular problem on heavy clay soils which crack, and there is much clay soil along the Goulburn River. Some of the vineyards there have suffered very severe losses recently, since young vines can become almost totally unproductive after only three or four years of infestation.

Phylloxera has not moved much in the last eighty years. In fact, it has never reached South Australia or Western Australia, though it was found in Queensland late last century. Just why it did not get to South Australia is uncertain. Interstate plant quarantine was introduced very early, and continues to the present day, but there are always irresponsible people who feel that they know better than legislators, so that it cannot simply be the result of plant quarantine. There are also considerable areas of vines on their own roots in heavy clay soils in South Australia. Whatever the reason, it has contributed to South Australia's dominance of the wine industry, at least as regards quantity, for approximately a century.

Education for wine-making

At the time of the establishment of Roseworthy Agricultural College, in 1883, the free colony of South Australia had been in existence for only forty-seven years, and the University of Adelaide for nine, yet in many ways the Agricultural College should have come first. South Australia had been the granary of Australia, on account of the good yields of wheat obtainable on the plains to the north of Adelaide, during the period of rapid population growth which followed the discovery of gold in the eastern states. However, yields of wheat had started to drop dramatically by the early 1870s, and other agricultural problems had also become evident.

The early directors of Roseworthy had a very difficult time, because they had both to run the College and teach agriculture, but the fourth principal, A. J. Perkins, was appointed to Roseworthy as government viticulturalist in 1892, and had had twelve years' South Australian experience before he became principal in 1904. A graduate of Montpellier, he introduced studies in viticulture and oenology soon after his appointment and established the College's wine cellars in the late 1890s. In fact, the dux of the course in 1896 was Leo Buring, a man who had a profound influence on the Australian wine industry until his death in 1962.

Scientific investigation of problems in oenology and viticulture had thus begun well before Australia became an independent nation, but it was not until the early 1930s that general agreement arose within the wine industry that a special course, adapted to the needs of Australia, should be established at one of the universities or agricultural colleges. Initially, there was no agreement as to the site of the course, some saying that it should be within the University of Adelaide, others saying that it should be somewhere along the River Murray, since this was where the most profitable grape growing was at the time. Luckily, A. R. Callaghan, the College principal, was an extremely vigorous and persuasive advocate for Roseworthy Agricultural College, and in November 1935 the South Australian Winemakers' Association sent a resolution to the Minister of Agriculture urging the establishment of a course at the College.

The minister accepted this urging because of both the strength of the support and the names of the supporters. Ron Martin of Stonyfell, Les Salter of Saltram, Oscar Seppelt, Thomas Hardy, Carl Angove, W. Smith, Sam Tolley, Ron Haselgrove, Karl Wiedenhofer, were among the supporters, and many of them were old students of the College, holders of its Diploma in Agriculture. Quite apart from the political backing, Martin offered a prize for wine tasting, Leo Buring one for the dux of the second year, and the Buring family offered a travelling scholarship in memory of one of their number.

It is of some interest that, just about the time that the Roseworthy course was being initiated, Herbert Kay, chairman of the Wine Board, was writing to the Registrar, University of California, Berkeley:

Dear Sir,

I have two sons aged 20 and 22 who are employed in my own wine-making business. They have good knowledge of the practical side of vine-growing and wine-making and they are anxious to have an opportunity of learning something of the scientific side of wine-making.

There is no oenological college in Australia, but I understand that there is one at your University. If this is so would you be kind enough to let me know

1 Can students take up a brief course in wine science – not to gain any degree or diploma but just to acquire knowledge?
If so, how long would such a course take?

2 What would be the approximate cost of such a course?

3 What would be the approximate cost of living for students?

If my information is wrong and the oenological college is not connected with your University, would you be kind enough to send this letter to the college which has such a course. Thanking you in anticipation.

Yours faithfully,
Herbert Kay

Half a century later, Herbert's son, who did not go to
Berkeley or even Davis, was surprised to learn of this letter,
but meanwhile Herbert's grandson had been dux of the
oenology course at Roseworthy.

When the course was established, teaching was partly carried out by two men bearing names notable in the industry.
Hickinbotham, father and grandfather of the Hickenbothams
now at Anakie, in Victoria, was one and John Fornachon, first
director of the Australian Wine Research Institute, was the
other. A Burge and a Kelly were among the first four
students, a Chaffey and a Seppelt in the second intake, though
that particular Seppelt was killed in the Second World War
and so is not one of the many Seppelts still in the firm. Wine
families have continued to support the College, not always in
the happiest circumstances. For example, when Hugo Gramp,
Thomas Hardy and Sidney Hill Smith were killed in 1938 in
an air crash on the way to a conference in Canberra, another
prize was established. More recently, as the College has
entered its second centenary, firms such as Penfold, though no
longer family firms, have continued to make substantial dona-
tions to support the College.

Some viticultural and related training was provided at
Dookie, in Victoria, for many years, and horticultural
research and education are carried out at the Universities of
Adelaide and Sydney. The major recent change has been the
introduction of strong wine-making courses at the Riverina
College of Advanced Education at Wagga Wagga, in New
South Wales.

This college opened its doors in 1971, but rapidly came to
serve both the Murrumbidgee and Murray irrigation areas,
with study centres at Griffith, on the Murrumbidgee River,
and Albury-Wodonga, on the Murray. At that time, the wine
industry was expanding strongly, and technical innovation
was widespread, so that local businessmen involved in the
wine industry saw the need for local education in oenology
and viticulture.

One of these was R. A. Potter, who was engaged in
improving wine-making technology at Griffith and was also
on the council of the new College.

As the wine industry expanded, Roseworthy was slow to
expand its well-established courses, so that pressure for a
second centre of wine-making education grew rapidly,

especially outside South Australia. This had to be different from Roseworthy, of course, so that it was decided at Wagga that they should capitalize on their developing expertise in external studies and in management and applied science. Thus, it was from the first planned that students could take their degrees while working full time in the wine industry. A lower-level course in viticulture was later established, in recognition of the lack of basic training in this vital area, and it too was aimed at external students.

The initial success of this new wine school was partly due to the need for more trained people in an expanding industry, but it was also attributable to the enthusiasm for, and involvement in, the wine industry of people such as Brian Croser, Tony Jordan, Max Loder and Don Lester, some of whom I shall be referring to again in subsequent chapters. And the fact that the course could be taken over a number of years while working full time (with occasional residential interludes at the College) meant that even from South Australia, relatively well served for research and training, wine-makers could enrol for the external degree. This particularly helps the proprietors of small wineries.

Thus, just like Roseworthy, Wagga has benefited from the fact that the leaders of the wine industry, unlike the leaders of many Australian industries, recognize the importance of scientific and technological innovation in their trade.

4

South Australia

South Australia was established by proclamation on 28 December 1836, in the name of His Majesty King William IV, who died soon afterwards, so that, apart from the first settlers in HMS *Buffalo*, the colonists were early Victorians. Not far from the spot where the colony was proclaimed, near Glenelg, seven miles from the centre of the city of Adelaide as it now is, Richard Hamilton established Ewell Vineyards before 1840. He was a wanderer, from Ewell in Surrey, though from a Scottish family, and had spent some time in New York before applying for land in the new colony of South Australia.

There is some controversy about whether Richard Hamilton or John Reynell first planted vines, but certainly Richard Hamilton arrived first, in October 1837, taking up land in June 1838, whereas John Reynell arrived in October 1838 and took up land in July 1839. However, this land had been taken up first by Thomas Lucas, and John Reynell married Mary Lucas soon after he arrived in Adelaide, so he could possibly have been in a position to plant vines as soon as he had land.

In the 'Paradise of Dissent', as Douglas Pike, Methodist moderator and first editor of the *Australian Dictionary of Biography*, called the free colony of South Australia, the way of the wine-maker was hard. When Walter Duffield sent a case of white wine to Queen Victoria in 1845 and was rewarded with a medal from Prince Albert, magistrates at Mount Barker, in the Adelaide Hills, fined him £10 for making wine without a licence. The Distillation Ordinance, under which such licences were issued, was very complex. For example, the building in which a still was housed had to be of stone with the

Clare

Watervale

Morgan

Riverland

Renmark

Tanunda

Nuriootpa
Angaston

Berri

Loxton

*Northern Adelaide
Plains*

Roseworthy

Barossa Valley

Springton

Adelaide

Southern Vales

McLaren Vale

Langhorne
Creek

KANGAROO ISLAND

ENCOUNTER
BAY

NEW SOUTH WALES

VICTORIA

Padthaway

Coonawarra

0   100
└────────┘ km

Mount Gambier

Wine-growing regions of South Australia

stones laid to a particular pattern, all tubs and pails had to be numbered and the door had to have two sets of locks and keys, one for the distiller, one for the Government agent. Since a licence cost £50 and was necessary for a wine-maker, then given the high frequency of failure at the time, this was a real disincentive to wine-makers. However, the demand for the product was there, and public drunkenness from over-consumption of ardent spirits was very frequent in the early days of the colony, despite its establishment by pious Dissenters, including large numbers of Methodists.

One can see how the industry developed in South Australia by following a few family fortunes. In time, these became the Australian wine industry's fortunes.

All around Adelaide, while it grew as a small colonial town, vineyards were established. In many cases, wine was for personal consumption only, but others saw further ahead. One such was a Scottish doctor, A. C. Kelly, from whose works I have already quoted. He made good wine to the south of Adelaide for twenty years until over-expansion and a break in the market forced him to sell up. However, the commercial acumen of Thomas Hardy, another early immigrant winemaker, allowed the vineyards to persist and prosper.

Christopher Rawson Penfold was probably the second medical practitioner after Dr Kelly to establish a vineyard in South Australia. Penfold arrived with his wife Mary and baby daughter in a 350-ton ship, the *Taglioni*, in late 1844 and took up a substantial property at Magill, four miles due east of the city centre. A great believer in the medicinal powers of good wine, Penfold brought with him grape cuttings from some of the notable wine areas of France. In particular, he brought Grenache, from the Rhône. Building or enlarging a stone cottage, which they called the Grange, and planting vines immediately, Dr and Mrs Penfold also established their vineyard in the same year, leading to the company's slogan, '1844 to evermore'. Penfold was not only a successful general practitioner and a fine wine grower and businessman, but also first chairman of the district council. Partly because her husband was so busy, Mary Penfold made the wine with the aid of Ellen Timberall, maid and companion. She was thus the first female wine-maker in Australia, a fact not always noted.

Despite the medicinal powers of wine, Penfold died at the age of 59 in 1870, and was succeeded in managing the firm by his wife and his son-in-law, T. F. Hyland. Within ten years of his death, the firm had twenty-four hectares planted in vines, mainly Mataro, Grenache, Pedro Ximenez and Tokay, and were buying over 200 tonnes of grapes from other growers. The vintage cellar was approximately twenty metres square, the storage cellar rather larger. When Mary Penfold died in 1892, Penfold was one of the largest wineries in Australia.

The Grange Cottage, from which the most remarkable of the

Penfold wines takes its name, was almost demolished soon after the Second World War, but was restored as a result of protestations by some members of the family, and opened for a time as a museum in 1949. It is no longer open to the public.

There were still over 100 hectares of vines at Magill at that time, and vintage went on until 1972, when all operations were transferred to Nuriootpa. When Tooth & Co., the Sydney brewers, took over Penfold in the early 1970s, the Auldana vineyard, which had been bought in 1942 from a receiver, was subdivided for building blocks, as small areas of land are called in Australia. Most of the Grange Vineyard itself has now gone the same way.

The Swan Valley wine-maker, Houghton, is making very good wines from a large vineyard of John Roche, in south-western Western Australia. It therefore seems a little odd that the reduction of the Grange Vineyard at Magill from a thirty-five-hectare vineyard, together with the winery buildings and the Grange Cottage itself, to a ten-hectare fragment surrounding the buildings, a development which 'released' 169 building lots, should be partly carried out by Roche, who is also a former lord mayor of Adelaide. The buildings are on the Register of State Heritage Items, but the vines and the land beneath them are not.

When N. S. Khrushchev made his famous secret speech to the twentieth party congress of the USSR in 1956, he attempted to end the cult of Stalin's personality. He did not fail completely, but in any case there was a recrudescence of the phenomenon in the last years of L. I. Brezhnev. Perhaps a personality cult is unnecessary in a long-established society where the system of government is taken for granted. The Australian wine industry is not yet in this happy state, where the vignerons know what to do in any given circumstance and wine buyers never know their names. The architects of the great cathedrals of medieval Europe are unknown, as (to all but a very few historians) are the great wine-makers who developed Claret, Burgundy, Hock, Sauternes, Sherry, Champagne, Port and all the others as we know them today.

In Australia, as the struggle to come to terms with a constantly changing market and a hostile climate continues, the wine-maker is a prince at least. Fortunately, because wine is such a civilizing and moderating influence, wine people, even those inflated to three or four times their original size by the press, remain relatively tolerable. Max Schubert is a man resistant to the pressures of publicity. He had to work hard for his success.

His career illustrates much of the history of the wine industry over the half century that he has been with Penfold, but some aspects of it could only have been possible within a family firm, and a rather old-fashioned one at that. When he joined Penfold, diseased wines were everywhere, and the problem was to keep them drinkable for at least three months, so that they could be sold. I have discussed these problems in the previous chapter.

Lesley Penfold Hyland gave Schubert his start, sending him to the School of Mines, as it then was, to learn chemistry. After the Second World War, he was promoted from laboratory attendant to wine-maker, and visited France in 1949–50.

Returning, and given some authority, he was able to make important changes. In viticulture, he ripped out the Grenache at the Grange vineyard itself and, in replanting there and elsewhere, changed the spacing to make the vines work harder. He began experimenting, inspired by what he had seen in Bordeaux. He wanted to use oak in the way the Bordeaux wine-makers use it, to add additional flavour and complexity in the most effective way, with small barrels of new wood, no larger than 300 litres, to allow increased area of contact with the timber and hence greater extraction of tannins from the wood.

Although Schubert aimed to make the best red wine in Australia, he also wanted the wine to be sold in relatively large quantities. The target was about 5,000 cases – hardly a third of Château Latour's – but this has only been reached in the best years, with very poor years allowing less than half as much to be made.

In 1952, Kalimna, in the Barossa, was Penfold's only source of Cabernet Sauvignon, and they could not persuade their contracted growers to plant it. They therefore had to use Shiraz, until then regarded largely as a reliable port variety. They had a number of individual vineyards growing Shiraz with particular, reliable characteristics which Schubert aimed to combine. The vineyards included one at Morphett Vale, now covered with housing, and others at Coonawarra, Clare, Kalimna and Eden Valley, and of course the Grange itself.

The technique used aimed to bring the various lots of fruit

in, crush them, run the juice off skins, cool in a heat exchanger, and then put the skins back. There had to be a little oxidation to develop complexity and flavour; totally protecting red fruit from oxidation could lead to instability later. Some sugar was retained when extraction had finished, then the wine would be put into new wood, where the malolactic fermentation would occur. During the development of Grange Hermitage, and indeed in all of Penfold's red wine-making, stuck fermentation was not a problem. Initially, fermentation would be at 15°C, then rise to 18–20°C, perhaps 18–22° by the end of fermentation. The juice would be left on skins for a week.

While some fruit from Magill has always gone into Grange Hermitage, it has gone into up to three other wines as well, St Henri and Bin 389 in particular, Penfold's top three wines in most cases, as Magill fruit has always reliably allowed really deep fruit flavour to develop. Initially, 40–50 per cent of Grange Hermitage was from Magill. At recent tastings, the second commercial release, 1953, has seemed the best, with 1963, 1952, 1955 and 1956 following in roughly that order. However, Schubert himself believes that the 1971 and 1976 will, when they are sufficiently old, equal the 1953. He made the wines to be enormous at first, so that as they aged they would become more elegant, never seeming overweight and always staying alive. In addition to their enormous depth of fruit, Schubert has always aimed at achieving absolute balance early on, since he believes that a wine with a fault will stay a faulty wine forever. Totally different from the much lighter, subtle yet earthy Shiraz wines of the Hunter or the huge, fruity examples from north-eastern Victoria, Grange Hermitage is a unique and outstanding Australian wine.

In 1909, the metropolitan vineyards of Adelaide were almost 1,000 hectares in extent, from fifty hectares each for Penfold and Auldana, at Magill, and Hamilton's thirty at Glenelg to vineyards of less than half a hectare at East Adelaide, almost in the city. Almost all of this has now disappeared; the map gives an indication of the remaining wineries. And there were vineyards in towns such as Maitland, Kapunda, Stansbury, Curramulka and Rhynie where none now survives.

In Australia, the years of the First World War began with a

Approximate boundary of built-up area

to Barossa & Clare

to Adelaide Plains

Main North Road

Tea Tree Gully

Modbury
Angove

Douglas A. Tolley

Torrens River

Norman

Adelaide

Seaview

Penfold's Grange

Uraidla

Glenelg

Woodley

Summertown

AUSTRALIAN
WINE RESEARCH
INSTITUTE

Mount Lofty

Piccadilly

Petaluma

0   4
km

South Road

to Southern Vales

Adelaide and Environs

devastating drought, one of the worst on record. Herbert Kay of Amery, in South Australia's Southern Vales, wrote to his brother in January 1914: 'My dear Fred, Many thanks for yours of 14 December. Things here are looking very dicky for the vintage, no rain, currants will be a poor crop, wine grapes mostly skin and seeds.'

On 5 February, he wrote again: 'I start vintage Wednesday 11th February and look forward to a very light one. The Mataro may save the situation but the Shiraz and Cabernet are shocking. Currants will be much lighter crop than last year.'

A few days later he was writing again to Fred:

'I was much interested in your account of the interview with Burgoyne [a wine shipper]. I hope they will treat us better in future but have no great faith though I do think both Cuthbert and Burney [staff of Burgoyne's] are fairer than the others we have dealt with.

I have sent away the 150 hogsheads to go per *Homeric* and have cancelled the other two shipments – I had to do it to secure hogsheads for the *Homeric*. I am very glad I have done it as the vintage is very early and my hands are full. We start currants tomorrow. Nine pickers are here. I expect two more tomorrow and three on Monday. If they turn up we shall be full handed, which is well and we must hurry if we are to save the Shiraz and Cabernet. The vines look awful, yellow everywhere except in the gullies. I tried Kell's grapes yesterday, nine and a half and beginning to shrivel, I told them to start picking on Monday, the density will be low but there will be some juice in them, of course if rain comes all will be altered but at present it looks bad.

Yields were indeed down: from about thirty-five tonnes of Cabernet Sauvignon to about twenty-one tonnes, the vintage starting halfway through February, so that one finds an entry: 'picking suspended until Monday owing to heat'.

For other wineries, the war was also a time of change. At Hamilton's, the two young brothers Eric and Robert took over a company run down during the war years.

It is said that over 1,000 gallons were made at Ewell in 1840, but Sydney Hamilton told me that, until the First World

War, 18,000 gallons formed the biggest vintage, so that 1,000 gallons from what must have been the first crop seems rather unlikely, unless Richard Hamilton had bought in a substantial number of grapes from unidentified growers.

Three of Richard Hamilton's sons went to Victoria, seeking gold, in the gold rush, but found it better to sell provisions to miners, and returned to South Australia in due course, their fortunes not made but hardly diminished.

Hamilton's increased substantially in size around 1860, but it stayed a relatively small family winery for many years. Mechanization came early, in the form of what was called a horse works, simply a horse-driven crown wheel and pinion which worked a crusher, labour being far too scarce for treading the grapes, whether by the white feet of laughing girls or the heavy leather thigh boots of Surrey yeomen.

Many remarkable techniques were tried out in the early days. For example, from a runaway French sailor in the 1870s Hamilton learned how to make a wine resembling the *vin de paille* of the Rhône, where the Grenache and Carignan grapes were laid on straw to dry them and concentrate the juice before crushing. With this technique, smaller quantities of stronger wine could be made, and better control could be exerted, for runaway fermentation was the norm in the hot Adelaide autumn and huge quantities of spirit were used to stop it. Hamilton's last vintage of this kind was in 1920, about the time a distillery was built.

By this time, most of the wines were fortified, both because of the problems with fermentation mentioned already and because fortified wines were what the market demanded. Beverage wines were regarded as fit only for weaklings. This at least meant that when a lower wine tariff, an effective subsidy to Imperial wines, was provided by the British government in about 1925, wineries such as Hamilton's were in a good position to export. However, before that they had seen a brief post-war boom and then a collapse in 1923. In the middle of vintage, in March of that year, Hamilton's, like most other vignerons, had had no orders at all.

For the first hundred years of export of wine from Australia to Britain, almost all of it was table wine. Although they travelled well, fortified wines were more expensive to make and attracted higher duties in Britain, so that they could hardly compete with Portugal or Spain. The treaty between

Britain and Portugal in 1916, which prevented the use of the words 'port' and 'madeira' to describe wines not from Oporto or Madeira, was also a great handicap. It was very easy to sneer at a wine labelled 'port type', and to assume that it was a poor imitation. It is no doubt partly for this reason that the inappropriate European names continue to be used throughout Australia, handicapping the development of meaningful regional names as well as inviting complaints from wine writers and European wine-makers.

After the war, the Federal Government, through the State Government, set returned servicemen up on small farms in many different areas, to aid the policy of closer settlement as well as to rehabilitate the demobilized soldiers. Some took up dairying, others wheat growing, still others grape growing, especially in the new irrigation areas along the River Murray. In 1924, the Australian government, noticing that soldier-settlers' blocks were producing a great deal of fruit suitable for fortified wine, introduced an export bounty. This itself was an incentive to export, but when the Empire Preferential Tariff gave its 50 per cent difference in excise for ten years, the possibility of dramatic increases in sales was soon realized. Later, the bounty was reduced by stages, but by then this new Empire trade was well established. This was despite problems such as that caused by giving six months' notice of intention to reduce the bounty in 1927, an announcement which was followed by wild hunting for cargo space on ships and for storage space in London. Imports into England in fact rose from less than nine million litres in 1926 to twenty million litres in 1927. Apart from creating an over-supply, these shipments did nothing to enhance the reputation of Australian wine, for they were not properly treated in bond, and much bad wine was sold. It was at about this time that the Australian Wine Board was created; in 1930, and soon afterward, under the leadership of Herbert Kay, it arranged for bacterial spoilage to be investigated, as was discussed in the previous chapter.

This time of over-supply of poorly cared-for wines is described indirectly in *Casanova's Chinese Restaurant*, where the narrator describes how he 'had bought the bottle labelled *Tawny Wine (port flavour)* which even Moreland had been later unwilling to drink. . . . Following a preliminary tasting, we poured the residue of the bottle down the lavatory.'

During this period, when the Australian wine industry was as usual struggling to find an identity and more importantly struggling with these problems of excessive shipments on consignment, a federal viticultural congress was held at Leonay, Emu Plains, near Sydney, in New South Wales, and on Friday, 4 October 1929, an al fresco Luncheon and International Wine Sampling was conducted. The location was symptomatic of an industry not controlling its own destiny; the centre of the industry was Adelaide, far from where important financial decisions were taken. The menu was heroic: 'brandied prunes; salt herrings; hot dogs; mustard dressing (kindly donated by the SPCA and mustard club); sliced fowl, ham, bully beef; Leonay asparagus; sauce vinaigrette (latter item provided by the United Vinegarons of Australia); cheese and salads; dessert; cafe.'

The wine list was even more remarkable: 'sherry; hock; Chablis; Sauternes; Claret; Burgundy; port and dessert wines and some *vins ordinaires* (presented by some ten more or less wine-growing countries of this universe). No restrictions on quantity.'

The Hocks included H. Buring & Sobels Ltd Springvale Riesling 1923, Lindeman Cawarra 1924, Eltviller Taubenburg Rhein 1919, and De Pury Victoria. Among the Burgundies were Burgoyne's (Victoria) 'sent on transport to England during war and subsequently returned', Gevrey-Chambertin (France, 1920), and Lindeman 1923, 'bottled in Scotland'.

The industry's ability to cooperate was at its best on such occasions.

The 1930s were quite prosperous times for the Australian wine industry, what was left of it after the depredations of phylloxera and the hard market times of the Edwardian period and the war, but the Second World War once more damaged it substantially; from 1941 to 1944, virtually no Australian wine at all was shipped to Britain.

When wine was once more exported to Britain after the war, it was at only 40 per cent of the 1939 level, which had been about 18,000 tonnes. Imperial Preference ensured some Australian exports, particularly of fortified wine, until Britain entered the European Economic Community.

The Barossa Valley

The Barossa Valley takes its name from Colonel William Light's participation in the Peninsular War; the mis-spelling no doubt

Barossa Valley

arose because signposts and maps were not being prepared in
large numbers by the time that Light died, and few of the
settlers were familiar with the Iberian Peninsula. Light was
the first surveyor-general of the new colony. His old comman-
der and patron, Lord Lyndoch, is commemorated in the name
of one of the towns in the Barossa Valley.

The fact that the Barossa was very largely settled by Germans came about in a curious way.

George Fife Angas, a rich and successful Scottish businessman and landowner, who was very active in promoting
the South Australian colony in London, saw it as providing 'a

73

place of refuge for pious Dissenters of Great Britain, who could in their new home discharge their consciences before God in civil and religious duties without any disabilities . . . a place where the children of pious farmers might have farms on which to settle and provide bread for their families.' However, the largest single group of pious Dissenters which Angas brought to South Australia consisted of Lutherans, led by Pastor Kavel, who were leaving religious persecution in Prussia, following the establishment of the national church there. A Particular Baptist, Angas had to grapple with his conscience before deciding whether to aid Lutherans but, in the event, the combination of the opportunities to promote the colony by bringing out more immigrants and to aid Dissenters was sufficient to sway him. The first group arrived in November 1838; by the end of 1847, over 2,500 had arrived.

Angas lent them a considerable amount of money, partly so that they could buy 2,000 acres at £10 per acre in the hills which were the sources of the Gawler and Rhine Rivers. (Like many other German place-names, this Rhine became the Para River at a time of anti-German feeling.)

After the 1848 revolution, the influx of immigrants from Germany increased greatly, in fact more than trebling over the next decade, so that when the colony was twenty years old over 7 per cent of the population were German immigrants. While a considerable number of the Germans were farmers, many were more familiar with mining than with wine, and worked along-side Cornishmen in the copper mines of Burra and Kapunda. Nonetheless, the community they created is notable because in it developed Australia's largest single wine-growing region.

Although the Barossa Valley was largely peopled by Ger-mans, they were not from wine-growing localities, and so it was a very long time before the promise of the higher areas for making good-quality Riesling became evident. Perhaps also the fact that railway workers wore heavy jackets and hats to work in the middle of summer and did not expect anything to be refrigerated, since the means had not been invented, also meant that robust red or fortified wines in fact suited the climate better, whatever their effects on the head. However, soon after the First World War, wine-makers such as Rudy Kronberger, an Austrian at Yalumba, and Sydney Hamilton, an Australian at Hamilton's, tried to make light, relatively dry white wines, feeling that a market for such wines must exist if they could only be made successfully. Yalumba Carte d'Or and Hamilton's Ewell Moselle were the results. For fifty years, Yalumba's Carte d'Or Riesling has had a considerable amount of Eden Valley Riesling in it, though the earlier ones, like Hamilton's Ewell Moselle, would have had many sherry varieties as their base. These have been reliable wines, blended to a standard for about sixty years, and one feels that they will go on in this way indefinitely, gradually becoming relatively more and more inexpensive compared with the current market favourites. It is in the area of making very reliable wines up to a quality and down to a price that the big Australian wine-makers excel.

Yalumba is one of the three big wine companies still in family hands, the other two being Hardy and McWilliam. However, Yalumba is rather different.

It was founded by Samuel Smith, a Dorsetshire brewer, who arrived in Adelaide in 1847, settling first at Klemzig, a German colony near the city of Adelaide. Soon, however, Smith needed to move further afield to establish himself, and he took a job with George Fife Angas eighty kilometres north-east, near what is now Angaston.

Having bought twelve hectares to establish a vineyard, Smith began to develop it at night while working for Angas during the day. It was not, however, that first small vineyard which established his fortune, but rather the £300-worth of gold which he got at the diggings in Victoria in the early 1850s. This allowed him to expand the vineyard and build his first winery. Within a decade, his wine was starting to sell well, as it has ever since.

The façade of the cellars is an imposing bluestone structure, two storeys high, with a large clock tower. It was built in the late nineteenth century, when Samuel Smith's son and grandsons expanded the business. When the grandsons retired, two great-grandsons took over, now with the surname Hill Smith, the name Hill coming from the family connection to the same Hills who had produced one of Australia's finest left-handed batsmen, Clem Hill, in the era before the First World War. There are now members of the sixth generation of the family working at Yalumba.

What has distinguished Yalumba from the other family dynasties is that it has kept one base, at Angaston, even though it has about 200 hectares of vines on the Murray as well as about the same amount in the Barossa. Thus, all its wine-making activities, from crushing to bottling and storage, are under one series of roofs.

Yalumba has always been successful in blending to a quality, whether in its Galway Pipe Port, its Galway Vintage Claret or its Carte d'Or Riesling. The Claret, a blend of Cabernet Sauvignon from Oxford Landing, on the Murray, Shiraz from the higher areas around the Barossa Valley and minor quantities of other varieties from the Barossa, is distinguished by the fact that a particular bottling of the 1961 vintage was described in 1966 by the then Prime Minister, the late Sir Robert Menzies, as the best Australian Claret he had ever tasted. Politicians' jokes tend always to be at other people's expense; few who subsequently bought or tasted the wine concurred in his judgement, though it was indeed a fair wine which lasted well.

In recent years, the best parts of Yalumba's 20,000-tonne crush have gone into special bottlings of reds with various family members' and others' signatures on them, and into their Pewsey Vale Riesling and other wines made from a vineyard in the cooler Barossa Hills, about 500 metres above sea level. The signatures have included that of a notable racehorse trainer, for the Hill Smiths have strong connections with the racing world. The skill of the makers and the large range of material from which they choose, was evident from Christabel Hill Smith's blend of Shiraz and Cabernet Sauvignon, made in 1974. Unlike most wines from that poor year, it had clean, elegant fruit in plenty, and a softness which made it attractive early. Later, better years have produced better, longer-living blends, but not so much better than their fellows with lesser labels. They typify what the Barossa should make.

Seppeltsfield is, like Yalumba, a family monument as well as the centre of a large wine empire now owned by the South Australian Brewing Company. In Seppelt's case, this embraces Château Tanunda nearby in the Barossa and vineyards or wineries at Qualco, on the Murray, and Clare, in South Australia, at Great Western, Clydeside and Drumborg, in Victoria, and at Barooga, in New South Wales.

The huge storage sheds for fortified wines and the old houses, distillery and winery buildings are flanked on one side by enormous car parks for the vast numbers of tourists who congregate at weekends and on the other by the creek into which winery wastes went a century ago. Well maintained and painted in the Seppelts' tasteful green and fawn, the village has a slightly melancholy air, a hint of Fatepur Sikri at times, because it is no longer inhabited by the army of workers the vineyard and winery required when Benno Seppelt was building them up. At vintage time, of course, it feels different, and the only peaceful spot is at the top of the nearby hill. Here stands the eclectically Greek family mausoleum, designed by one of the family, on which I can recall climbing in company with a small Seppelt when as little boys we waited for someone who was working down below.

Although founded by a German immigrant in 1850, Seppelt saw its biggest expansion in a later era, buying Clydeside at Rutherglen just before the First World War and Great Western in western Victoria at its end. Drumborg was planted in about 1960 to provide cold area fruit, and Clare over a decade later for similar reasons. Today, Seppeltsfield is the centre for fortified wines, both sweet and dry, which have consistently been among the best in the country. The DP series of Australian sherries is particularly good, for example. The 'fino' is light, dry, clean and yet full of flavour, having just the right quantity of aldehydes and related compounds. At Château Tanunda a range of very reliable table wines is made. During the many years when such wines were out of favour, the Greenock Sauternes, made mainly from Sémillon, were reliably fruity, though never quite luscious enough.

Not all Barossa wineries are as large as Yalumba, Penfold, Kaiserstuhl or Seppelt, but some aim to grow very rapidly. Two long-established South Australian beverage companies were brought to the stock market in 1983. A comparison between them illustrates some of the problems of the Australian wine industry.

Woodroofe, a family-owned soft-drink company founded in 1878, had had a declining market share but good brand acceptance when it was taken over by two vigorous entrepreneurs in 1980. Within three years, they had increased the profits from about $250,000 a year to over $1,250,000, and the company was floated off with an issued capital of $8,000,000, the 50-cent shares having an asset backing of 35 cents, with forecast earnings of about 17 cents a share and dividends of 9 cents a share. The company was well received by the market.

Two very enterprising young wine-makers, Grant Burge

and Ian Wilson, had been working together successfully since the mid-1970s, making good wines at the Southern Vales Cooperative, despite its descent into extreme financial difficulty culminating in liquidation. Some time before this, they had acquired, with other businessmen, a firm called P. T. Falkenberg, a century-old winery near Tanunda selling wines as Krondorf, and had once more begun to make quite exceptionally good wines. Virtually every wine they have made since 1978 has won a medal in a state capital wine show, and most of them have won trophies or gold medals. Their brick-built winery in the Barossa is one of the ugliest, but the unimpressive façade hides some of the most modern equipment for controlled low-temperature fermentation of all wines. It can crush 2,000 tonnes of fruit per annum and is designed to accept both mechanically harvested and hand-picked fruit. Like many other makers in South Australia, Burge and Wilson grow only a little of their own fruit, but buy in high-quality material from Clare, Coonawarra, Eden Valley and elsewhere to make a small range of very fine wine, the Eden Valley Riesling and Coonawarra Cabernet being particularly good. They have also bought Merrivale, at McLaren Vale, a financially unsuccessful maker of good, clean wines of the type discussed on pp.95–7.

When Krondorf was brought to market, it was to have an issued capital of $4,000,000, with an asset backing for each 50-cent share of 36 cents, projected earnings per share of about 12 cents, and dividends of 4 cents per share. Such a profit was indeed achieved for the first year of operation, on sales of about $4,500,000.

Initially, the market received Woodroofe far more enthusiastically than Krondorf. Evidently it expected a better financial performance from a maker of carbonated drinks and mineral waters than from a maker of fine wine. This was despite the fact that Woodroofe is competing with enormous companies like Cadbury Schweppes and Coca Cola, whereas Krondorf, like many other medium-sized makers of fine wines, should have an established market niche quite separate from that occupied by the major companies, such as Penfold and Lindeman. Furthermore, the price of good fruit is currently very low in real terms, so that a winery which does not have to grow most of its own fruit, and therefore make a large capital investment in land, should be in a position to perform very well in a financial sense, just as it is making very fine wines. A year later, the market had reversed its initial appraisal, but twenty years after the wine boom began, everyone recognizes that wine-making, for all its charm, is not an easy way to quick fortune. A year further on, Krondorf, battered by the discounting of even its best wines, was acquired by Mildara.

Because the Barossa has been Australia's largest dryland wine-growing region for so long, and also because it has too much sunshine to be regarded as ideal for making the best table wines, it has few very small wineries. Chatterton (1969) and High Wycombe (1976) are the only ones crushing less than fifty tonnes.

In the 50–100-tonne class are Barossa Settlers (1983), Holmes Estate (1973), Gnadenfrei (1980) and Mountadam (1984). Holmes Estate is in higher rainfall country outside the Barossa proper and should have good long-term prospects. Gnadenfrei is run by Malcolm and Joylene Seppelt and sits beside the little church where the characteristic palm trees of the Seppelt family begin, a mile before the Seppeltsfield itself. Malcolm is the first Seppelt to stay in the wine industry and establish himself independently of the large, family-controlled company, B. Seppelt & Sons Ltd, recently acquired by the South Australia Brewing Company.

Mountadam is small, but it has been established in the Barossa hills by David and Adam Wynn, father and son, who have between them great experience and current scientific expertise. In the future, using only thirty hectares of a 1000-hectare property, the Wynns will enlarge their crush to 200–300 tonnes, a very large proportion of which will be Chardonnay, with some Pinot Noir and Cabernet Sauvignon, as well as the Riesling already mentioned. It can be confidently predicted that their Chardonnay and Riesling will be outstanding, given the quality of wines made from their fruit in the early 1980s by Jeff Anderson at Roseworthy Agricultural College, and the quality of Wynn's High Eden Riesling, established in the Eden Valley nearby by David Wynn when he was running Wynn Winegrowers before its takeover by the Sydney brewer, Toohey's. As Adam Wynn puts it:

Good wine-making is being careful, observant and gentle and in a small winery you have the perfect opportunity to apply these principles. What is different about the way we operate is that the winery, although having all the toys and equipment which any wine-maker could ever desire, has been built with gentleness, flexibility and the traditional methods in mind. So this vintage [1984] I was making some Chardonnay in the typical Australian stainless steel manner and some in the barrel-fermented Burgundian tradition. You will get no prizes for guessing which is the vastly superior wine.

There are six wineries in the 100–500-tonne class: Basedow (1896), Hamilton (1839, but the move to Springton, in the Barossa hills was made between the two World Wars), Karlsburg (1971), Lindner's St Hallett (1918), Rockford (Tanunda Vintners) (1980) and Veritas (1955).

Basedow was a small family-owned winery which was sold to a group of small investors in about 1970, since when it has greatly improved and become one of the best of the traditional Barossa makers. Its reds have little or none of the cooked-fruit taste so characteristic of the warmer areas. St Hallett is a family-owned winery which has always made thick, rich ports and other fortified wines which last for many years without a great deal of development but which has more recently begun to make a surprisingly well-balanced, fruity Shiraz, more like a Rutherglen wine than a Barossa wine in its overpowering flavour and longevity.

In the 500–1,000-tonne class are Bernkastel (1932), Henschke (1850), Hoffman (1870), Karrawirra (now Red Gum Vineyard) (1969) and Wilsford (1928).

Bernkastel wines I have found to be rather light in character. For example, 1970 was a very big year, yet the 1970 Claret (Shiraz and Mataro) was tolerable in 1973 and over the hill by 1975, and the 1970 Cabernet Shiraz Mataro, which was well balanced and clean with some Cabernet character in 1975, was thin and dull two years later. The winery is a slightly fantastical castle.

Henschke changed its nature from just another German winery to one of the most interesting in South Australia during the twenty years that Cyril Henschke was wine-maker. Using much less new oak than most other aspiring fine wine-makers, and also aiming at softer wines than most, he made his Shiraz-based Hill of Grace and Mount Edelstone

Barossa Hills

— two of the most sought-after wines of the 1960s and 1970s.
Despite their softness, some of them have continued to improve
for a decade, though enjoyable when only two or three years
old. I recall his 1968 Mount Edelstone as a velvety Shiraz in
1978, where it had been spicy five years before. Henschke also
made dry whites of original character and surprising staying
power. His 1965 Sauvignon Blanc, for example, still had a
fresh, grassy nose, deep flavour and a light dusty finish in 1973,
and the same year's Ugni Blanc, though past its best, was
fading slowly and still enjoyable in 1978.

Hoffman, like Henschke, now has the fourth or fifth generation in charge. The current family member in charge, Bruce
Hoffman, whom I recall as a gliding instructor rather than a
wine-maker, makes reliable table wines and outstanding ports
blended of Shiraz, Grenache and Mataro.

In the 1,000–5,000-tonne class are Château Rosevale (1962),
Leo Buring (1945), Hardy's Siegersdorf (1921), Krondorf (1860),
Liebich's Rovalley (1919), Saltram (1900) and Yaldara (1947).

Château Rosevale is most notable for 'Vin-Spa', a sparkling white. It is sold in beer bottles with crown seals for the price of beer but with twice the alcoholic strength, so that it is ideal for making a fruit cup or punch absurdly strong by eliminating the need for soda water or lemonade.

Leo Buring's Château Leonay is part of Lindeman, which is owned by the Australian subsidiary of the American tobacco company, Philip Morris. However, the name commemorates a notable figure in the wine industry. Buring came from a wine-growing family, so after being dux of Roseworthy in 1896, he studied further at Geisenheim and Montpellier before starting work in the industry. He worked at Rutherglen and Great Western before joining Penfold in 1902, for whom he made their first bottle-fermented sparkling wines at Minchinbury, near Sydney. He stayed with them until 1919. Overall, he worked in New South Wales for more than twenty-five years, including a period when he ran Lindeman for a creditor bank, so that when he returned to South Australia in 1945 he was one of the most widely experienced as well as successful people in the industry. The winery which he bought from the Hoffman family had been built at about the time he left Roseworthy, but he added the rather ugly castellations as he expanded the business. After his death, Lindeman bought what was by then a substantial but struggling company. It makes better whites than reds, with fruit from Clare and Coonawarra as well as the Barossa. In fact, those made by John Vickery for more than a decade from about 1963 probably represent the best Australian Rieslings to be made on a large scale as yet. Crisp and fragrant, they have successors in the Leasingham Rieslings of Stanley and many other similar wines, but they have yet to be surpassed by any wines from Clare, Eden Valley or Coonawarra.

Saltram was begun very early as a partnership between the Salter and Martin families, H. M. Martin of Stonyfell eventually taking it over. While Peter Lehman was in charge, it made exceptional full-bodied red wines, even blends such as Shiraz and Tokay, as made in 1972, but after several changes of ownership, it has less of a following than previously. One sees its Mamre Brook Cabernet-Shiraz blend, the flagship of the Stonyfell-Saltram line, quite heavily discounted in bottle shops, such is the competition in the over-supplied red wine market. Mamre Brook is thus good value, but one tends more to recall the reds of the late 1960s and early 1970s which in the early 1980s were fine examples of the old style, having an abundance of fruit, a tannin finish, and a sulphur-derived bottle stink necessitating as much breathing as any wine from the Hunter or McLaren Vale. The whites have not been as good as the reds.

Peter Lehman has continued to make wine very successfully since leaving Saltram. For Masterson Wines, called after the television-famous gunfighter, Lehman has made very reliable wines from grapes which growers have been unable to sell elsewhere, sold under his own name, while for Primo Caon, an Adelaide wine merchant, he has made good wines from Pinot Noir, Cabernet Sauvignon and Sémillon. The Pinot, with none of the depth of flavour of the best Yarra Valley examples, is delightful young and may age gracefully.

Château Yaldara is a family firm which actually has a château, a simulated Georgian-Victorian structure built in stages over the last twenty years. It houses a remarkable collection of Victoriana, including a large academic painting of 'The First Tiff' or perhaps 'The Reconciliation' which a cousin of mine inherited but could not house. The wines vary from odd to reasonable and are relatively modest in price. The odd ones include a sweet red table wine, the reasonable a clean, light, dry, bottle-fermented sparkling wine.

Seppelt is the only firm in the Barossa crushing between 5,000 and 10,000 tonnes a year. This is about half of its Australian production.

Tollana (1888), Wolf Blass (1973) and Yalumba each crush between 10,000 and 20,000 tonnes a year. Tollana is the brand name of Tolley Scott & Tolley, which was established for wine-making and distilling by the Tolley family and which after one or two intermediate owners has belonged for about twenty years to the Distillers Company of the UK. Tollana does not have a high market rating, so that its well-made but unexciting table wines represent good value for money. Like other big distillers of brandy, the firm had to reorientate itself somewhat when the preferentially low duty on brandy as against other spirits was 'harmonized' around 1970.

Wolf Blass is a German-speaking immigrant wine-maker who might have been expected to improve Australian whites, but who has used his remarkable palate to make and blend prize-winning wines of whatever kind the judges currently

seek. As there is general agreement that the standard of
wine-making is much improved, some of the credit is probably
Blass's. I can recall obtaining from a club in 1976 a special
blend of two prize-winning 1974 wines made by Blass, and
initially being most disappointed by the brown colour and
lack of integration of fruit, tannin and oak, yet over three or
four years the wine came together into an outstanding Barossa Cabernet-Shiraz blend. It is now a soft and charming
wine, despite a lingering slight excess of oak. Blass's gift for
publicity has not earned him universal admiration, but he has
nevertheless introduced many to the pleasures of better wines
than come in flagon or plastic bag; his influence, on balance, is
benign.

Two wineries crush over 30,000 tonnes: Penfold Kaiserstuhl
and Orlando (1847). The development of Penfold's red wines I
have already discussed briefly, but they deserve further
thought. Because of the effects of oak, pressing and a very
little oxidation, their firmness, richness and lasting abilities
make them atypical of the Barossa, where the best purely
local makers have usually sacrificed some intensity of flavour
in striving for elegance and an absence of jamminess. Penfold
has sought flavour and balance. The Grange sometimes hints
at cooked fruit, one bottle of the 1966 having this attribute
tasted in 1979, for example, in contrast to the 1964 and 1965
tried at the same time. By 1985 this jammy taste had depar-
ted, even when the wine was tried after a day when the
ambient temperature had exceeded 40°C, and the 1966
Grange was a superb wine – rich, complex, elegant, with a
flavour of mulberries and cream. The Bin 389 is lighter and
always avoids jamminess, though it is considerably less complex and long-lived. Particularly good years have been 1969,
1971, 1972, 1975 and 1977. The cheapest of this set of closely
related wines is Koonunga Hill; on sale everywhere and
drinkable when only two or three years old, it represents an
attempt to make the house style available cheaply without too
much loss of quality, an attempt largely successful.
Kaiserstuhl was established in 1931 as the Barossa Cooperative Winery and struggled for many years with the inherent
problem of cooperatives: concentration on production rather
than marketing. Eventually a decision was made to appoint a
really outstanding manager, and in the decade or so that he
was there, Keith Smith, with no background in the wine

industry, turned Kaiserstuhl into a financial prize, which was won by the Adelaide Steamship Company through Penfold Wines in 1981, in the face of very strong competition from Thomas Hardy & Sons. The joint company appears to have an outstanding combination of red wine-making and mass marketing skills, but the market seeks mainly white wines. Several Kaiserstuhl products are among the top ten of bottled wines in terms of sales throughout Australia, mainly tank-fermented sparkling whites.

Almost the only red wine to make the charts is Orlando's Jacob's Creek, a blend of Cabernet Sauvignon, Malbec and Shiraz. A light, fruity wine which has won many prizes in the 'commercial' (that is, high-volume) classes of the shows, Jacob's Creek is blended to a style and a standard from fruit which can originate anywhere. The Gramp family, who established Orlando and guided it through its first 110 years, were early users of cold fermentation, *cuve close* sparkling wine-making, centrifugal filtration, gas blanketing of fruit to prevent oxidation and other techniques for making wines clean, fresh and drinkable very young. Thus, the takeover in the early 1960s by Reckitt & Colman of the UK has been more of an aid to marketing than to wine-making. Jacob's Creek is to be found everywhere, even in fast food chains which have licences. It is now sold in the UK as William Jacob from Colmans of Norwich.

As might be expected, Orlando also makes very fine wines in much smaller quantities. Its Cabernet Sauvignon, from various sources, is always good. Its Auslese Riesling is not made every year, but in the early 1970s a few cool summers allowed wines to be made which are at their peak when a decade or more old, with a rich yet delicate, honeyed nose, luscious fruit on the palate and a lingering yet fresh finish. Its white Burgundy, made from Chenin Blanc and Madeira, has been reliable year after year, much better in many years, such as 1967, 1968, 1970 and 1977. The earliest of these was still fine in 1983, though somewhat madeirized. Such wines are made from the 5 per cent of its crush which Orlando grows, or from a few selected suppliers in cooler areas.

Adelaide

Until very recently, as I have outlined, there were substantial numbers of wineries, and considerable areas of vines, within

the Adelaide metropolitan area. However, they have disappeared rapidly, Stonyfell after a change of ownership
from Dalgety to Seagram, Hamilton to build a new university, others less notable leaving no trace. Now there are only
five, apart from hundreds of backyard makers who probably
only sell to their friends. They are Norman (1853), crushing
1,000 tonnes a year; Patritti (1926), crushing 500 tonnes; Seaview Champagne Cellars (1904; formerly Wynn's Romalo),
making over 40,000 cases of sparkling wines a year from
base wine fermented elsewhere; Woodley (1856), crushing
over 1,000 tonnes; and Penfold's Grange, which is being
reconstituted to make about 2,500 cases from the fifty tonnes
of fruit which will come from the remaining fragment of the
vineyard.

Patritti is a family-owned winery with forty hectares in
the Southern Vales. It buys in much of its crush and makes a
wide range of wines with Italian overtones. It has been inno-
vative in seeking to make a light red wine drinkable soon
after vintage, the 'April Red' mentioned previously, but less
successful in selling such wines. I shall discuss such attempts
further when looking to the future.

Norman has vineyards at Angle Vale, to the north of
Adelaide, with its winery closer to the city. It also takes fruit
from other growers and has experimented successfully with
varieties such as Traminer and Pinot Noir. The wines are all
carefully made and good value for money, but rarely reach
peaks of excellence.

Woodley had its greatest days as a maker of fine wine
when a substantial part of the production of Coonawarra was
sold under its elaborate labels, which were among the most
attractive in the trade. The proprietors, David Fulton and
then Tony Nelson, an Austrian wine-maker with experience
in France before coming to Australia to avoid Hitler, were
much more alive to what might be done with good fruit than
the makers who drew their fruit from the hotter areas and
made mainly fortified wines. However, Woodley has belonged
for several years to Industrial Equity, a corporate raider, and
while the labels of the 'Queen Adelaide' red and white wines
are elegant and distinctive, the wines are merely reliable; its
recent sale to Seppelt may herald better times. It is sad to
reflect that the façade of the winery was modernized at one of
the many inopportune moments for such renovation which

the post-war period has offered. Parts of the buildings are hidden behind plane trees, however, as are its last few square metres of vines.

Northern Adelaide

Tea Tree Gully, less than twenty kilometres north-east of Adelaide, in the foothills of the Mount Lofty ranges, is no longer regarded as a notable wine-growing area but, in the early 1860s, Archdeacon G. H. Farr established a vineyard at Brightlands, his property there. Other neighbours did likewise, and when Dr William Thomas Angove established his practice at Tea Tree Gully in 1886, he emulated his neighbours and planted a vineyard, making his first wines in the archdeacon's cellars. He later bought another property at nearby Hope Valley and built his own cellars at the start of this century. He called his Tea Tree Gully vineyard St Agnes, and sold his wines under this name.

By the time that Dr Angove built his own winery, his oldest son Thomas had graduated from Roseworthy, and when all three sons were working for the firm, they took it to the Murray River, first to the Renmark Irrigation Settlement, which had been established in the late 1880s, and then to Lyrup, another settlement south-west of Renmark on the river.

As with Yalumba, Seppelt, Lindeman and other large firms, the move to the River was to provide a source of reliable, high-sugar fruit, which could both be made into wine and also provide the base material for distillation. For Angove is most notable for its brandy, its vermouth sold under the name of Marko, and other fortified products. Its Shiraz port has many admirers. For example, the 1968 was a rather rough wine when young, as is not unusual, but softened and developed steadily so that from 1978 to 1983 it was rich and yet restrained, drinkable well past mid-winter in Adelaide.

When the state government compulsorily acquired 100 hectares of vineyards at Tea Tree Gully for some additional suburban sprawl, Angove lost its main source of unirrigated material, so that most of its 15,000-tonne crush is now from the river. A family-run vineyard, it will no doubt surmount this obstacle, which will certainly not be the last act of government vandalism perpetrated against the wine industry.

Not far away, in Hope Valley, the Tolley family has a larg

operation, crushing over 5,000 tonnes, about half of it bought in. The firm was established by Douglas A. Tolley in 1892 and labels its wines 'Pedare', after the sons Peter, David and Reginald Tolley. Possibly the name contributes to the under-valuing of the wines by the market. Whatever the reason, its port is a fine old rich, fruity wine which is outstanding value, its Cabernet Sauvignon and Cabernet-Shiraz blend very reliable and its Traminer neither bitter nor blowsy, common faults in Traminers from the warm areas.

Less than thirty kilometres north of Adelaide, on feature-less flat plains which receive less than 500mm of rain a year and which, because of over-zealous pumping in the past, have a problem with salt in the water table, is an unlikely group of wineries using the most modern techniques to make some very good wines.

One of these is Roseworthy Agricultural College, where experimental wine has been made for most of the present century. For a long time, under the leadership of Bob Baker, it was notable for its fortified wines, especially *flor*-influenced wines of the sherry type. More recently, as the industry and teaching needs have changed, Roseworthy has changed too and crushes about 100 tonnes of fruit from almost every area in South Australia for the large range of table and fortified wines and brandy to which I have already alluded. The table wines extend from student project wines, sold in screw-topped bottles and made from odd varieties grown at the State Department of Agriculture's experimental station, to out-standing Chardonnays made from the Wynn family's Mount-adam vineyard high in the Barossa Range, before Mountadam's own first crush in 1984.

Primo Estate is probably the most notable. Working closely with Roseworthy, the Grilli family have tried techniques like double pruning, whereby the vines are pruned after they have flowered, so that they flower again and harvest is up to a month later than normal. This avoids the searing heat of February and March. As well as an excellent Cabernet made by this method, Grilli has produced a very fine botrytis-affected Riesling. In fact, in late 1983 I had a wine circular from a club which offered the 1983 Primo Estate Beerenaus-lese in half bottles for the equivalent of $180 a dozen bottles. In the same newsletter, the 1980 Château Coutet (Barsac) was offered for $150 a dozen. The Primo Estate wine was very carefully made: Riesling and Traminer grapes were sprayed with *Botrytis cinerea* culture, in a controlled atmosphere, after harvest, and the grapes were crushed after the mould had grown for some weeks. The wine was certainly very sweet, and had intense flavour, but to me at least lacked a little acid on the finish to balance the lushness. In consequence, it is hard to see why such a wine should command a 20 per cent premium over one of the best Barsacs – albeit from a secondary year.

Anglesey Wines was established as Angle Vale Wines in the mid-1960s and took its present name in 1978 after a financial reconstruction. Like Primo Estate, Anglesey crushes between 100 and 500 tonnes a year.

Gordon Sunter established a very small operation in the early 1980s.

One of the most interesting aspects of this area is that, because of the salt in the underground water, the vines have to be irrigated with sewage effluent from the huge sewage treatment works on the coast at the improbably named Bolivar – given this name in a flush of nineteenth-century enthusiasm for the Liberator. Indeed, many of the vineyards have to be irrigated almost continuously in order to keep the salt at bay. For this reason, and because the area is very close to Adelaide and ideal for building Australian dreams – detached single-storey houses, each set on a twentieth of a hectare of land – in enormous numbers, it is unlikely that the area will ever become important. In 1984, a promising new-comer, Gawler River Wines, sank under the weight of its financial obligations, a gloomy portent, perhaps.

Adelaide Hills

The Adelaide Hills form the only high-rainfall cool climate of South Australia. The elevation of 400–700 metres and rainfall of 700–900 millimetres combine to make grape growing an exacting task which should reward skill and patience but which was not favoured when palliation of disease and frost was impossible rather than difficult. The land also slopes very steeply and is expensive compared with most potential vine-yards. Vignerons will have to be rather different from the old norms.

Petaluma is certainly a different kind of winery. Its location

89

is unusual, in what used to be prime market gardening land at an altitude of about 650 metres, just behind Mount Lofty, in the Adelaide Hills, but at first sight it looks conventional enough: well-tended young vines with turf down the rows, olive-green sheds at the bottom of the hill; but a closer inspection shows that the spacing between the rows is only about two metres, compared with the Australian norm of about three metres, and the vines themselves only a little over 1.5 metres apart down the rows, compared with almost two metres. There is drip irrigation throughout, but the yield of about twelve tonnes per hectare means no sacrifice in quality, since there are twice as many vines per hectare, and they are having to work rather harder than usual to produce the grapes. Pinot Noir and Chardonnay only have been planted, to complement vineyards at Coonawarra and Clare, and make a sparkling wine by the champagne method, but labelled rather severely Petaluma Tiers, the Tiers being the old name of this part of the Adelaide Hills.

When one reaches the winery, one notices that it too is different. A few stainless steel fermenters are visible above the crusher, but most of the stainless steel tanks are shrouded in insulation and covered with plastic-clad pressed sheet steel. Over twenty tonnes of liquid nitrogen and the same amount of liquid carbon dioxide are used a year for cooling, and what one is actually looking at is a totally insulated winery, freed from the vagaries of climate. Grapes can be picked into plastic-lined pallet cases, which can then be stored in a cold store, so that even the picking and crushing season can be extended, at least for a couple of weeks.

Everything looks very simple and is the result of a great deal of planning. Brian Croser, whose label Petaluma is, has planned and built a number of wineries, and established his label half a decade before he had a vineyard, and almost ten years before he had a winery of his own. With his partner, Tony Jordan, he has a consulting company, Oenotec, which provides the most modern and advanced advice to about twenty wine-makers. More importantly, they take their own advice.

Taking in only the best fruit, and handling it as carefully as possible, they will have expended about $3.00 (in 1983 terms) on a litre of juice by the time that it is fermenting. Such high costs demand absolute control over all stages of the wine-making process, and this is what the insulated winery gives them.

Only a few wines are made: a Riesling, from the best fruit from Coonawarra, Clare and Margaret River in Western Australia; a Chardonnay, first from Cowra in New South Wales, then including Coonawarra fruit, and eventually to include Adelaide Hills fruit; a Cabernet mainly from Coonawarra; and a sparkling wine.

Fermentation is, of course, at very low temperatures; the red wines are begun at perhaps 10°C and increased to 15°C, with the cap of skins, which is held in the middle of the fermenter, controlled so that it does not get too hot (a bit over 20°C). No sulphur is used in the red wines and very little in the whites. Croser believes that physico-chemical fining removes flavour, and that the best fining agents are time and gravity, so that the must may be held at very low temperature for some time after crushing in order that it may fine itself. One might ask to what extent this large-scale self-fining replaces the six or seven rackings and finings which are used during the *élevage* of a classed growth Bordeaux, given that Croser's low-temperature undisturbed process is so very different from traditional handling.

Investigation by the Australian Wine Research Institute some years ago showed that about 70 per cent of all Australian red wines spontaneously underwent a malolactic fermentation. Such a chance is not good enough for Petaluma. In June to July, a malolactic culture of specially selected *Leuconostoc oenos* is seeded into the wine, and the malolactic fermentation is completed. In some years, such as 1979, 1980 and 1982, the wine requires no filtration, but this cannot always be achieved.

The wines which require wood treatment, the Chardonnay and the red, are now being held in French oak barriques in the Ashton cold store, not far from the winery, at 2°C. This is an almost completely new departure in the wine world, but the end results speak for themselves. The reds, when released at about three years old, are dense, vigorous, crimson wines showing tremendous Cabernet fruit and minty herbaceous bouquet, with the oak already well integrated, and yet the wine obviously has the potential to improve for a decade or more. Tasted a couple of years before bottling, they are purple as well as crimson and have the same characteristics but in super-abundance. Croser calls them aggressive, but they are too elegant for this word to be appropriate.

The Rieslings have much more of the mouth-filling flavour which one associates with German whites rather than with Australian whites. Although the Riesling boom is over, the wines remain exceptionally good and, for those who do not necessarily follow fashion, they are starting to become more reasonable in price. This is Australian wine-making at its best.

Other wineries and vineyards are under establishment in the Adelaide Hills, mostly near Lenswood in country which has grown apples, cherries and other fruit requiring a cold winter for fruit-set. Stephen George, whose parents established Skillogalee at Clare, Geoffrey Weaver, one of Hardy's young wine-makers, and Tim Knappstein of Enterprise at Clare, are among the new growers, most of whose plans were set back by the devastating bushfires of Ash Wednesday, 1983. Early wines from Weaver's Ashbourne label and from George have shown great promise, though Weaver's 1981 Cabernet Sauvignon used Coonawarra, not Adelaide Hills, material; the skill is there and in time so will be the fruit.

Southern Vales

Vineyards were established to the south of Adelaide from 1838 onward, as we have seen. South-east of Reynella, around what is now McLaren Vale, Dr Kelly saw the possibilities and moved to exploit them, followed by Thomas Hardy, who was the dominant grape-buyer by the end of the century.

The early 1890s saw many successful wine growers begin in business. Growing exports, widespread drought in the pastoral and extensive agricultural country, and the defeat of phylloxera all combined to make grape growing and wine-making look attractive from many different points of view.

The Kay Brothers' story begins in an 'Australian Rough Diary for 1891 No. 4': on Monday, 2 February 1891, we find the entry, 'Entered into possession at Amery Section 514, 515, 516 and 740. Rose, Bert and Fred arrived about 6.30. Stock, brown horse "Darkie", roan horse "Roanie", four swarms bees, six hens, furniture per M. Weber's wagon 19.45.' The property was well established, for there were still mulberries to pick, and on Ash Wednesday, 11 February, we find the entry,

0 —— 6 km

Adelaide 20 km

Torresan

Happy Valley Reservoir

Marienberg

St Francis

Field River
Reynella

Hardy-Reynella

Glenloth
Horndale

Light's
Coolawin
(Norman)

Patritti

Christie Creek
Morphett
Vale

Trennert

Christies
Beach

Old
Clarendon

Port
Noarlunga

Hackham

Onkaparinga River
Chapel Vale

Elysium

Blewitt
Spring

Coriole
Seaview

Seaford

Kay Bros'
Amery

Maglieri

Oliverhill

Woodstock

Moana

D'Arenberg

Settlement

Berenyi
Ingoldby

Taranga

Merrivale

Fern Hill

Ryecroft

Palladio
Southern Vales
Cooperative

1

3
2

6
7
4

5

McLaren
Flat

Cambrai

Maslin
Beach

McLaren
Vale

8

9

Middle Brook

Pirramimma

Wirra Wirra

Pedlar Creek

Noon

Richard Hamilton

1 Hardy's Tintara
4 Tinling
7 Daringa Cellars

2 Manning Park
5 James Haselgrove
8 Maxwell

3 Chalk Hill
6 Genders
9 Hazelmere Estate

Southern Vales

'Counted trees and vines – hill patch 1,829 vines, 101 blanks; flat patch 1,957, 149 blanks; cuttings 1,545.' On Friday the thirteenth, one finds, 'Began hoeing vineyard'; on Saturday, 'Continued hoeing vineyard.' Sunday was the day of rest for these devout Unitarians. On Monday, 'Finished hoeing hill vineyard and began flat.' On Tuesday, 'Finished hoeing flat vineyard.'

In late July, one finds, 'Carted three dray-loads of vine cuttings from Tintara 25,800 Shiraz, 5,000 Reisling [sic], 10,000 Carbonet [sic]'; next day, after half an inch of rain, 'Jarvis began plowing hillside vineyard. Began planting in fallow paddock – planted 452 Shiraz.' The planting went on until early September, Frontignac, Mataro and Carignan being among the varieties. On Tuesday, 29 March 1892, is the record of the first grape harvest: 'Picked wine grapes and carted to Mill 4¾ cwt. Picked Muscatells [sic] and put partly on cow shed roof and part on house roof. Memo grapes were 4¼ cwt black (Mataro and Grenache), ½ Sweetwater.' The record of the first vintage appears on Friday, 15 April: 'Made wine from Doradillo grapes one and a half gallons must.' The 'Mill' to which the grapes were carted in McLaren Vale would have been Hardy's Winery; in April the following year one finds, 'H. K. went to McLaren Vale to arrange with Kelly about grapes, agreed to sell him twenty bushels wheat.' These black grapes were delivered to the mill also, this year over one tonne.

The cellars were built in 1894 and 1895, and the first real vintage took place in 1895, with everything scarcely finished by Thursday, 7 March: 'Moved press into cellar, burnt out bung holes, took head out of 300 gallon cask, began making plunger, cutting wood, began picking in windmill paddock.' The next day, 'finished picking in windmill paddock, 4¾ cwt. Shiraz and ¾ cwt. Carbernet [sic] . . . crushed first cask of grapes.' Vintage was more strenuous then than now, and equally hectic. Wood-cutting, racking-off casks, picking, crushing, greasing the dray wheels, and even cleaning up the cellar on the occasional Sunday: so the work went on. Picking finished on 11 April, but work on the wines went on through the autumn and winter. In July, on Sunday the fourteenth, one finds the entry, no less laconic than usual, 'cellar roof blew off'. The following day, 'took cellar roof to pieces and carted to pig sties and barn, put iron on roofs of new pig sties and little sty. Began repairing cellar.' In 1896, cellar work was set down as 'before vintage: men 71 days; vintage: men 672 days, horses 24 days; after vintage: men 491 days,' all this for about fifty tonnes of fruit.

The view from Amery, Kay Brothers' homestead, is splendid. Situated on a ridge, it looks south and south-east to the gentle curves of the Willunga hills, a uniform set the tallest of which is Mount Wilson, south-west to the sea. At the bottom of the hill, behind tall pines, is the old Tintara vineyard, planted more than a century before, its Sauvignon Blanc grapes contributing to Hardy's fine dessert wines, the 1965 blend with Sémillon still a fine wine in the 1980s, though with rather a bottle stink.

On soil which is mainly red-brown earth over limestone and ironstone, Amery has grown Shiraz, Cabernet Sauvignon, Sémillon and Rhine Riesling successfully for many years. The quiet Cud Kay, of the third generation on the property, has made many fine examples of the staple blend, Cabernet-Shiraz, notably in 1964, 1967 and 1971. More recently, his son, Colin, has begun to make lighter wines, the Pinot-Shiraz being relatively successful, but the Cabernet-Shiraz remaining the wine of choice.

Despite the neo-brutalist shed which obscures the old, rambling cellars built down the slope to take advantage of gravity in handling the wine, the vineyard is one of the most welcoming in an area which saw too much whimsy, tax-dodging and general incompetence during the wine boom. The Kays have a kind word for everyone, saying, of a straight Mataro made by a competitor, 'Yes, I think that he does about as much as you can with Mataro.' Their own have been grubbed out.

Only three Southern Vales wineries fall into the very small (25-tonne) category – Dridan's Skottowe Estate (1975), Dyson (1977) and Fernhill (1975).

Dridan made some excellent Shiraz wines, the labels an attraction by themselves – for he is one of South Australia's most successful artists – before he moved his interest and his wine-making to the Old Clarendon Winery in about 1983, a gallery, restaurant and tourist trap which also makes and sells a range of red and white wines. It is too early to assess the interaction between attracting customers and making good wine.

Fernhill makes one of the area's best Shirazes and a good crisp Riesling.

In the next category, 25–50 tonnes, are Berenyi (1964), Daringa (1974), Donolga (1976), Hugo (1980), Manning Park (1983), Noon (1969) and Trennert (1971).

Berenyi makes extraordinary red and white wines from Grenache. He picks the grapes when they are very ripe and lets wild yeasts ferment them dry. Volatility and aldehydes give them the character of sherries or madeiras and they are very high in alcohol. I do not understand them.

Manning Park, formerly the property of the nearby Merrivale, which is now part of the Barossa's Krondorf, is almost in McLaren Vale itself. Owned by the proprietors of St Anne's vineyard, near Ballarat, in Victoria, it offers rich, full-flavoured wines which avoid the sulphurous stink associated with the area.

Makers of 50–100 tonnes are Cambrai (1975), Elysium (1975), Maxwell (1979), Oliverhill (1970), Richard Hamilton (1972) and Settlement (1968).

Cambrai has as its wine-maker and proprietor Graham Stevens, who was very successful when wine-making successively for d'Arenberg in the 1960s and Coriole in the 1970s. He is an outstanding wine-maker with an open mind: he has made a rich, deep-flavoured and durable blend of Cabernet Sauvignon and Pinot Noir, uses Grenache well, makes an enjoyable, rapid-maturing Zinfandel, uses wood well in his sweetish, full-bodied whites and make a dense, purple port of great quality.

Settlement was set up as a partnership between a medical practitioner and an Italian wine-maker with a flair for publicity and incredibly powerful but balanced red wines, made partly with fruit from the vineyard's own sandy slopes above McLaren Flat, partly from any source of good fruit. In the past, this has included Coonawarra, but now Settlement's own vineyard at Margaret River, in south-western Western Australia, is supplying very fine Cabernet Sauvignon, and these wines should get better and better.

Makers of 100–500 tonnes are Coriole (1967), Genders (1968), Estate (Hazelmere) (1980), Maglieri (Gully) (1972), Marienberg (1966), Merrivale (1972), Palladio (1974), Pirramimma (1892), St Francis (1970), Taranga (1973), Wirra Wirra (1969) and Woodstock (1970).

Estate Wines, formerly Hazelmere, like Marienberg and Elysium, has had a female wine-maker, not a rarity in Australia but still relatively unusual. However, at the latter two wineries, the makers are also proprietors. Hazelmere is, like the Old Clarendon Winery, intended to be a centre of attraction and entertainment, with restaurant and accommodation as important as the well-made Cabernet and Chardonnay. Its first vintages have been very good, but changes of wine-maker and owner occurred only a few years after its establishment, so that style and direction may change.

Pirramimma was a long-established maker of fortified wines which took some time to adjust to the disappearance of this market but which is now making some of the most elegant reds in the Southern Vales, even a carbonic maceration wine for instant consumption. With those of Kay Brothers, Hardy and Osborne, Pirramimma's earlier red wines typified the area's style – rather dirty but with plenty of flavour for those prepared to wait.

Wirra Wirra is established in an ironstone building rebuilt on the ruins of a winery begun in 1902 but successful for only a few years. The Trotts, who run it, are related to the Johnstons of Pirramimma and were among the earliest to begin to make clean, fresh red wines in the Southern Vales, using Shiraz and Grenache together well, and making a Cabernet which might well have been mistaken for one from a much cooler area. They also make a 'Hand-Picked' Riesling which displays the strength, sweetness and fruit to be expected from a very good Auslese indeed. Whites from the area have always had flavour; they now sometimes have finesse as well.

Woodstock, like most of the larger wineries in the area, makes wine from others' fruit as well as its own – for example, one of the more unusual of the botrytis-affected wines of 1984, using Riesling and Chenin Blanc from Clos Robert, a large vineyard without a winery.

In the 500–1,000-tonne class are only Coolawin (now part of Normans) (1969), d'Arenberg (1928), Kay Brothers (1890), and Ryecroft (Wilkinson) (1985). All are more notable for their red wines than their whites, and they hover in the difficult scale where national sales are necessary but national advertising is impossible.

In the 1,000–5,000-tonne class are Reynella (1838) and

Seaview (1850). Reynella belongs to Thomas Hardy, the giant of the area, and Seaview to the Adelaide Steamship Company. In this category until 1980 was the Southern Vales Cooperative, first established in 1896 as a proprietary winery, belonging to Penfold from 1911 to 1965, expanding by buying the Horndale Distillery from Gilbey in 1968, and then collapsing in 1981. Wine is still made there, from some of the same grapes which Burge and Wilson, later of Krondorf, in the Barossa, used so successfully in the mid 1970s, but it is no longer a major winery.

Finally, crushing over 5,000 tonnes of grapes before one counts Reynella or Houghton in Western Australia, there is Thomas Hardy. It has stayed family-owned and controlled in an era when this has become not only difficult but unfashionable, and has, as is said in Australia, quoting a former rural Deputy Prime Minister, 'Black Jack' McEwen, 'bought back a bit of the farm,' acquiring Emu Wines, parent of Houghton and Valencia, in Western Australia, from British interests and Reynella from an overseas-influenced tobacco company. Acquisition by the original Thomas Hardy, at a low price in 1877 (following a decade of economic difficulty), of Dr Kelly's pioneering Tintara vineyard had been one of the most successful investments in the wine industry. Sale of the 27,000 gallons of good wine made by Dr Kelly paid for the entire purchase as the economy recovered and the population grew. The acquisitions of a century later seem likely to be just as successful.

Family control has allowed moves into new areas, with management and wine-making gradually incorporating more outsiders. The wines are consistent, rarely reaching the greatest peaks, though the company wines won many prizes. Its brand names, such as Nottage Hill Claret, St Thomas Burgundy and Old Castle Riesling, are very reliable, and some of its more recently developed wines, using fruit from Keppoch or Coonawarra, in the south east of the state, have been very good indeed, though its use of Pinot Noir has yet to impress.

Both Hardy and Reynella have always made very good fortified wines. Now, in Reynella, Thomas Hardy has a winery which long made a complex, rich Cabernet Sauvignon with a very small following, a wine which improved for many years, twenty-year-old examples clearly different from, yet not disgraced by comparison with, similarly aged Clarets of good years. That these wines will still be made, given Hardy's respect for tradition, one feels certain.

Langhorne Creek

Langhorne Creek is a very small area, possessing less than 150 hectares of grapes, no more than a dozen growers and only two vignerons – Potts Bleasdale, founded in 1862, and Bremer Wines, Potts's junior by more than 110 years. Nonetheless, its fruit has long been recognized as having a distinctive character, best described as earthy. Stonyfell has made a powerful tannic long-lived wine called Metala, from Cabernet Sauvignon and Shiraz grown at Langhorne Creek, for many years, Lindeman has similarly made a Shiraz-Cinsault blend, and Wolf Blass has used Shiraz from the area to provide the fruit and tannin for many a prize-winning blend. Metala remains fruity and earthy almost indefinitely, the 1966 hardly changing between 1974 and 1984.

Yet it has been the Potts family, their vineyard named Bleasdale after a temperance advocate who recommended wine for moderation, which has established both the area's name and its special method of ensuring good yields in a dry area near the slowest-flowing part of the Murray River. They built sluices which allow them to divert the winter floods of the Bremer River, a minor stream, on to the vineyards. It is probably fallacious, though of course appealing, to relate the earthiness of the wines to the annual inundation with silt.

The most interesting Potts wine is their Malbec, at its best soft, scented and fruity, improving for up to eight years. They also make an attractive dry wine from Verdielho, rather watery and characterless when young but developing a good, rounded flavour after three to four years. However, much of their 1,000-tonne crush, half of it bought in, goes into tank-fermented sparkling wines which sell at about half the price of the bottle-fermented product and are very widely taken, mixed with orange juice, round swimming pools on Sunday mornings.

Bremer Wines, which grows about twenty of its fifty-tonne crush, is no threat to the identification, in the wine buyer's mind, of Potts and Langhorne Creek.

On the Angas River is Temple Bruer, run by the former

Langhorne Creek

distillation instructor of Roseworthy Agricultural College.

At Currency Creek, not far away, is Santa Rosa (1968), also very small. Its late-picked Riesling is a wine with considerable fruit but little finesse. The wines have improved recently with the aid of Brian Barry of Clare. Near Middleton and other beaches is Marklew Wines, another small producer begun by a medical enthusiast.

Clare

As explorers moved north from Adelaide, they also became settlers. John Horrocks, one such, had his servant establish a vineyard at Hope Farm, Penwortham, near Clare. Horrocks had been born at Penwortham Hall, in Lancashire, and called his new village after it. Horrocks also provided vines in 1840 to George Hawker, an important pioneer of the Merino sheep industry, but Horrocks himself did not live to see the wine industry established, for he was shot by his camel in 1846. It kicked his gun as Horrocks handed the weapon to a servant. It was probably the first camel imported into Australia, from Tenerife, in 1840. It had given great trouble in the Clare district, frightening bullock teams, and on the expedition to the north of South Australia on which Horrocks was killed, biting one member of the party and one of the goats taken for provisions. The camel itself was shot as a punishment after Horrocks's death, Edward Gleeson, who gave Clare its name, being one of those appointed to execute the animal.

Gleeson established another of the very early vineyards at his house, called Inchiquin. The house remains, but the name is attached to a flagon port made by the local cooperative. Gleeson peppered the district with Irish names, so that there is today, for example, a Donnybrook Tea Garden.

As well as the Lutherans who left Germany after 1848 and who established the Barossa wine industry, Roman Catholic Germans came to South Australia at about the same time and some headed further north. Austrian Jesuits set up a church at Seven Hills, to the south of Clare, and later a college, to educate the many Catholics in the area, and one of the Jesuits obtained vines from Bungaree, the Hawker property north of Clare. These were planted in 1851; by 1858, the seven acres in production supplied sufficient grapes for 1,000 gallons of wine and sixty of brandy.

Barry's St Clare

Hutt River

Clare

Enterprise

Clarevale Cooperative

Stanley

Wendouree

Robertson

Sevenhill Cellars

Sevenhill

Skillogalee

Mitchell

Penwortham

Paulett Wines

Polish Hill
River

Quelltaler

Watervale

Watervale Cellars

Mount Horrocks

Skillogalee Creek

Fareham Estate

Taylor's Château
Clare Valley

Auburn

Jeffrey Grosset

0   5
└──────┘ km

Adelaide 110 km

Clare Watervale

With plenty of labour from the congregation, fine stone cellars were built, cut into the side of the hill and roofed with arched stones. Initially, only altar wine was made, but over the years, though altar wine remained important, a range of table wines and temporal fortified wines was made as well, fermentation occurring in big slate tanks, the stone coming from the nearby Mintaro slate quarry.

The community has stayed small but there has been a succession of only seven cellar-masters from the first in 1851 to Brother John May who was appointed in 1972. The first two were Austrians, followed by an Irishman, a Swiss and two Australians.

The fine stone church of St Aloysius reminds one that, like most of the wineries of north-eastern Victoria, this one is not open for tasting on Sundays. On other days, the visitors can try a range of strange whites – for example, a very dry one made from Tokay, often oxidized, and rather better dry reds, perhaps the most interesting being one made from Cabernet Sauvignon, Shiraz and Grenache, called simply Dry Red, restrained, well-rounded and faintly like a Rhône wine, with a lightish colour, a deep flavour and a strong finish. In 1976 and 1981 it was particularly good, but it is always reliable.

Several wineries were started before 1870, but only the Jesuits' and Treloar's Prospect survive, the latter, established at Watervale in 1865, now called Buring and Sobels Quelltaler. Buring and Sobels, Germans from the Barossa Valley, bought it in 1889 and established a reputation for good sherry, good Riesling and a lighter red than most in the district. One of the Sobels family is still involved in running Quelltaler, but it is now a part of Remy Martin.

By 1900, the Clare area was defined as the strip of relatively high country from Auburn in the south to Stanley Flat, just north of Clare. There was also a vineyard near Riverton, slightly to the east, but it no longer exists.

Four wineries at least were established in the 1890s. Koonowla and St Andrew's were built near Auburn in 1896, but they disappeared, though the buildings remained, as did a few growers. Only in the 1970s did wineries return to Auburn. The Stanley Wine Company was formed in 1894, the winery in an abandoned jam factory within the Clare town boundary. Alfred Basedow, of the Barossa wine family, was the first manager and wine-maker. Between 1900 and 1912, one of the proprietors, Joseph Knappstein, rescued Stanley from the effects of a wine slump by travelling to Europe himself to establish a market for the company, and by 1912 it was a Knappstein family concern. It was sold to the H. J. Heinz Company in 1971, though a member of the family is still involved. By then it was becoming very well established for making fine white wines and elegant fruity reds, much of the credit in its last years as an independent company going to Tim Knappstein, who had been dux at Roseworthy, and who has since established his own winery in the old Enterprise Brewery, also within the town of Clare. By the time it was sold, Stanley was very large for the area, its crush of 4,000 tonnes in 1972 being of the same order as the entire crush of Hunter Valley grapes. It is now moving its production base to irrigated fruit, the major centre to be at Buronga, in New South Wales. The crush there is 30,000 tonnes.

Tim Knappstein has rapidly established himself as one of the area's best makers of both reds and whites. His wood-matured Sauvignon Blanc is one of the first of many aimed at the Pouilly Fumé style, and still one of the best, and his Cabernet Sauvignon has more balance and firmness than one expects from this area.

Just south of Clare, A. P. Birks began wine growing as a hobby on his farm in 1895. By 1903, he was ready to sell his wine and in that year sold 1,500 gallons. His son Roly had his first vintage in 1917, and in 1977 a big party was held in the cellars to celebrate his sixtieth. By then, the winery had been sold, first during the mining boom to the Fitzpatrick brothers of Sydney, who also had the Seymour Winery in Victoria. Later, after some financial vicissitudes, more sympathetic proprietors acquired the winery, and it has been during their time that the winery has stabilized as the last maker of the really big red wines for which the area has been known, so that Wendouree is rather like Bailey, in north-eastern Victoria. The Shiraz, at its best, is a complex wine full of smells like crushed ants, blackberries, mint and cedar wood, bright purple in the glass but turning one's teeth black. 1976 was a particularly good year for this wine. 1983 and 1985 also show great promise, the wines being similar to good young Hermitage, perhaps less complex than Côte Rôtie. As 1983 was generally disastrous at Clare, the 1983 Shiraz is an outstanding achievement. As the makers produce these traditional wines with rather more finesse than ever before, they also experiment: one such experiment is the first fortified Riesling to come out of the area – indeed, perhaps the first in Australia or anywhere else. Quite a delicate wine, with strong Riesling character and yet a certain grapiness, it is an experiment which should be pursued by someone.

Between 1900 and 1970, only two wineries, the Clarevale Cooperative and Jim Barry's St Clare, were established. The Cooperative, however, was established twice, collapsing within a year and then beginning again just at the start of the Depression, in 1930. The winery, like Stanley's, is in the town, in the old coaching stables of Hill & Company, local affiliate of Cobb & Co., of romantic gold-fields association. The initial members were small grape growers, mostly returned servicemen on small blocks, debt-ridden and struggling. With government support, the Cooperative persisted through the years of rationing during the war. After the war, when fortified wines were in demand for export, it was more successful but, when the need came to modernize, to make table wines, its debt grew too great to manage, and control was taken to the Barossa by Kaiserstuhl, which itself was then acquired by Penfold.

St Clare, just north of the town, was started by Jim Barry after twenty-two years at the Cooperative as wine-maker. With careful control over his fruit quality, which was impossible in the Cooperative, he rapidly established himself as a maker of good, rich, fruity reds – the 1970, 1971 and 1973 Cabernet-Shiraz blends all developing very well into the early 1980s.

In the 1970s, seven wineries were established in the Clare area. Taylor Brothers of Sydney established Château Clare Valley Estate on the Wakefield River near Auburn in 1973, the aim being to make the best Cabernet Sauvignon in the area. They achieved immediate success, just in time to catch the red wine slump and the white wine boom. An extensive grafting programme has achieved a better balance of varieties, but the white wines have yet to demonstrate themselves to be as good as the red. Robertson Wines (now Heritage Wines) was established in about 1975 and Skillogalee, Enterprise, Mitchell and Fareham Estate at about the same time or a little later.

Skillogalee and Mitchell, quite near each other, with vines

growing at an altitude of about 450 metres above sea level, make elegant whites and robust yet restrained reds. Indeed, the 1980 Mitchell Cabernet is one of the best reds from the area over quite a few years, the Riesling fine every year.

In the early 1980s, Jeffrey Grosset established himself in a disused butter factory at Auburn, where he is making some of the best Rieslings in the area. At about the same time, the Mount Horrocks Winery and Watervale Cellars were set up a little further north, and Polish Hill River and Paulett Wines to the east.

The Mount Horrocks wines of Watervale have no connection with the explorer other than that the grapes are grown near the slopes of Mount Horrocks, a modest hillock to the north-east of Watervale. At least one member of the Horrocks family, however, has enjoyed them, as he told me, though he was surprised to see a winery with his name on it. The wines are made by Jeffrey Grosset of Auburn, but later the proprietors, the Ackland brothers, will make their own. (Such cooperation is by no means unusual in this friendly industry.) The Horrocks wines are very similar, therefore, to the Grosset wines. This makes them among the more elegant wines of the Clare area. The 1982 Cabernet-Merlot is a purple-crimson wine, soft yet with enough acid to make it last for roughly a decade, and with great charm in both smell and taste. The Sémillon shows what can be done with this variety in Clare: drunk in the year of making, it was crisp, fresh, fruity and slightly sweet but with a long acid finish, so that one could be confident it would last. Taken with Tommy Ruff, a small, slightly sweet South Australian fish, it was far superior to Angelo's Sundown 1982 Sémillon from the Granite Belt, in Queensland, which was soft and oxidized and seemed to show slightly too much oak treatment.

Apart from the local makers, Penfold, Seppelt and Wolf Blass all have substantial plantings in the area, and Clare fruit is used by many other makers, particularly the large blenders like Lindeman, to provide fruit and body to wine from thinner, lighter areas in good years and bad.

Only four wine-makers crush less than fifty tonnes: Watervale Cellars, Paulett Wines, Mount Horrocks and Grosset.

In the next smallest category, 50–100 tonnes, are Fareham Estate, which is also a contract bottler for wine from the McLaren Vale and Coonawarra areas as well as Clare,

Robertson (Heritage), whose founder was notable for the pan-ache with which he sold a range of wines of limited distinc-tion, and Polish Hill River, whose Riesling is a good example of the area's style.

Enterprise, Mitchell, St Clare, Sevenhill and Wendouree all crush between 100 and 500 tonnes.

Quelltaler and Taylor's Château Clare Valley crush between 1,000 and 5,000 tonnes.

Clarevale and Stanley both crush between 5,000 and 10,000 tonnes, though Clarevale's crush has declined since Penfold-Kaiserstuhl took over its management and re-directed fruit from the river growers to Nuriootpa, in the Barossa, where much irrigated material is already handled by the larger company (since Kaiserstuhl merged with the Waikerie Cooperative some years before).

Coonawarra

The Coonawarra area was settled by graziers from Tasmania in 1837, the year after the Colony of South Australia was established. However, John Riddoch and his family, the Scot-tish farmers who established grape growing at Coonawarra, did not arrive in the south-east of South Australia until 1861. There Riddoch acquired a property called Yallum Park, which he extended by buying land whenever possible until in 1881 he held 50,000 hectares freehold and almost 200 square kilo-metres leasehold.

Riddoch decided that closer settlement would be very profit-able, and determined to form the Coonawarra Fruit Colony. In setting this up, he took the advice of an old Scottish gardener called William Wilson, who was one of the great-grandfathers of the now celebrated vigneron, Owen Redman. In 1890, about 100 4-hectare allotments were offered for working men to grow fruit, at £100 each. The terra rosa soil was chosen for this subdivision. One of the reasons that gardeners like terra rosa soil is that it has a naturally good tilth; this ease of working would have been even more important a century ago.

The scheme collapsed with the bank crashes of the early 1890s. Despite this, Riddoch pressed ahead with plantings of vines and fruit trees. Indeed, by the end of the century over 100 hectares had been planted, of which about a half was Shiraz, one third Cabernet Sauvignon and less than 10 per

South-east South Australia

cent Pinot Noir. The first wine-maker was Ewen McBain, a
Roseworthy gold medallist.

Initially, fruit prices were high: Cabernet Sauvignon was
bought by the winery for £7. 10s. a tonne, but within a few
years, as Riddoch was unable to sell the wine, its price had
dropped to £5 a tonne, and the more prolific, lower-quality
Grenache only £2 a tonne. This was in 1903, two years after
John Riddoch's death. Some of Riddoch's descendants still
graze sheep in the area, but they own none of the wineries.

The family of Redman, the name most characteristic of
Coonawarra, came to the area just after Federation. They
worked in the vineyards and on the land during the long era
when first all the fine red wines that had been stored in the
shearing shed on the Katnook station and later any young
wines were distilled. First, Château Tanunda, which is now
part of Seppelt, bought the winery as a distillery, and later
another South Australian distiller, Milne, notable more for its

Australian whisky, ran the vineyard until 1946.

When Bill Redman bought forty acres, some of it planted to vines, in 1908, he had worked in the winery for six years. He knew he could make good wine but not sell it, so he offered it to Douglas A. Tolley, of Hope Valley. For several years, this was a satisfactory market, until Tolley found that English buyers would not take his wine after they had tasted Redman's. However, Redman was able to sell his wine to Colonel David Fulton, who owned Woodley Wines, and Fulton persuaded Redman to start making light, relatively low alcohol but high acid wines, to aim at the true Claret style rather than the rich, strong wine which was taken for granted as the normal product of the Australian industry. Such wines would also avoid the cooked fruit flavour so often found in Australian wines.

During the 1920s and 1930s, other attempts were made to start wineries at Coonawarra, but they all ended in failure. Despite this, the Redmans were able to sell their wines successfully through Woodley throughout the 1930s. Buyers did not know that they were getting Coonawarra wine but everyone was happy.

After the Second World War, a dramatic change overtook Coonawarra, though nobody noticed at first. Indeed, prospects at first seemed so poor that the Milne brandy and whisky firm wanted either to sell out to Redman or to buy Redman out, but Woodley, led by Tony Nelson, knew the secret of its success and urged the Redmans to stay out of any deal.

In the event, S. Wynn & Company, which had appeared likely to buy Château Comaum, as Riddoch's property was now called, did not do so, and Woodley, now controlled by Tony Nelson, took it over.

Soon afterward, problems arose between the Redmans and Woodley, and the Redmans went their own way. This time, S. Wynn & Company did buy Coonawarra. It was the time of the Korean War wool boom, when good grazing land reached extraordinary prices, so that it was a courageous step to buy a vineyard to enlarge and improve it. The decision was made by Samuel Wynn, with strong encouragement from his son David, and though it was the Redman family which had continued to make good wine throughout the bad times, it could be said that it was David Wynn who brought about the revivification of Coonawarra. He named the Riddoch winery

Wynn's Coonawarra Estate, promoted the area, and brought in Ian Hickinbotham, Coonawarra's first qualified wine-maker and the son of Alan Hickinbotham, who had established the oenology course at Roseworthy.

The Wynns had well-established vineyards at Modbury, not far north of Adelaide, and sparkling wine cellars at Magill, so Coonawarra was a major change, far-sighted and characteristic of the family.

Samuel Wynn, born Solomon Weintraub in part of what is now the USSR, came to Australia in 1913. As his name implied, he had grown up in a wine-making family, but the persecution of Jews in the Russian Empire of the time meant that when young Wynn and his new wife arrived in Melbourne, their financial resources were tiny. What Wynn had in abundance was business skill – insight, energy and foresight. Towards the end of the First World War, when he had saved a little over £100, he bought his first property, a small wine shop in Bourke Street. Within two years, he was able to buy a restaurant to which he had been supplying wine. Soon afterwards, he expanded to become a wine merchant on a large scale, participating in the fortified wine export trade in the late 1920s. At about the same time, he changed the name of his restaurant to the Café Florentino, and as an Italian restaurant it expanded and became more successful.

On his buying trips to South Australia, Wynn had become interested in the affairs of Roseworthy Agricultural College, buying its wine in bulk and selling it in Melbourne. Thus, when the first wine students of the College went on a tour of the eastern states in 1938, the Café Florentino was a highlight of the trip and, if they had taken it to heart, the advice which he gave them would certainly have helped them to sell wine: 'Firstly, the wine-maker must carefully consider the tastes of the consumer. Secondly, the wine must be attractively bottled and neatly labelled – not over-colourful. Thirdly, the wine must be well balanced and palatable. Fourthly, the wine must be crystal clear, and in this respect it is preferable to run the wine through a polishing filter prior to bottling.'

Wynn's Coonawarra reds were quite outstanding in the 1950s and early 1960s, but as production rose and as much Coonawarra wine could be sold as was made, quality seemed to suffer a little. Happily, recent vintages have been better than those made around 1970, though less austere and restrained than the established style. The current wines are good without being outstanding, the 1979 Cabernet Sauvignon, for example, being a deep-coloured, rich-flavoured wine with sufficient of everything to improve for many years from a good starting-point. Compared over dinner with Château La Tonnelle 1977, a minor Bordeaux wine from a poor year, the Wynn wine showed much more fruit, a little of the minty character typical of Coonawarra's best, and rather less balance than the Claret.

The temptation to produce a great deal of tolerable wine rather than restrict fruit production and improve wine quality is ever present at Coonawarra. Everyone seeks to plant on the productive terra rosa. Indeed, so firmly is terra rosa established in the public mind as something to be sought after that there was a racehorse with this name running in 1983 in South Australia.

Not everyone has been able to find terra rosa at Coonawarra. In 1972, John Greenshields and Sue Andrews bought a small isolated patch north-east of Coonawarra, after they had been unsuccessful in a twelve-month hunt for this coveted soil in the Coonawarra region itself. Like many other vignerons in the area, they had their vineyards planted under contract by the Coonawarra Machinery Company, normally called Katnook, but more unusually they did so because they were themselves working in Papua New Guinea.

Planting, like so many others in the area, Cabernet Sauvignon, Cabernet Franc, Merlot and Riesling, they have already begun to make wines of the same character as the general Coonawarra style. In terms of wine, the partners, who are a neurophysiologist and an architect, are working well in the regional tradition, aided by the skills of the Oenotec consultancy. Even though they are a little isolated from Coonawarra, the area is so large now that they may be regarded as part of it.

In essence, the Coonawarra growers would join W. H. Auden 'In praise of limestone':

'If it form the one landscape that we the inconstant ones
Are constantly homesick for, this is chiefly
Because it dissolves in water. Mark these rounded slopes
With their surface fragrance of thyme and beneath
A secret system of caves and conduits . . .
. . . what I hear is the murmur
Of underground streams, what I see is a limestone landscape.'

It is hard to know where the search for terra rosa will travel next. Kangaroo Island, close to the South Australian coast and less than 100 kilometres from Adelaide, has a maritime climate, cool autumn, 600–750mm of rain a year, falling mainly in the winter and early spring, and quite large areas of terra rosa soil. Perhaps it is a candidate for the seekers of good red earth. In 1984, the only licensed maker of alcoholic beverages on the island was making mead at the north-eastern corner of the island, diagonally opposite the most suitable vineyard country.

In the 50-tonne class are Bowen Estate (1972), Hollick Estate, Penowarra and Zema Estate, and Leconfield (1975) is only slightly larger. Most of the vineyards at Coonawarra, however, have taken advantage of the abundant underground water to grow as much fruit as possible on the limited area of terra rosa.

Leconfield was started by Sydney Hamilton when he was in his late seventies, as he had become bored with limited vintage advisory work after his retirement from the long-established family firm in 1955. He had talked to Bill Redman about soils and sites and bought a derelict farm at Penola on a spot where Redman had told him, 'You couldn't go wrong.' All Hamilton was worried about after this was sufficient underground water, and when a boy found a cave in the limestone on one corner of the property, he knew it was hardly worth testing, since there must be plenty of water there. After this, he indeed did not go wrong. His Riesling has not been universally liked, as he gave it almost as long in new wood as his Cabernet Sauvignon, which broadens the flavour and removes some of the fresh fruit character. I find it quite attractive in its full-bodied way. The Cabernet, however, has been very successful – less austere and more fruity than the area style established by Redman. In 1981, Sydney Hamilton's surgeon nephew Richard took over, ending Sydney's wine-making career after sixty-two vintages.

Crushing between 100 and 500 tonnes are Brand's Laira (1966), Redman (1966) and Terra Rosa (1970). Owen Redman started his Redbank winery after he had sold the family winery, Rouge Homme, to Lindeman in 1965 and retired in 1982, leaving his sons to take over. At Redbank, he continued to make the same relatively light, firm, graceful Shiraz and Cabernet Sauvignon that he had followed his father in

Kidman ◆

Glenroy ■

Redman ◆

Brand's Laira ◆ ■ Coonawarra

Penfold ◆

Wynn ◆ ◆ —— Zema Estate

Lindeman's Rouge Homme ◆ ◆ Mildara

Katnook ◆ ◆ Hungerford Hill

Leconfield ◆

◆ Bowen Estate

◆ James Haselgrove

◆ Hollick Estate

■ Penola

0   2
└────┴ km

Coonawarra

making after 1946, when Bill Redman retired. The Shiraz, which is labelled Claret, is a spicy wine dominated by its firm acid finish and is probably a better wine, in terms of what can be done with the grape, than the Cabernet; many, indeed, would compare the Shiraz with Bordeaux rather than with the Rhône. They are both very good, however. Redman has always used more art and less science than most of the other makers, so that quality has varied from bottling to bottling, in vintages as distant in time as 1966 and 1981. However, his remain distinctive wines of great merit, reasonably priced for their high quality.

Brand makes rather similar wine at Laira, close by, as befits a Redman son-in-law. In addition, there is a clean, fresh, acid rosé using some Grenache, which reminds one that this difficult style can be very successful in sympathetic, careful hands.

Penfold crushes between 500 and 1,000 tonnes, mostly Riesling and Shiraz to go into its Bins 231 and 128 – reliable, widely available wines of the type which the big companies must supply. Light and unforthcoming in Australia, the 1978 Bin 128 tasted quite berry-like in England in 1984 compared with many Crozes-Hermitages, an example of the fact that fruit flavour is the great strength of Australian wines, but taken for granted when one is in Australia. Penfold began planting in about 1960, as did Hardy and Seppelt at Keppoch, not many kilometres north.

There are five firms crushing between 1,000 and 5,000 tonnes a year: Hardy, Hungerford Hill (1971), Katnook Estate (1975), Mildara (1955) and Seppelt. Hungerford Hill, which also has vineyards in the Hunter, was a public company taken over in 1983 by a combination of Melbourne and Sydney interests, the former, associated with Katnook Estate, presumably wanting the Coonawarra part, the latter the Hunter. Because it has thus been divided, Hungerford Hill's true potential at Coonawarra may never become clear, but it had in fact failed to establish itself in the top rank in the public mind, so that its best wines were bargains; indeed its Cabernet Sauvignon wines from 1978 to 1982 may stay in this category where they are to be found, for they are all good examples of the firm yet fruity Coonawarra style usually associated with Mildara.

Mildara had its origins at Mildura, on the River Murray in

Victoria, to be discussed in the next chapter. It came to Coonawarra in 1955, through its management's recognition that elegance in table wines was not to be found along the River. The wines from Coonawarra are well made, softer and richer than those of Wynn, Rouge Homme or Redman.

Katnook sells small quantities only under its own label, crushing fruit and making wine for many others, as well as developing its own vineyards. What is labelled Katnook is therefore outstanding, especially the whites: Chardonnay, Sauvignon Blanc, Riesling and Traminer are all very good, the Chardonnay exceptional in its depth of flavour.

Lindeman has expanded Rouge Homme greatly since buying it in 1965. Indeed, it is now probably the largest producer in the Coonawarra-Keppoch area, having over 1,000 hectares of vines. In order to ensure high quality from this area, Lindeman has identified individual vineyards, some of which lie along the road from Coonawarra to Adelaide, such as 'Limestone Ridge' (and the slopes of any such should be good for grapes, of course) and 'St Cedd's', after the small, pink-washed Anglican church of the area. The wines are very well made, and recently-graduated agricultural scientists find Rouge Homme a good place to work because things are done so carefully. The Pinot Noir from the area is a good example of the result: attractive, cough-elixir nose, clean varietal palate, soft finish, but with none of the depth of flavour or promise of development of, say, the best Victorian Pinot wines.

The Riverland

The big wineries, Penfold, Seppelt, Orlando and Yalumba especially, take fruit from the Riverland, both from their own vineyards and those of others, and buy wine from the River cooperatives, but for the most part their wine-making operations on the River are small.

Irrigated grape growing looks easy when one walks through, or rather under, the huge canopies borne down by tonnes of swollen berries, but it is not. Penfold, for example, determined in the late 1960s to develop a large vineyard near Morgan. It bought a large tract of elevated land, to avoid frost, and later noted with some pleasure that it had very little sandy soil, so that nematodes would not be a problem. However, the vines had to be planted into what was nearly solid

Riverland

rock, and every summer there has been a struggle to keep the water up to them, as they do not have normal root systems. Further, they must be given nutrients with the water, since so much of the nutrients becomes rapidly unavailable on entering the soil. In the early 1980s, the vineyards were drastically reduced to the least troublesome few hundred hectares, and the enterprise is now reliable and productive, a tribute to Dianne Davidson, Penfold's first vineyard manager, originally an academic plant physiologist and appointed after the company was 120 years old.

When the first irrigation settlements were established around the turn of the century, the sandy alluvial flats and related higher ground were chosen, and it is from such flood- or spray-irrigated vineyards, rather than the trickle-irrigated modern vineyards, that the bulk of the area's 200,000 tonnes of fruit comes.

Along the river in South Australia are no more than a dozen independent wineries, ranging from small to vast.

There are two very small ones. County Hamley (1974) is unusual in that it takes its 100 tonnes of fruit from the Adelaide Hills and the Southern Vales rather than from close at hand, and makes a wine called 'Semichon' by putting fresh grapes into the previous year's wine and fermenting the result to dryness. Bonneyview (1975), which has a view of the brackish Lake Bonney, crushes a little over 100 tonnes and makes a number of very reasonable fortified wines, especially from Shiraz.

Lubiana (1959) crushes over 1,000 tonnes and makes a wide range of table and fortified wines. All the other Riverland wineries crush more than 10,000 tonnes.

Angove is unusual in growing one-third of its 15,000 tonnes. Much of this has always gone towards its highly successful 'St Agnes' brandy. However, after the tax advantage which brandy had over other spirits was removed in the early 1970s, Angove has been forced to move more towards table wines, as well as its popular Marko vermouth, a consistent prize-winner in the flavoured fortified wine classes.

Renmano (1918) is about the same size as Angove, and is successful in the very large 'bag-in-a-box' market, which I shall discuss later. The Barossa-Waikerie Cooperative (1953), also about the same size, is now part of Penfold-Kaiserstuhl, and supplies much of the latter's bulk wine needs.

The Loxton Cooperative crushes over 20,000 tonnes and sells over 15 million litres. It has been quite active in introducing new technology to the Riverland, such as the brimstone process. This is the addition of a large quantity of sulphur dioxide to grape juice so that it can be economically stored until six or eight weeks before wine is needed in the market-place. At this time, the sulphur dioxide is stripped out of the grape juice with hot nitrogen, yeast is added, a controlled fermentation is carried out, and the wine is racked, stabilized, polished, packed, shipped and sold. It is a masterpiece of delay, allowing fermentation facilities to be economically used throughout the year.

The Loxton Cooperative also makes quite small quantities of wine of some interest. I have, for example, tasted a clean, fresh yet tannic dry red made from St Macaire, a minor Bordeaux variety, which suggested that Riverland grape growers should be looking further afield for different varieties, and not simply growing the same as have been proved suitable for the cooler areas.

The Berri Cooperative (1918), its marketing associated with Renmano for some years, followeed by a full merger in 1984, has the largest single winery in South Australia, but it may be that Lindeman's Karadoc, in northern Victoria, taking irrigated fruit from much further up the Murray, is now the biggest in Australia. Whatever the case, Berri-Renmano will crush about 50,000 tonnes each vintage. Before the merger, Berri made some excellent early-maturing red wines, even some which have won trophies at the major shows, an example being the 1974 Cabernet Sauvignon, which, though perceptibly thinned, was clean and drinkable in 1984. The fresh, lively, fruity whites are meant to be drunk young, whether made from Trebbiano, Riesling, Chenin Blanc or Muscat Gordo Blanco.

5

Victoria

Although there was a vigneron among the Tasmanian businessmen who were so important in the establishment of the colony at Melbourne, he does not seem to have promoted the vine there. Perhaps this was simply because his Tasmanian vineyards were sufficient to occupy him. In any case, others soon recognized that the climate was ideal for good wine growing. Vineyards were planted all around Melbourne.

As settlers spread out, so they took vines with them, and wines were made experimentally in many places, successfully in most, profitably in quite a few. This is hardly surprising, as Victoria, the most southerly of the mainland states and the best watered, has few areas where fruit cannot be grown. Initially, of course, many vineyards were planted which were rendered unproductive by frosts, because there were no climatic records to guide the growers. Later, the American fungal diseases, for which no effective treatments were known, became important and finally phylloxera arrived, fresh from its European triumphs. During the first half-century, however, outstanding wines were made, wines good enough to arouse the French to accusations of cheating – French wine in colonial bottles – when the newcomers won prizes at many of the mid-Victorian expositions.

The Yarra Valley: history revived

The first vineyard in Victoria seems to have been planted by Donald and William Ryrie in 1838 at their station (large grazing property) called Yering, on the Yarra. They were

Victorian Regions

followed by others soon after and the surrounding area, called Lilydale, had 100 acres under vines by 1848, 3,000 by 1870. In 1873, Trollope wrote:

> There is now on sale in Melbourne, at the price of, I think, three pence a glass, – the glass containing about half a pint, – the best *vin-ordinaire* that I ever drank. It is a white wine made at Yering, a vineyard on the Upper Yarra, and is both wholesome and nutritive. Nevertheless, the workmen of Melbourne, when they drink, prefer to swallow the most horrible poison which the skill of man ever concocted.

Trollope's 'poison' was cheap brandy, not the local beer. It is not clear with which Yering he was so pleased, for, in addition to Ryrie's Yering wines, there were also those of Paul de Castella's Château Yering and Baron de Pury's Yeringberg.

The de Castella brothers, Charles Hubert and Paul Frederick, were born two years apart in the 1820s, at Neuchâtel in Switzerland. Hubert was an architect and also spent five years in the French army. Paul, on the other hand, worked in a bank for four years and then went to England to learn English and English business ways.

Paul was the first to come to Australia, in 1849. The following year, he bought Yering station from Donald and William Ryrie. The most important part of its 12,000 hectares was a ten-year-old, four-hectare vineyard planted by the Ryries. Over the next few years he relinquished most of the property to the government but increased the vineyard to forty hectares. Despite his lack of direct training in viticulture, he was very successful in winning prizes at many of the Victorian exhibitions, as was his brother Hubert, who had arrived in Melbourne in 1854 and worked in partnership with Guillaume de Pury. After various false starts, Hubert, like his brother, bought a part of Yering station and called it St Hubert's, eventually establishing over 100 hectares of vines there.

A thoughtful man with a great fondness for Australia, he lauded his adopted country in his two books about Australian wines and vineyards, *Notes d'un vigneron Australien* and *John Bull's Vineyard*. When he returned to Switzerland in 1886, he left his eldest son, François, in charge. François was destined to have a great influence on the Australian wine industry for, as chief viticulturist to the Victorian Government, he was most effective in overcoming the problem of phylloxera, though he saw his own vineyard dwindle and disappear like the other Yarra vineyards. Although there is a hamlet called Castella on the map, north of Lilydale, most Australians today know the name because of the success of the marathon runner, Robert de Castella, who is a grandson of François.

Most writers of the time, and judges at exhibitions in Europe, are agreed that this area produced the closest Antipodean approximations to the wines of Bordeaux. It was therefore disastrous that phylloxera, frost and competition from the more productive South Australian vineyards destroyed this area as a vignoble in the succeeding fifty years. Yeringberg's last vintage was 1924, after which the area fell into desuetude.

Happily, in the 1960s, when table-wine consumption started to increase dramatically, and when improved winemaking really began to make its presence felt, a number of small wineries were established or, in one case, re-established. The de Pury family had kept Yeringberg and replanted it with the best varieties, Pinot Noir and Cabernet Sauvignon. By the mid-1970s they were making light, elegant wines with great finesse. The 1975 Pinot, for example, consumed when eight years old, had a quite remarkable amount of Pinot character and an elegant, developed nose yet was merely pink in colour; a deep colour might have been expected. The Cabernets of the same year, and the ones immediately preceding and following it, were firmer wines, with more complexity but still with the same remarkable delicacy.

A New Zealander, Bailey Carrodus, who had trained at Roseworthy after learning about wine-making in his native country, began Yarra Yering in the later 1960s. Returning from Europe, he found Australian wines unsatisfactory, lacking 'complexity of flavour, continuous flavour right through the palate, an aftertaste which stays in the mouth', and decided to make wines which would match this standard. He chose land which had never grown vines but which had an appropriate northern slope unlikely to suffer the severe frosts which have troubled the area throughout its cultivation. Calling his wines simply Number 1, which is Cabernet

Yarra Valley

Sauvignon-based, and Number 2, which is Shiraz-based, he set out to make wines of the complexity and intensity which he saw in the best French wines. Extreme volatility was a problem for a number of years, but in more recent times he has achieved his aims. A firm believer in the French tradition that the best fruit will make the best wine and that high technology will never substitute for good fruit, he has been quietly influential in setting the styles of the best southern Victorian wines.

More recently, he has made Chardonnay and Pinot Noir. These are superlative wines. I tasted the 1982 Chardonnay with smoked eel in late 1983 and it was full of rich fruit and powerful acid, yet disciplined, so that it will open out and improve for many years. The 1981 Pinot Noir, tasted blind with a 1978 Nuits-St-Georges, was recognizably in the same class; I was surprised and delighted.

Land values have scarcely altered in the Yarra Valley since the revival of the wine industry there. Standing at the top of the Middletons' vines at Mount Mary, one can just see why. The broad valley is lush, rich pasture in all directions, the townships of Coldstream and Yarra Glen almost completely invisible, the wooded hills in a big circle from south-west to south-east, clouds hiding Mount Donna Buang, to the north-east. Aberdeen Angus cattle munch their way slowly along, up to the clod or at least the silverside in the ryegrass, phalaris, fescue and cocksfoot. No other vineyard is visible. Certainly a north-eastern slope is best in this cold area, but the nineteenth-century vineyards were on hillocks and outcrops above the river and the streams, between ten and fifty metres in altitude above them, and were over 800 hectares in extent. John Middleton will point out where they were.

His site is perfect and on the gentle, grey-black, sloping soil, cultivated rather than sprayed because of the near-certainty of build-up of even the most reliable herbicide, he has over eight hectares of Chardonnay, Sémillon, Sauvignon Blanc, Muscadelle, Pinot Noir, Cabernet Sauvignon, Cabernet Franc, Merlot and Malbec. These last four varieties go into what he calls his Cabernets. An enthusiast's enthusiast, he is concerned with every aspect of vineyard management and winery practice, from the technical to the magical.

The wines are a tribute to this informed enthusiasm. If there is a better Chardonnay in Australia, it has escaped my

attention. Full of honeyed flavour, peaches and citrus perceptible to nose and palate, solid to the finish, attractive young
yet durable, wines such as this best of Australian Chardonnays are largely more obvious, open wines than white Burgundies at this stage of their development. The Pinot Noir is
equally outstanding in the eyes of most judges. The 'Cabernets' is exceptional. The proprietor admonished me for my
South Australian palate when I expressed almost unmodified
rapture over the 1981 version: 'All those great strong phenolics hiding the fruit; you South Australians are only
impressed by excess.'

'But it will be such a fine wine in a decade.'

'Yes, but the usual Mount Mary has better balance, the
fruit isn't hidden, and the development is equally good.'

'How are the real Clarets usually when they are two years
old?'

Wines like these would have everyone beating a path to his
door, so John Middleton does not have cellar-door sales: 'Then
I can enjoy the visitors.'

Diamond Valley has been a marginal electorate for some
time in Federal politics, but it is also the name of a good small
winery in the Yarra Valley. It has vineyards at both St
Andrews, in the Diamond Valley, and near Seville, in the
Yarra. It is also a rare example of the brewing industry
having a benign influence on the wine industry, since it was
started by three men who had worked together as research
scientists with the Carlton & United Brewery in the 1960s
and who aimed to use their technological skills to make fine
wines. They started planting in 1976 at both locations and
now have about twelve hectares growing virtually all the
high-quality varieties: Cabernet Sauvignon, Merlot, Cabernet
Franc, Malbec, Chardonnay, Traminer, Riesling, Pinot Noir –
they are all there. And the wines are exceptionally good,
although very hard to find.

Crushing less than twenty-five tonnes are Bianchet (1979),
Kellybrook (1966), Prigorje (1983), Wantirna Estate (1963),
Warramate (1977) and Yeringberg (1862–1924, 1969). Kellybrook also makes as much cider as wine, indeed began as a
cider-maker. Its success in this endeavour is a further indication, if such were needed, of the cool climate of the Yarra
Valley.

In the 25–50-tonne class are Mount Mary (1971), Seville

Estate (1971) and Yarra Burn (1976). Seville Estate is owned by John Middleton's former partner in medical practice, but its wines are not of the exceptional quality of Mount Mary's, though very good.

The 50–100-tonne class is as yet the largest in the Yarra and contains Château Yarrinya (1971), Diamond Valley (1976), Fergusson (1968), St Hubert's (1838–1920, 1968) and Yarra Yering (1969). Yarrinya achieved rapid success in the late 1970s, when it became the first Victorian wine to win the Jimmy Watson Trophy for the best one-year-old red wine at the Melbourne Show, a prize hitherto the exclusive preserve of South Australian makers. Yarrinya's wines are well made, and though in my view not by any means the best the Yarra has to offer, they are still very good, especially the Pinot Noir, and quite good value. The winery is an unsuccessful evocation of a Norman keep and lacks charm.

Fergusson is a very successful business, having a large restaurant with the ability to cater for coaches and parties. For this reason, and also because he makes wine from irrigated fruit from north-western Victoria, the founder, Peter Fergusson, has come in for much criticism. This seems unreasonable, as he has attracted both custom and publicity to the area. Furthermore, his Yarra wines, which are clearly indicated to be such on the label, are good, though they need rather more breathing than most of the others from the Yarra.

Gippsland

Australia's first successful cheeses of the Camembert type came from Moe, in Gippsland. In fact, much of Gippsland is good dairying country, the rain spread somewhat more evenly through the year than in most of southern Australia. The pattern of the winds is also different, south-westerlies less dominant, and the result is quite high relative humidity during the summer as the grapes swell and ripen. This should lead to better fruit, as should the cool, late vintage.

Because the climate seemed so propitious, a small number of intrepid growers began planting in the 1970s. They had little by way of history to guide them, as Gippsland had never seen extensive vineyards in the past. So far, there are few wines available to assess how right those growers were. Golvindah (1971) was one of the first to be established and is the

Gippsland

only grower to crush a significant quantity, around fifty tonnes from ten hectares of mainly white varieties. The wines are
variable.

The others all crush less than twenty-five tonnes: Carrick
Springs (1978), Coalville (1978), Djoandah (1980), Lulga
(1970), McAllister (1975), Nicholson River (1978), Parish
(1975) and Tanjil (1975). Most have planted Bordeaux
varieties, but Parish has only Chardonnay and Pinot Noir, to
make sparkling wines.

Geelong

Near the You Yangs, odd little hills which leap out of the
plain north-west of Geelong, is Anakie. The winery was begun
by the Maltby family, but for all kinds of reasons is now leased
and run by the Hickinbotham family. The Hickinbothams are
eclectic wine-makers of great experience and competence.

The Anakie vineyard itself, found by following the Fairy
Park signs to a Jack-and-the-Beanstalk castle on top of a rock
and going straight past it, is a well-laid-out vineyard more
than 100 metres above sea level on a north slope. The Cabernet Sauvignon is outstanding, as one might expect from the
man who made so many well-regarded Coonawarra wines for
Woodley Wines in the 1950s, or from his son, Stephen, who
has been trained in Bordeaux as well as Australia, but I could
not detect any botrytis character, despite being advised in
advance of its presence in the 1982 wine. Most makers would
probably have despaired of making tolerable red wine from
mould-affected grapes; the Hickinbothams have made a very
good one. The Chardonnay is also very fine, in the same class
as the best from the Yarra Valley: intense fruit character,
despite its youth, so that the figs and peaches and other
strange characters mix well with the lemony oak. Tasted
much too young, the 1981 and 1982 examples are obviously
fine wines of the future.

Carbonic maceration, the technique whereby grapes are
fermented whole under pressure, then allowed to expand, so
that the crush is self-generated and pigment extraction is
very gentle, is something the Hickinbothams have made their
own. It produces extraordinarily fruity yet well-balanced
wines, which are true to variety but charming as a class. A
1976 Saltram Cabernet Sauvignon from the Barossa, for

example, was, at six or seven years old, as clean and fruity as a year-old River Cabernet Sauvignon, yet with depth and balance. The Hickinbothams' wines are even better: the 1984, made from Cabernet Sauvignon, Shiraz and Grenache, slipped down easily; the 1983 made from Tarrango, was similar to Brown Brothers' Tarrango, but cleaner and fresher; and the earlier years, made from more durable and interesting varieties such as Shiraz, are similarly easy to enjoy in hot weather yet possess some staying power. The Hickinbothams' process, trademarked 'Cab Mac', has been sold to Mitchelton, in northern central Victoria, so that it will be more widely used for its freshness and its undemanding palatability.

Lightness is not all, however: Hickinbotham's Tasmanian Riesling, from Meadowbank, near Hobart, has great depth and complexity of flavour, just like a mouthful of melon. Consumed with lasagna, the 1982 Riesling had sufficient flavour to demand attention, unlike a 1982 Plantagenet Riesling from another new area, Mount Barker, in south-western Australia, which was an elegant, slightly floral Riesling with plenty of staying power. (A wine, moreover, as the label informs one, picked as late as 3 May 1982 at 31.1° Baumé, pH 3.08, and total acids of 8.3 grammes per litre.) The Hickinbotham wine, despite the crush being almost two days after picking, is deep and round and durable, almost raisiny in its Riesling intensity, thick with a hint of quinces, a fifteen-year wine.

Other wines from the same team have as much interest. The Elgee Park Cabernet Sauvignon, made from the Myer retailing family's grapes, grown on the Mornington Peninsula, on the other side of Corio Bay, is a simpler wine than the Anakie Cabernet, similar in style yet firm and long lasting. (Elgee Park is now making its own wines.) The Shiraz has a regional herbal character, claimed by many to be that of the bay tree.

Yet a doubt remains: wine-makers are indulging themselves in making superb wines from outstanding fruit. Can an industry be based on such activities? Are there long-term prospects, despite the exceptional merits of the makers and the wines? In describing an industry, one is hard put to it to make any reasonable predictions.

When Idyll Wines was established in 1966, it was the first

Geelong

new vineyard in the Geelong area since the nineteenth century. This meant that the owners, the Seftons, a vet and a social worker, had to learn for themselves. Most Australian viticultural and wine-making expertise relates to hot or moderate areas and Geelong is very cold, harvest often finishing in May. Fortunately, as every visitor to the winery finds, the Seftons are people of almost overwhelming enthusiasm and resource, and though there are now about ten wineries in the

Geelong area, Idyll is still the first winery most visitors to Geelong would think of seeing.

It is situated very close to the main Ballarat railway, and as one enters the property one passes an old stone station-master's house, which belongs to the winery. The winery itself, however, is not made of the local black basalt, but of the much more traditional galvanized iron over a steel frame. This was all built by the wine-maker, just as he made his own bottling and labelling line.

There are twenty hectares of vines, about 70 per cent planted to Cabernet Sauvignon and Shiraz. The red wines from these are firm, long-lasting wines typical of the colder areas of Victoria. The Traminer, of which as many as three vintages may be available at any one time, is an exceptionally clean and elegant wine for this variety.

Prince Albert Vineyard, established in 1857, was successful until about 1885, when it was one of about fifty vineyards destroyed by phylloxera, temperance and competition. Replanted with Pinot Noir in 1975, it is now only two hectares in extent but may be expected to yield very fine wine in due course, given the area's high reputation when it was a virtual Swiss colony a century ago.

In the 25–50-tonne category are Bannockburn (1973) and Tarcoola (1972). Slightly larger is Anakie, and Idyll is the largest in the area, crushing a little over 100 tonnes (and exporting red wines to Switzerland and Germany).

It is surprising, given the outstanding quality of the Anakie wines and the best of those from Idyll, that Geelong attracted so few hopeful vignerons during the wine boom of the 1960s and 1970s compared with the other lost vignobles. Surprising, that is, until one has felt the bitterness of winter and the frosts of spring, the dismal climate, compared with most of Australia's grape-growing regions. Yet, when one widens the comparison, the air nimbly and sweetly recommends itself.

The Western District

Grapes will grow everywhere in Victoria and many of the best regions were discovered and developed in the nineteenth century, but new ones are still being established. In the early 1960s, in search of more fruit for its bottle-fermented sparkling wine, Seppelt began to plant a large number of

Western District

different varieties at Drumborg, some 180 kilometres south-west of Great Western. The volcanic soils are very fertile and rainfall and temperature patterns are not unlike those of Champagne. Many of the varieties tried have not ripened satisfactorily, but a range of cold-climate varieties, such as Sylvaner, Müller-Thurgau, Riesling and Chardonnay, are producing good wine. These wines are made at Great Western, so that Seppelt's move to the district did not immediately initiate a new area.

Since then, however, two wineries have been established, Crawford River, near Condah, and Cherritta, near Branxholme.

Crawford River is about forty kilometres north of Drumborg, in a slightly drier area with fewer problems of fungal disease but a similarly cool climate. Indeed, very severe frosts are the main problem and can coincide with drought, as in 1982–3. John Thomson, the proprietor, established the vineyard in 1975, much encouraged by the success of Drumborg. With relatively high yields from his three hectares of Riesling, three of Cabernet Sauvignon and one of Merlot, he is in the fortunate position of so many of the small Victorian wineries of selling out mainly by mail-order very soon after he makes his wines available each year. His Cabernet is surprisingly rich for a wine from such a cool area, his Riesling much lighter. Like a number of the south-western Western Australian wineries discussed in Chapter 7, Crawford River is part of an enterprise, not the whole: the establishment costs were carried by the rest of the enterprise and the development costs are still being met in the same way. As John Thomson put it: 'If I were solely a vigneron and waiting for my first feed I would be losing weight.'

Making wines of similar character to those of the Geelong area and Drumborg, these new vineyards have little to fear unless fashion changes and austere, elegant, lively table wines are no longer sought after. Phylloxera remains the more obvious threat. Almost all the vines have been established on their own roots, though Crawford River will have an 'insurance block' on hybrid root stocks once its existing plantings are completely established.

Cherritta is of similar size and makes wine of variable quality, reflecting the problem of establishing a new area. At their best, the wines show considerable promise, reflecting the area's climate and Roseworthy-guided care in wine-making. Established in 1969 by the Sobey family on a family property, Cherritta's vineyard now consists of a little less than ten hectares of vines, mainly Shiraz and Riesling, with Cabernet Sauvignon and Chardonnay just beginning to bear.

Great Western

Great Western, between Ararat and Stawell, was first planted by two French brothers-in-law, Jean Pierre Trouette and Emile Blampied. With cuttings from Geelong they began St Peter's, near Ararat, in the late 1850s. This vineyard prospered for some twenty years, its wines being exhibited successfully in Europe, but did not survive the century.

Joseph Best began the vineyards which have persisted until

Great Western

today. He and his brother Henry had made money out of supplying the gold miners, and Joseph was able to start planting his vineyard at Great Western in 1865. Henry planted on the Concongella Creek a year later.

Joseph's vineyard was a great success and when he died, unmarried, in Queen Victoria's golden jubilee year, 1887, Hans Irvine bought it for £12,000.

The Bests made wines from a wide variety of grapes, not always knowing what they had received as 'Mixed Trouette' from St Peter's. However, Shiraz, Malbec (Dolcetto) and Pinot Meunière have survived to make fine distinctive wines. After Henry Best died in 1913, his son carried on only until 1920, when he sold Concongella to Frederick Pinchon Thomson, who owned St Andrew's and Fairview vineyards. Thomson paid £10,000 for the vineyard and the name 'Best's Great Western Wines'. Through many vicissitudes, including near bankruptcy at the start of the Depression, they have continued to make wine at Great Western. They have also made products like 'Best's Baby Bubblie', carbonated party wines with a sound base and a rapid fizz.

134

Irvine would not have approved of Baby Bubblie. As he wrote,

> Notwithstanding expressed opinions to the contrary, I am confident that in several districts of Australia champagne wines can be produced that will compare favourably with the best champagne wines in the world.

He brought out Charles Pierlot and others from Europe to make sparkling wines from Pinot Blanc and from a grape which for a long time was known simply as 'Irvine's White' but which is now known to be Ondenc. The gold miners had shown how easy it was to make drives through the soft rock of the area; their tunnels were used for sparkling wine manufacture, providing ideal conditions for maturation: constant humidity and almost constant temperature. When Irvine's first sparkling wines were deemed acceptable by the future first Governor General of the Commonwealth of Australia, it was a triumph of vision and pertinacity.

Irvine himself stayed in Australia until 1918, when he sold Great Western to his old friend Benno Seppelt and retired, having no son to succeed him. For the next forty years, despite the decline in the Victorian wine industry, Seppelt's Great Western was relatively prosperous on account of its position in the sparkling wine trade and because of the influence of the notable wine-maker and manager, Colin Preece. In the 1930s, Preece made very fine wines which wine-makers of today, such as John Middleton of Mount Mary, recall with pleasure, and in the 1950s, as table wines started to become popular, he developed Chalambar Burgundy, Moyston Claret and Rhymney Chablis as house styles. Initially, these were premium wines, mainly made from Great Western fruit, but now, with fruit from everywhere, they are simply reliable.

Today, Seppelt's Great Western is very similar to Seppelt's Seppeltsfield. It is huge; it is geared for coaches; it makes, very competently, enormous quantities of acceptable wine; equally, it is not a place which everyone would like to visit. The drives through the soft granite are still there, and indeed have been extended, and are still very important in making the Seppelt sparkling wines. However, the fact that Great Western is close to the heart of the pleasure-seeking area means that Seppelt has had to cater for the mass market. A few wines, some of them called 'Old Shaft House' wines, are sold at Great Western only, but the special sparkling wines are very similar to the ordinary Great Western sparkling wines. A Chasselas sold only at Great Western is not as attractive as Best's Chasselas, and the 'Old Shaft House' port is no better than many of Seppelt's north-east Victorian wines. Many outstanding red wines have been made by Seppelt from local fruit: the 1962 Cabernet Sauvignon, an outstanding wine, firm, elegant and distinctive. Quantities were always small, and the area's exceptional reputation grew from the assiduity of Great Western's discriminating admirers.

Many of the newer Victorian wineries illustrate the difficulty of making white wine of merit in small quantities, yet produce exceptionally good red wines. Near Ararat, on the slopes of Mount Chalambar, Macrae's Montara is such a winery. The 1979 Shiraz, consumed with cevapcici, reminded one of six tasters of peanut butter, but no one else admitted to remembering what this smelt like. Others noted the peppery nose, the berry flavour and the splendid balanced finish. The 1980 Pinot Noir was even better. A Tulloch 1978 'Valley-Selected' Shiraz was flabby and over-oaked by comparison.

Boroka (1969) is the smallest winery in the area, crushing less than fifty tonnes. Montara (1970) crushes between fifty and 100 tonnes. Best crushes a little over 100 tonnes of its own Great Western fruit, most of its production coming from north-western Victoria. Seppelt's Great Western processes local fruit, its own and others', and fruit from Drumborg, about 60 per cent of its 5,000-tonne crush being bought in.

Bendigo and Central Victoria

Australia does not have a very violent history. The aborigines were for the most part neither numerous nor well-organized enough to provoke major battles as they were slowly dispossessed of the better lands and broken by disease, cheap grog and Christianity. The last organized 'punitive expedition', or lynch-mob murder of aborigines, took place only fifty years ago in central Australia but, like most of its antecedents, it was a low-key affair. For this reason, the few outbreaks of organized violence have a great symbolic role in our history. One of these is the Eureka Stockade. This took place on the Ballarat gold-fields, but the trouble which caused Eureka was common to all the gold-fields.

Gold was discovered at Bendigo in October 1851, and by December a correspondent in Geelong wrote to the *Argus* in Melbourne, 'If the women and children would only go to the diggings we might placard Geelong with "this town to let".'

In 1851, over 200,000 ounces of gold were mined, in 1852 476,000 and in 1858 662,000. Returns were so great that many initially ignored Governor La Trobe's proclamation of 16 August 1851 that the Crown had the right to all the gold in Victoria, and a miner's licence to 'dig, search for, and remove gold' would cost £1 10s. per month, the price of half an ounce of gold in Melbourne.

Some remembered, including some republicans. On 8 December 1851, over 14,000 miners assembled to hear Captain John Harrison, a noted 'red republican', denounce La Trobe and the charges. The licence fee was to have been increased, but the meeting prevented this.

In fact, the Government was hardly profiting by the licence fees; it had spent £600,000 to administer the gold-fields, and the licence brought in only £474,000. Despite this, agitation continued, as yields fell off at the fringes of the greatly expanded diggings. Revolution seemed to be near in the winter of 1853, but did not come. The licence fee was reduced, and all seemed calm when a new enemy appeared: the industrious Chinese.

The mood of insurrection was stronger near Ballarat, and it was here, on 3 December 1854, that the Eureka Stockade was set up, by what was originally the Ballarat Reform League, essentially Chartist in tone.

It was led by Peter Lalor, an Irish republican, and Raffaello Carboni, an Italian opera-writer. Troops had been hunting unlicensed diggers near Lalor's Eureka shaft, where he was working 40 metres below ground, and Lalor proved himself a natural leader in the moment of crisis.

Twelve thousand diggers gathered under their blue-and-white Southern Cross flag on 30 November, and Lalor called on the men to arm to defend themselves: 'We swear by the Southern Cross to stand truly by each other to defend our rights and liberties.'

Fifteen hundred diggers joined a day later in the defence of the Eureka digging, around which a stockade was thrown up. But over the next day, miners drifted away, and when the troops and police attacked at 3.00 a.m. on 3 December, they could only kill about thirty miners and capture 100.

Lalor was wounded and lost an arm, but was not captured. Hidden at Geelong by his fiancée, he returned to Bendigo later in 1855, and was elected to the Assembly in November. He showed in parliament that the 'independence' he had sought in the Stockade was freedom from oppression, not from the British crown as such; in fact, he became quite conservative, defending landowners' rights.

Throughout the gold rush, vineyards were growing near Bendigo, not always well tended. Each time a new discovery occurred, a new rush developed, and vineyards were neglected.

Even the Germans, who developed most of the vineyards in the 1850s, would flee, against the urgings of the leaders of their community, but despite this the names of Bruhn, Kahland, Fuchs, Grosset, Pohl and Griefenhagen rapidly become notable in the area. These Germans, like those who established the Barossa Valley, in South Australia, were sturdy dissenters who had come to Australia because of the revolutionary ferment at home. They made good grape growers, though rarely from wine-growing areas. By 1870, 60,000 gallons a year were produced. As late as 1890, 700 tonnes of grapes for wine made 90,000 gallons, though almost half the production of the 1,000 acres was used for eating.

François de Castella's remarks on the Bendigo wine industry in 1890 are much as could have been written of the Australian industry in 1960, at the start of the wine boom:

The climate of the Bendigo district is warm, but not excessively so, and is intermediate between that of the Yarra Valley and Rutherglen; it is, therefore, capable of producing lighter wines than the latter place, although, as a rule, the wines produced are not of a very light description. Some that I tasted were excellent, and were remarkable for their bouquet and freedom from what is known in France as *goût de terroir*; they are mellow, round, and possess good keeping qualities. The kinds grown are chiefly the Red Hermitage, Carbinet [*sic*],

Kerang

Bullock Creek

Murray River

Echuca

Loddon River

Serpentine Creek

Rochester

Elmore

Serpentine

Glenalbyn

Inglewood

Kingower

◆ Waterwheel

Bridgewater

◆ Blanche Barkly   ◆ Passing Clouds

◆ Balgownie

Marong   Bendigo

Maiden
Gully

◆ Château Le Amon   ■ Heathcote

Maldon   Harcourt

◆ Harcourt Valley

Maryborough   ◆ Castlemaine

Malmsbury

Virgin Hills   ◆ Knight's Granite
Hills

◆   ■ Kyneton

Lauriston

Daylesford   Kilmore

Melbourne 85 km

Central Victoria (1)

Sauvignon, Burgundy, Mataro, Grenache, Dolcetto, and
one or two others, though to a limited extent, for red
wines; whilst for white, the principal varieties are Riesling, Chasselas, Pedro Ximines [sic], Madeira, Ver-
deilho [sic], Gouais, White Hermitage, Frontignac, and
many table varieties. Although the white varieties are,
as a rule, suitable, this is not entirely the case with the
red, the Shiraz or Red Hermitage meeting, in my
opinion, with an undue amount of favour, and such
varieties as the Mataro, Carignane, Dolcetto, etc., being
more or less neglected. Were the latter cultivated to a
greater extent, the resulting wines would be lighter and
better suited for the European market.

Yet in late 1893, phylloxera was discovered at Emu Creek,
near Bendigo, and since the only government-approved treatment was eradication, vines were torn up for a two-mile
radius, and as the more productive South Australian vineyards gained access to the protected Victorian market after
Federation in 1901, the industry collapsed. By the First World
War, it was dead.

Its revival in the 1960s was inevitable, given the quality of
the previous century's wines. At Balgownie, near Bendigo,
Stewart Anderson, a pharmacist who used to play the bassoon
in the Adelaide Symphony Orchestra, is making some of the
best wine in Australia. Like so many others, he began
planting Cabernet Sauvignon and Shiraz in the late 1960s,
then later Pinot Noir and Chardonnay. Ever since the wines
became available in the early 1970s, drinkers have been
delighted with them, especially the Cabernet Sauvignon.
Wines from this area can have excessive fruit character, as
compared with those of the more southern vineyards, but
Balgownie does not have this problem. The Cabernet is a very
fine wine, even when only a few years old, with balance and
soft velvety fruit yet enough acid and tannin to improve for a
decade. Having no successor, Anderson has sold Balgownie to
Mildara, making the wines more widely available. It is to be
hoped that use of the name 'Balgownie Cuvée' for wines made
from fruit other than that grown on Balgownie will not
demean the label.

Located at Kyneton, not far from the state forest and only
an hour's drive from the Yarra Valley, on rolling land which

had never really been tested for vines, Virgin Hills was started by a Melbourne restaurateur, Tom Lazar, who wanted, like many others, to make the best red wine in Australia. With the first two vintages in 1975 and 1976, he seemed well on the way towards his objective, with dense, powerful, purple wines combining Cabernet Sauvignon, Malbec and Shiraz to give an intense fruit palate with a long, strong finish. If later vintages had improved on this, they would have been fine indeed, but the 1977 smelt and tasted like carbolic acid, and the 1979 had, when only four years old, something of the balance and feel, but not the strength, of an old Delaforce Port. The vineyard has suffered from financial difficulties, but under new ownership, it is beginning to strike its initial form again, and with mature vines the results are outstanding. In addition, for confirmed bottle-watchers, it has one of the most attractive labels in Australia: Virgin Hills, the year, Produce of Australia, and Tom Lazar's signature in a broad octagon.

Tasted from wood, Virgin Hills' recent wines are remarkable. Both the 1983 and 1982 are deep crimson, with barely a hint of purple, and tremendous, aggressive tannin and acid but with so much fruit in the middle that it is not overwhelmed by the tannin and acid, but is still clearly perceptible. These wines will last well over a decade, after they become drinkable at three or four years of age.

Even though Tom Lazar is only involved in a consulting capacity with what is now the Domain Gilbert, many of his ideas linger, quite apart from the fossilized hulk of his restaurant, lurking in the trees a little distance away from the winery. The maturation cellar is beautifully simple and works very well: a large excavation in the slope below the winery was roofed with rough timber, black plastic and galvanized iron, and covered with a few feet of earth. It maintains a uniform temperature, ideal for the wine and for cellar work in the height of summer.

The vineyard's location on a sandy loam hill overlying quartz, between a state forest and the defunct gold-mining town of Lauriston, was recommended to Tom Lazar by the Victorian Department of Agriculture but, while the wines are outstanding, in other ways this spot is a viticulturist's nightmare. Yields have never reached three tonnes a hectare, and the wine-maker now tells where the grapes are ripe by where the crows are attacking most fiercely.

Most of the vineyards in the heterogeneous region near Bendigo are very small, crushing much less than twenty-five tonnes: Blanche Barkly (1972), Château Dore (first established in 1866, then replanted in 1975 by descendants of the de Ravin family, who began it), the Leamon family's Château Le Amon (1973), Harcourt Valley Wines (1976), Mill Vineyard (1980) and Passing Clouds (1974). Le Amon, close to Balgownie, is making good reds in similar mould in its concrete block château, but like so many small makers has much work to do on the whites. Passing Clouds makes a Pinot Noir with the strong varietal attributes but little resemblance to Burgundy which characterize so many Australian Pinot Noir wines.

Slightly larger, crushing 25–50 tonnes, are Knight's Granite Hills (1976), Virgin Hills (1968) and Zuber (1972). Knight's wines are very good indeed but less distinctive than Virgin Hills. Remarkably, for a vineyard planted so recently and at 550 metres above sea level to obtain a cool microclimate, Knight's plantings included Palomino and Crouchen.

Balgownie and Waterwheel both crush between 100 and 200 tonnes, but are otherwise very different – Waterwheel wines having some of the characteristics of the better wines of north-eastern Victoria.

A flour milling company, Waterwheel, at Bridgewater on Loddon, has the small winery as one of several enterprises. The wines are erratic in quality, but at their best are very good. Taken at lunch with a salad which included many radishes, their 1982 Cabernet Rosé was sweet with clean fruit but no nose, in contrast to a 1980 Grenache Rosé from Biltmore, in the Granite Belt, which was ultra-dry, clean with a strong Grenache nose and a hard finish. The 1983 Chardonnay was lacking in fruit when compared with the Roseworthy 1982 Chardonnay enjoyed at the same time. The 1981 Cabernet Sauvignon, however, which required a great deal of breathing, was a wine with plenty of backbone as well as attractive stalky fruit.

The Pyrenees are attractive hills, mostly gently rolling country which was once thickly wooded. Now, most of the timber is on or around the steeper hills and occasional cliffs which gave the area its name. Certainly the triangle between Avoca, Moonambel and Redbank, which contains most of the Pyrenees wineries, is not mountainous: there are signs pointing proudly to distinctive peaks a few hundred metres above sea level, the same height as the Great Dividing Range at its southern extremity, not far away. The wines do not conform to Hilaire Belloc's prescription for true Pyrenean wine: none of them tastes of tar.

The first winery in the area was Château Remy, established by Remy Martin in 1963, with advice from Colin Preece, who had been responsible for so much of Seppelt's good wine from the 1930s to the 1950s. Originally, the aim was to make good brandy, since at that time Australian brandy was protected against both imported brandy and other locally-made spirits. When the rules were changed, and the brandy glut began, Château Remy was re-directed towards bottle-fermented sparkling wines. These are big wines, with some fruit flavour as well as much yeast, distinctive as well as enjoyable. Made from White Hermitage (Ugni Blanc) and Chardonnay, they rest for three years on the yeast, and the bead is very fine for an Australian sparkling wine. A vintage is only declared if the year promises exceptionally well; 1982 was such a year, and the wine will be released in 1987. To judge by results so far, this wine will be well worth seeking out. The big, thick reds are sold as 'Blue Pyrenees', a label more striking than handsome.

The Château, or *chai*, consists of an abruptly shaped building set among stringybarks, big cellars dug into the hillside behind. Inside the winery, the tall still and its appurtenances stand covered with dust – such is the state of the brandy industry.

Mount Avoca is a smaller winery nearby, making deep-flavoured wines of considerable merit, the lightest, a Shiraz, representing particularly good value for money, though the Cabernet is a better wine, as is a heavier Shiraz.

Redbank is more a maker than a grower, taking fruit from some of the better growers nearby and making very fine wines. That made from Redbank's own fruit, 'Sally's Paddock', a blend of Cabernet Sauvignon, Malbec and Shiraz, is excellent. Like so many of the cool-area wines, these reds need time to show their outstanding quality but are so enjoyable young that few have the patience to keep them long enough.

Taltarni, which has one of the most distinctive labels in Australia, an exotic haloed figure on a buff background, also makes some of the best wine in Victoria. American-owned

Central Victoria (2)

with a French wine-maker, Dominic Portet, it generated much bemused discussion with its first few vintages, which were so thick and tannic that people responded as they had to Grange Hermitage twenty-five years before: 'Can this man be serious?' But he was, and so are the wines. The Cabernet Sauvignon has quite remarkable depth of flavour, the 1976 and 1977 vintages slowly coming into balance by late 1983. The Malbec is much softer, the 1981 vintage drinkable in a tooth-blackening way at the same time. Not content with these reds and some good still whites, Portet has also made some very acceptable sparkling wines – the white 'Cuvée Daly's' and pink 'Taché Brut', widely available, are both good value for money.

Summerfields (1974) crushes less than twenty-five tonnes a year, Redbank (1973) between twenty-five and fifty tonnes, of which about ten are grown on the property. Warrenmang

(1974) crushes an amount similar to Redbank but grows most of its own fruit, the Cabernet in particular being very good. Mount Avoca (1970) crushes about 100 tonnes. Château Remy (1963) and Taltarni (1972) both crush about 500 tonnes.

Not far to the south is Ballarat, near which there are a few small wineries. St Annes (1970) crushes less than twenty-five tonnes, Home and Landrigan's Yellowglen between fifty and 100 tonnes.

Yellowglen, which merged into Mildara in 1984, is making some of the best sparkling wines in Australia. At a site some 450 metres above sea level, it grows a range of varieties, from Sylvaner to Shiraz, but its future probably lies with Chardonnay and Pinot Noir, for the sparkling wines which it has made, using irrigated Chardonnay from the Murray and varieties such as Chenin Blanc from the Pyrenees, have been very good. Some were made by Neil Robb, of Redbank, but Landrigan, who first came to Australia from France to work at Seppelt's Great Western, is now the wine-maker. The wines, when relatively young, show a good pale straw colour, a fine bead and a good deal of yeast.

North-eastern Victoria

In the late 1880s, the Victorian government decided to encourage the wine industry. In 1889, there were less than 5,000 hectares under vine, but as a result of a bonus of £5 per acre to anyone who would plant and cultivate vines, by 1895 there were over 12,000 hectares, most of the increase being in the north, particularly around Rutherglen. Additional encouragement to growers was provided by P. B. Burgoyne, an English wine merchant who made a fortune out of Burgoyne's Big Tree Burgundy and other similar products.

In the Australian depression of the 1890s, new wineries had difficulty enough, but when phylloxera struck the area in 1899 it was the crowning blow. Furthermore, after Federation, fashion changed and the heavy red wines of the area were no longer in such demand. However, sweet fortified wines came into favour.

Cheap fortified wines sold well on the domestic market and wine-makers began to build up stocks. Over time, as they blended to a style, they realized just how exceptional these fortified wines were, particularly the whites. Whether

145

NEW SOUTH WALES

Lindeman
St Leonards
Corowa
All Saints
Wahgunyah

VICTORIA

Chambers
Rosewood

Morris's Mia Mia

Fairfield

Murray Valley Highway

Seppelt

Stanton & Killeen

Gehrig Bros

Jones

Buller's Calliope

Rutherglen

Campbell

Murdering Hut Creek

Barnawartha

Black Dog Creek

Chiltern

Diddah Diddah Creek

Gayfer

Springhurst

Hume Highway

0   4   8
km

Melbourne 250 km

Wangaratta

North-eastern Victoria (1)

labelled Frontignac, Muscat or Tokay, the well-made ones are almost always outstanding.

The young wines have strong fruit character and a marked raisiny flavour, but as they age, particularly in old wood, they become much more intense, with an extraordinarily lingering richness and astringency. Bailey, Campbell, Lindeman, Morris, Chambers – they are all fine wines. Stanton and Killeen is one of the few wineries of the area which has produced a vintage Muscat, a wine of much greater freshness than most of the blended ones, but it is not clear, because of the rarity of such wines, that there is a place for vintage Muscats as there is for vintage ports. Seppelt, with its enormous stocks, is another company which makes, at the top of its range, a fresh Muscat, despite it being a blend of many years' wines.

The combination of the Australian wine consumer's rejection of fortified wine, the loss of the Imperial Preference, the movement away from sweet wines and the briefly-imposed tax on fortifying spirit at the time that it is added to the wine, which may be a decade before the wine is sold, may damage the Victorian Muscat industry irreparably, to the discredit of all concerned. These wines are worth seeking out as something which Australia has made which, like Phar Lap or Don Bradman, is the best of its kind in the world.

The classic table wines of the area echo the fortified wines' attributes: they have vast body and fruit flavour. They develop very slowly but at their best very gradually exchange subtlety for immensity. In recent years, lighter styles have been aimed at, such as Campbell's Rutherglen Red, but they do not match the lighter wines of Bendigo or the Pyrenees and certainly do not approach the lighter Rhône wines, as one might have hoped.

The road from Wodonga to Rutherglen runs through rich pastoral and cropping country. In late winter, it is a flat, bright green. Every flooded creek or river swirls round huge river red gums, the water a muddy grey. Every soggy paddock is full of ibises, straw-necked or white.

The first winery to which one comes is Gehrig's, an unspoilt agglomeration of tin sheds and beautiful old golden brick buildings, old machinery surrounding trees near the buildings.

Next comes Morris's, on Mia Mia Road, a neater collection

of buildings, but still with galvanized iron as the predominant structural material.

On Highway 16 is 'historic' Fairfield House, with its rather Mediterranean-looking winery. The house itself is a fine example of late Victorian country architecture, such as can been seen around Melbourne and Adelaide. On a gentle slope on the opposite side of the Highway is a fine stone building looking rather like a monastery. The locked gates and unused drive suggest that it is no longer a thriving community.

Closer to Rutherglen, there is a turn-off to Mount Pryor, and in the opposite direction the Jones Winery, a collection of sheds in green-painted crumbling brick and galvanized iron, from which surprisingly fine Shiraz wines sometimes come.

In Rutherglen itself, on quite a different scale, is Seppelt's tank farm, its Clydeside Winery. This is large-scale professional wine-making. From the old buildings backed by so much stainless steel have come many very fine fortified wines, a distinctive lighter dessert wine called Barooga Sauternes, made from Ondenc (Irvine's White), and many fine regional Shirazes, even a few Pinots with intense, rich fruit and no Burgundy feel to them at all. In 1984, Clydeside was closed down for economic reasons; one would have preferred that sentiment would prevail.

Continuing on to Echuca, almost opposite each other are Campbell's 'Bobbie Burns' Winery and Stanton and Killeen's. Campbell's is a curious mixture of new façade, old, well-kept tin sheds and stainless steel, carefully set well back from the other buildings. Like all the other wineries in the area, it has much small wood and large wood, much of it close to the roof, for this is the source of the superb Muscats of the north-east, this hot summer, cold winter treatment. Old equipment, like a disused polished copper pot still, lies about carefully, to give the impression of continuity and tradition, but this is a winery which has had quite a deal of capital expenditure in the recent past. The atmosphere is friendly: one is pressed to try everything, even wines that are unavailable for purchase but of which a few bottles remain.

Further on, on the road to Echuca, a turn-off takes one to the fortress-like All Saints Winery, its rear rather like the front of Fairfield.

Because of the extremely rapid expansion of the Victorian wine industry after 1850, as compared with the much longer, slower development of the New South Wales and South Australian wine industries, as well as its subsequent collapse, the vegetation of the little surviving islands of wine in Victoria carried far more strange relics than are found in the industries which survived in better shape. Thus, at All Saints there is a strange grape called Rutherglen Pedro Ximenez, now known to be Dourado, and what is called a Chablis is made from this; the 1982 wine shows none of the fatty rich coarse fruit of Pedro, as one finds it in South Australia. Indeed, the wine has a clean, hard finish, like licking a carving knife, a finish which characterized the 'Riesling hocks' of the South Australian Southern Vales in the 1950s and 1960s.

Further on still, one comes to the Goulburn River, which can be followed to Château Tahbilk.

Continuing still further towards Swan Hill and Ouyen, one passes Mystic Park and Lake Boga, irrigated vineyards supplying Brown Brothers, at Mildara, and Bests, at Great Western, with reliable fruit in substantial quantity.

But one should have made a detour to Château Tahbilk.

R. H. 'Orion' Horne was of the type who came to Australia to make his fortune. As he wrote,

A sultry haze broods o'er the silent bush,
And horse and ox move slow through steaming dust;
In each man's face is seen the feverish flush
Of hope, or of success; the ceaseless thirst
For gold . . .

urged him too, but prospecting was one of the few enterprises he did not try. He acted, he stood for parliament, he wrote, he tried to promote companies, and he saw that viticulture was important. The Goulburn Vineyard Proprietary Company was to be formed to grow vines and make wine on the banks of the Goulburn River, on the Moorilim run; Horne was made honorary secretary on 16 March 1860, and he also wrote the prospectus for the public issue of shares: 'The Wines of the Rhine and the Moselle can certainly be equalled, but in some instances will be surpassed, by vintages of the Goulburn, the Loddon, the Campaspe . . .' Three months later, following the unexplained death of one of the other promoters, Horne was promoting the Tahbilk Vineyard Proprietary Company, Tahbilk being the run adjacent to Moorilim. J. P. Bear, one of the

North Central Victoria

other promoters, recommended advertising for 1,000,000 cuttings.

Twenty-five men were needed to work the square mile of the Tahbilk run, and less than six months later 150 acres were cleared and sixty-five planted. Horne himself planted the first vines, but his connection with Tahbilk lasted less than two years. As he put it in another poem, he vanished 'in the yellow Wog-Wog', but within a decade the company, now the family company of the Bears, was producing and shipping as much as 50,000 gallons a year, with 100,000 in storage. Advanced plant and French wine-makers ensured quality, though a vast range of wines was attempted: Riesling, Verdielho, Pedro, Muscat, Shiraz, Cabernet, 'Burgundy', Gouais and 'Aucerot', and a sweet white wine called 'Pascorata'.

Thomas Hardy visited in 1881 and advised the South Australian practice of wider planting of vines for ease of working. Irrigation also was sought by François de Coueslat, the wine-maker, but was not available.

The name Château Tahbilk was adopted in the late 1870s, and as such it has continued, though declining towards the end of its first half century through the same problem as affected a number of other Australian agricultural properties: an absentee landlord. When the Purbrick family bought it in 1929, Tahbilk had less than fifty hectares of vines, of which thirty were old. Marsanne, now one of its notable wines, was part of the new planting. Phylloxera had affected the vineyard, but it had survived, a rarity in Victoria.

Despite the Depression, Eric Purbrick reconstructed much of the winery and out-buildings, replanted the vineyards, then went off to the Second World War. Afterwards, wine sealed into the wall of the old winery by Bear in 1876 was taken out and tasted: the red was drinkable, the white not. Wine of the 1960 vintage was sealed into the wall by the Prime Minister of the day (and other days), R. G. Menzies. One suspects that the 1960 white will last better than the 1876.

Tahbilk is a Victorian institution, a major tourist attraction and a maker of very fine wines. It has made exceptional wines, at different times, from Riesling, Shiraz and Cabernet Sauvignon. The Cabernet, at its best, which is quite often, is a big wine, ruby in colour, with strong berry fruit and a firm finish, yet with elegance as well as power. Early in changing from European names to grape names for wines, the proprietors have seen fashion follow them.

Near Château Tahbilk are Osicka and Mitchelton. Not far north is Tisdall, to the south Seymour.

Tisdall has two vineyards, one irrigated near Echuca and another, Mount Helen, at about 500 metres above sea level. Wines from Mount Helen are usually very good.

Mitchelton was established as a fun parlour as well as a winery, with a tower, to be seen on its labels, which is a kind of parody of Tahbilk's Australian vernacular (i.e. corrugated iron) pagoda. It had trouble with flooding from the Goulburn

North-eastern Victoria (2)

River soon after its establishment and more recently has had a severe outbreak of phylloxera, endemic in the area. Despite all this, it makes good wines, segregating them from its bulk wines by calling the latter 'Thomas Mitchell'.

Osicka (1955) crushes less than 100 tonnes, Seymour (1968) between 100 and 500, and Tahbilk (1860) between 500 and 1,000, Mitchelton (1969) and Tisdall (1975) over 1,000 tonnes.

From Rutherglen, one could have gone south to Glenrowan. Glenrowan is part of Australian history and also part of Australian myth, for it was here at about 5.00 a.m. on Monday, 29 June 1880, that Ned Kelly, Australia's most famous bushranger and bank robber, was captured, wearing forty kilos of armour made from plough mouldboards. Opinion is sharply divided as to whether he was a typical Irish victim of British injustice or, as the Australian historian M. H. Ellis said, 'One of the most cold-blooded, egotistical, and utterly self-centred criminals who ever decorated the end of a rope in an Australian gaol'; either way, he is part of popular myth, so it is only appropriate that the winery associated with Glenrowan, Bailey's, should itself be legendary.

Cooled to −271°C, liquid helium climbs out of a glass and down the outside. At room temperature, Bailey's Shiraz wines leap out of the glass and take the drinker by the throat. They are quite exceptional in flavour and high in alcohol, usually over 13 per cent. Unlike most Shiraz wines from warm areas, however, but similar to the ones from Clare, they are very clean: it is just the immense body of blackberry fruit that makes the tongue furry and sticks the teeth together. Diacetyl, which gives hot-area wines their buttery smell, is a substance which is more often found in wines after, rather than before, the malolactic fermentation. Very small quantities, two to four parts per million, enhance flavour, while amounts much greater than this detract from it: Bailey's wines rarely show this trait. In this, they may be contrasted with similar wines from Bungawarra, in Queensland's Granite Belt. The standard 1980 Shirazes from both vineyards were enjoyed with pizza, and the Bungawarra definitely showed some diacetyl, whereas the Bailey simply showed the enormous body of bramble fruit already mentioned.

Bailey's is a very old-established winery; it was ten years old when Ned Kelly was captured, and some of the alcohol under the influence of which Ned and his gang were when arrested may well have come from Bailey's wines. During the wine boom of the late 1960s and early 1970s, the winery was taken over by Davis Consolidated, a maker of gelatine, which in turn has been taken over by a maker of starch and related products, Fielder Gillespie. After these changes, the wines have remained the same, partly because of the dedication of a long-serving wine-maker, H. J. Tinson. Bailey's HJT Shiraz is a wine to be sought out and enjoyed on very cold winter nights.

There are only three very small wineries in north-eastern Victoria, where yields are high even from vineyards with very limited irrigation: Jones (1888), Markwood (1970) and Mount Bruno (1970). Markwood was started by a member of the Morris family after Morris's Mia Mia had been sold to Reckitt & Colman, whose major winery, Orlando, was also bought at about the same time. Markwood's wines already show their distinguished provenance.

Crushing from fifty to 100 tonnes are Stanton & Killeen (1925), Excelsior (1868), Monichio (1962) and Phillips's Goulburn Valley Winery (1908–66, 1978). Excelsior was the first vineyard in the Shepparton area, and has remained in the hands of the family of its founder, Trojan Darveniza, ever since. However, it seems that the best days are past for Shepparton, which awaits a revival, another François de Castella, who ran Château Dookie for a decade at the turn of the century on behalf of a creditor bank before the change in wine tastes and markets eliminated it, like so many Victorian wineries.

Most of the vineyards crush between 100 and 500 tonnes: Bailey (1870), Booth's Taminick (1893), Buller's Calliope (1921), Campbell (1870), Chambers' Rosewood (1860), Gayfer (1913), Gravina (1972), Gehrig (1858), Morris's Mia Mia (1859) and St Leonards (1860).

Booth's Taminick is a winery with very few products, and its best wine is perhaps its Shiraz, most of which has been sold in the past to Wynn for its 'Ovens Valley Burgundy', a wine which has also included some material from Bailey and elsewhere. It is a very reliable, fruity wine which reminds one of hot summer afternoons without tasting cooked. It was not disgraced by a number of 1978 and 1979 Rhône wines when we tried the 1980 in England in 1984. However, it was being retailed there at a little over twice what it costs in bottle shops in Australia, a good illustration of the difficulty a high-cost country like Australia has in competing with lower-cost countries, a problem which would exist even without the EEC's discriminatory import rules and taxes. Comparing the Booth 1980 Shiraz with the Wynn version in Australia in 1983, the most obvious difference was that Wynn's was cleaner and less rich, with no sediment, clearly the result of adhering to Samuel Wynn's rule about taking the wine to the consumer only when it is brilliant to the eye.

Chambers's Rosewood is another old family winery which has continued to use odd grapes, for example Gouais, which is part of the blend in a firm white wine rather lacking in fruit but lasting very well.

Apart from its excellent fortified wines, Morris's Mia Mia makes a fine inky Durif with backbone and fruit to let it last a decade without tasting old.

The three biggest wineries in the area, all crushing between 1,000 and 5,000 tonnes, are All Saints (1864), Brown Brothers (1889) and Seppelt's Clydeside (1886, but Seppelt's only since 1914).

Brown Brothers have been among the great successes of the industry over the last twenty years. I first recall noticing their blend of Cabernet Sauvignon, Shiraz and Mondeuse, a reliable, fruity wine of considerable complexity and a cleaner finish than many comparably priced wines from McLaren Vale or the Barossa. However, the Browns were among the earlier of the medium-sized established wineries to realize the possibilities of cold fermentation and related techniques for making good wines from fairly warm areas. They were also interested in trying different varieties and styles, with the result that they make a bewildering range of wines rather well. Their whites, made from everything from Riesling to Muscat, are fruity, attractive, well-balanced wines. Their reds include the blend I have already mentioned and small batches of everything from Tarrango to Barbera.

Of particular interest is their move to develop vineyards at higher altitudes, for cooler ripening. Koombahla, south of Milawa, is only a few hundred metres above sea level, but both the Cabernet Sauvignon and Chardonnay reflect the advantages of the area. The 1979 Cabernet, for example, is a big, rich wine with strong berry flavour, but none of the earthiness which has characterized the wines from Milawa itself. Whitlands, nearby, is at about 800 metres altitude, and appears likely to suit early-ripening varieties like Pinot Noir and Chardonnay. Given the quality of the broad-flavoured Chardonnay from Koombahla, the Whitlands wines should be much in demand when they begin to appear in the late 1980s.

Brown Brothers have been helpful to others developing new high-altitude vineyards. They made the first vintages for Delatite (1970) at Mansfield within viewing range of Mount Buller, in the Victorian snowfields. A young graduate of Roseworthy now makes a range of wines which includes excellent, deep-flavoured Rieslings for her family-owned vineyard, having called Brian Croser to her aid in her own first vintages.

Seppelt mainly makes wines for fortification and bulk sales in this area but has also produced very good dessert wines typical of the district and surprisingly good Pinot Noir in the late 1960s and early 1970s. Possibly a hotter fermentation was allowed, running up to the 30–40°C peak used in Burgundy, thereby producing wines of strong character and depth of fruit. I recall preferring both the 1969 and 1970 to Robert Mondavi's Napa Valley 1970 Pinot Noir in the winter of 1975.

The Murray: north-western Victoria

There are small wineries along the Murray, but the impression one retains is hugeness. Towering stainless-steel tanks, vast concrete blockhouses, cavernous tin sheds supported by massive red gum beams: old, like Mildara, at Mildura, or relatively new, like the Loxton Cooperative in South Australia, they verge on grossness. Tasting areas must have large capacity and remind one about the licensing laws, for the tourists are there for the river first, the wine later.

Mildara's tasting room has huge illustrations simulating the atmosphere of a winery of the 1880s: they do not match the present winery in anything but size. The wines do not match the room, either: those from the river tend to have a little sweetness, but those from Coonawarra are elegant, restrained, and firm, smooth though they are when young, compared with Redman's or Brand's. Mildara's skills have changed with the times, but those developed to make sherry and port when these were demanded have persisted: their 'George' and 'Supreme', bone dry and smoothly dry, both with

North-western Victoria (1)

some *flor* character, remain among the better Australian sherries. If the climate – physical, social and economic – changes so that sherry is once again drunk in large quantities, Mildara will still be there to benefit from it. Meanwhile its extensive Coonawarra vineyards, its acquisition of Hamilton, and its association with William Grant & Son Ltd, which owns 15 per cent of Mildara, give it an extraordinary range of products to meet changing tastes. Mildara is a survivor.

More than a survivor, in fact: it has risen from the dead twice. Founded as Château Mildura in 1888 by the Chaffey brothers, who pioneered large-scaled irrigation in Australia, it was bankrupt within five years and George Chaffey left the country, returning to north America.

William Chaffey remained, but could not sell his wine or brandy and by 1908 the winery was shut, and all vines had been grafted over to drying grapes, still the largest outlet for vines in Victoria seventy-five years later. But as the wine industry changed to meet the demand for fortified wine, Chaffey was ready and, with a new company, bought the assets of Château Mildura.

In the slump just after the First World War, the company

157

again became insolvent and yet another company, this time called Mildura Wines but still chaired by Chaffey, took over the assets in 1922. It prospered in the artificial export boom of the later 1920s, and in the 1930s began, under Ron Haselgrove, to make good fortified wine as well as good brandy.

After the Second World War, Haselgrove saw that a table-wine market would develop, and began to move to meet it, buying material from many sources, principally McLaren Vale, with some from the Hunter. But their key move was to Coonawarra, to ensure supply, in the 1950s. Much had been bought from Bill Redman of Rouge Homme, but others wanted his wine. The land Mildara bought cost £3,500 for twelve hectares, in 1954 a very high price, but their first commercial Cabernet Sauvignon, made in 1963, is still a famous wine. Nicknamed 'Peppermint Patty' because of the intensity of its minty fruit character, at twenty years of age it tasted like a good five- or six-year-old wine. The company has yet to repeat this success, but its wines are always very good.

Mildara crushes over 19,000 tonnes of grapes a year, but little more than 5 per cent comes from its slowly and carefully acquired 200 hectares at Coonawarra and twenty-five hectares at Eden Valley. It now has some sixteen hectares of vines at Yellowglen, at Smythesdale, and thirteen at Balgownie, with further development potential, and Krondorf will increase its production by some 5 per cent.

Mildara's net profit after tax has only been about 2 per cent to 7 per cent of its sales of $25 million a year, 2 per cent to 9 per cent of shareholders' funds in recent years, despite its premium wines, its efficient management and its range of agencies, such as Pommery & Greno, which are far less capital-demanding. This illustrates again the problems of the industry.

Nevertheless, its Sauvignon Blanc and its Cabernet Sauvignon from Coonawarra, and its skill in handling enormous quantities of good fruit, make it one of the best of the medium-to-large wine companies. Its recent acquisition of Balgownie, Krondorf and Yellowglen give it a remarkably balanced coverage of the premium wine market. If the different characters of these smaller companies can be maintained, Mildara's expansion will benefit wine-lovers as well as its shareholders.

There are very few small wineries along the Murray in the area which is also called north-western Victoria. The smallest

North-western Victoria (2)

is Capogreco (1976), which crushes less than 100 tonnes, and the next smallest Robinvale (1976), which crushes between 100 and 500 tonnes, about half of it bought in, to make wines with a Grecian model, for the proprietors are of Greek origin. In passing, quite a few Australian wineries have tried fermenting wine in pine to make retsina, and the results certainly taste of pine, but somehow under Australian skies quite as blue as those above the Mediterranean, these wines seem tainted rather than enjoyable. Chatterton, in the Barossa, makes a wine called 'Obliqua', a kind of white port stored in casks made of messmate (*Eucalyptus obliqua*), a native hardwood, but the result is interesting rather than a portent of things to come.

Best of Great Western established a vineyard, St Andrews, at Lake Boga in 1930 to supply fruit more economically than it could be grown at Great Western. It now takes almost 1,000 tonnes from the area, about half from St Andrews.

Crushing between 1,000 and 5,000 tonnes are Bonnonee (1974), Buller's Beverford (1952) and Fairefield (1968). Beverford was established by Buller's in the same way as Best's St Andrews. Fairefield is a cooperative.

Mildara (1888) is the giant of the region with its 19,000 tonnes, plus.

6

New South Wales

The early history of wine growing in New South Wales is the early history of Australian wine growing, discussed in Chapter 2. Despite this start, New South Wales was never the dominant wine producer. While its range of climates includes some adverse enough to produce good wine, like the Hunter Valley, the problems of disease from summer rainfall and poor fruit set in a dry spring meant that the first colony became a large-scale producer when it was no longer a colony, after Federation, through development of the irrigation areas on the Murrumbidgee and Murray Rivers after Victoria and South Australia had established large areas of both dryland and irrigated vineyards.

The Riverina College of Advanced Education at Wagga Wagga set up an oenology course some forty years after Roseworthy, well after the revival of the Hunter Valley and Mudgee and the establishment of the Upper Hunter. Even then, the problems of fine wine growing in summer rainfall country have hardly been the main priority, given that students come from all over Australia, as they do to Roseworthy.

Looking ahead, wine growing seems unlikely to expand in New South Wales, as against Victoria, Tasmania and Western Australia, despite the attraction of the nation's largest market, Sydney.

The Sydney area

Captain William Minchin, an Irish army officer, first set out for New South Wales in March 1797, but the prisoners in the female convict transport *Lady Shore*, in which Minchin was in command

New South Wales

of the troops, mutinied and Minchin, his wife and others were cast adrift off the coast of Brazil. When he returned to Britain, he was able to explain the problem away and once more set out for New South Wales, arriving the following year.

Despite sharing the experience of a mutiny with Governor Bligh, Minchin was one of the officers who took a prominent role in the rebellion in Sydney in January 1808, though his true part in this unpleasant episode has never been satisfactorily clarified. Remaining in the army, Minchin saw service in the American War of 1812–15 but not with much distinction. When he retired in 1817, he returned to New South Wales with his family and received a land grant of 400 hectares in 1819. This he named Minchinbury, but he did not live long enough to enjoy it. After his death in 1821, wines were made from vines which were planted by his wife and daughter and extensive vineyards were planted and cellars built.

Expansion continued until phylloxera struck at the end of

the century, and in 1899 the vineyard was destroyed. Before this, Leo Buring had made the first sparkling wine there, and he stayed on until 1920, so that he was manager for the first eight years for which Penfold owned the property. Buring was followed by a French champagne maker, and it was over the forty years that Penfolds had vines on the property that Minchinbury became a major Australian name for sparkling wine fermented in the bottle. In fact, Minchinbury was the first Australian winery to use the transfer method, which is to say that after the secondary fermentation of about fifteen months, the wine is disgorged into stainless steel, filtered, liqueured and rebottled.

Although the last vintage was as recent as 1980, from the 1950s onwards the vineyards were gradually running down, and the sale of the vineyards for building blocks marked the rule of the accountants, following the takeover of Penfold by Tooth & Co. Today, the old cellars are a dismal sight, despite the developers' assurance of their 'preservation as an historical asset' at the time of the first subdivision of the land.

There are still three small vineyards and wineries within what to the visitor seems the never-ending sprawl that is Sydney: Richmond Estate (1967), crushing less than fifty tonnes, and Camden Bridge (1974) and Cogno Brothers (1964) crushing less than 100 tonnes. Camden Bridge is of particular interest because it is on the Nepean River, just opposite the Macarthurs' Camden Park, where much early vineyard experimentation went on, with some success. A range of wines is made from most of the major varieties, and the early vintages show considerable promise, though the area will never become a major source of good wine, given its proximity to Sydney and the consequent high value of the land for residential purposes. Cogno Brothers is north of Camden and makes, among other wines, a Barbera. As I have mentioned, it is surprising how rarely Australia's Italian wine-makers use this variety.

The Hunter Valley

The Hunter has a big-city offshoot's feel about it. The restaurants are not simply good where they are good, they are smart. Only two-and-a-half hours by road from Sydney, not so close as Clare to Adelaide, let alone the Swan to Perth or Lilydale

to Melbourne, it seems part of Australia's only metropolis.
Hungerford Hill, Arrowfield and some of the other larger
wineries have taken advantage of this to add touches of big-
city boutiquery to their grounds, so that one can do more than
merely taste wine, talk or wander around looking at things.
Hungerford Hill has what it calls a 'Wine Village', in fact,
where one can spend a fortune without leaving the premises –
or buying any wine.

Between Cessnock and Pokolbin is Bellbird, with a much
improved hotel, and there is also the Hunter Valley Wine
Society's old wine saloon, where a modest, changing, well-
thought-out range of wines is shown. We found on a visit once
something similar in St Emilion, but did not determine
whether it was purely for profit or partly for information. The
Hunter Valley Wine Society is both.

Tradition is important in the Hunter. Charles King founded
Mount Pleasant in about 1875, and it was already well estab-
lished when his sons sold it to the New South Wales Wine
Company soon after the company was founded in 1896. The
NSW Wine Company was John Augustus O'Shea, an Irish-
man with a French wife; it was formed in an era when titles of
this kind were coming into fashion: United States Steel,
Standard Oil, Patrick Auld's Australian Wine Company in
London. However, John O'Shea was setting up a wine busi-
ness for his sons.

One son, Jack, went to the war and never really became
involved in what was only large enough to support one man.
The other son, Maurice O'Shea, completed his education in
France after leaving school in Sydney, and returned to Mount
Pleasant.

There he became a legend, for his sense of humour, his
cooking, his kindness, but above all for his wine. He was
exceptional in Australia in using very small batches of grapes
from particular small blocks in the vineyard, so that he knew
just how the fruit would finish and how the wine must be made.

He would take fruit from Tyrrell, Elliott and some smaller
growers, as well as his different blocks at Mount Pleasant,
and make wines with Christian names – Philip, Elizabeth and
so on – blending carefully and usually succesfully, whether
red or white. After the McWilliam Brothers bought him out,
they allowed him to continue in this way, and some of the
names are still used, though O'Shea died in 1956. The quality

Hunter Valley (lower Hunter)

is not the same, however: the wines are representative Hunter wines, no more.

O'Shea's was the French approach, but he did not have the immense backing of local knowledge that centuries of wine growing leaves, so that he was experimenting. At their best, his were wines of exceptional elegance for Australia and yet had great staying power, similar in style but not flavour to the best Burgundies. They occasionally surface at auctions, and fetch very high prices, for they are still reminders of a remarkable wine-maker. As old Sydney Hamilton said,

'The Hunter isn't any place for good wine. Only three people made good wine there – that French chap, Lindeman's and one I forget.'
'French chap?'
'Yes. O'Shea. And how he did it in a tin shed with a dirt floor and a roof even I' – he is a very small man, physically – 'could touch, I'll never know. But he did.'

Mount Pleasant is still a beautiful spot, with gentle slopes down to the winery, small, reasonably neat winery buildings and the wooded curves of the hills beyond, but it has changed a lot since Maurice O'Shea died. He had used close planting in the European manner, and McWilliam pulled out every second row, giving it a more orthodox Australian appearance, especially as further vines were planted and a new winery built of the giant-shed kind, replacing O'Shea's small shed, L'Hermitage. Total plantings are now well over 100 hectares, and the crush is about 1,500 tonnes, divided equally between red and white.

One of the reasons that the styles have changed is that McWilliam, like every other big company, likes to be able to offer a continuous service. That is, rather than release a dozen quite different wines over the course of a year, it prefers to offer two or three throughout the year. It therefore offers the Philip Hermitage every year, even in outstandingly bad years like 1971, whereas others, such as Charles, Robert, Frederick or O.P., are made or sold only occasionally. The Philip Hermitage is said to have the largest sale of any Hunter red wine, so that magic has given way to reliability. McWilliam has made some exceptionally good wines from the Pinot Noir which O'Shea planted in the 1930s, blended with Shiraz: its

Pinot Hermitage. The elegance of the Pinot Noir is particularly evident in the 1978 wine, which may still be available in unfrequented bottle shops, but over the years the combination of the two varieties has made for balance, depth of flavour and cleanness and lightness of finish.

Ben Ean is Lindeman's winery in the Hunter Valley, but it is also the name of its 'Moselle', a wine, which, while it is now losing its preeminence, has for many years been the wine which has sold more bottles than any other in Australia. A clean, smooth, fruity, sweet white wine, it is made at Karadoc, near Mildura, in north-eastern Victoria. The predominant grape is Sultana, but others, such as Muscat and Trebbiano, contribute to the fruit flavour.

It was introduced by Lindeman in the mid-1950s when Ray Kidd, who was given a centenary award of achievement by Roseworthy Agricultural College in 1983, realized that Hamilton's Ewell Moselle, with a simple label and the same attributes of clean, fruity flavour and some residual sweetness, was a wine which people were starting to buy in increasing quantities. For a decade, sales of Moselle rose at about 50 per cent a year, a rate which could not continue indefinitely, of course, but which was succeeded by more steady growth. In marketing parlance, Ben Ean is now a mature product and in recent years has been overtaken by several of the sparkling wines of the Penfold-Kaiserstuhl combine as the biggest-selling bottled brand-name. It introduced an extraordinary number of people to wine and was one of the attractions to Philip Morris, the American tobacco company, when it took over Lindeman during the great Ben Ean growth phase.

Lindeman has traditionally used other old local names for well-made brand-named wines. Coolalta is a Shiraz-based wine of light fruit character which is given considerable oak treatment yet retains balance and flavour for about a decade, the 1965 and 1966, for example, drinkable in the mid-1970s. Porphyry is the name for two levels of dessert wine made predominantly from Sémillon. The ordinary Bin 36 has been a useful wine, at its best when about five years old, whereas the four-digit bin-numbered Porphyries have been among the best Australian dessert wines. Four digits signify high price and, usually, exceptionally high quality. This applies to dry wines, usually old Hunter Shirazes and Sémillons as well.

If the Hunter sometimes seems much closer to Sydney than it really is, this is because of its Sydney orientation. When Murray Robson set up the Robson Vineyard in 1973, he called it the Squire Vineyard, after the Squire shop which he had had in Sydney. He saw that the Hunter Valley was the 'number one wine-retailing area in Sydney,' as he put it, and made fine wines of distinctive character. He saw further that with large numbers of visitors, he could develop a reliable mailing list, and that if he made only very high-quality wines in very small quantities he could carve out a market niche for himself.

All this planning, of course, would not have achieved its present success unless the wines had been very good. This they are. Recently, noting in Robson's list that the 1979 Pinot Noir should be drunk now, we compared it with a 1976 Echézeaux from Prosper Maufoux. An unfair comparison, some would say, but on the other hand the best Hunter wines are quite often claimed to be the equal of the best Burgundies. The two wines were indeed in the same style, but there was more complexity in the Echézeaux, and more integration of the different attributes. Nonetheless, the Hunter wine was a fine Pinot, true to variety and showing scarcely a trace of the traditional Hunter earthiness.

The Robson Vineyard is like something out of Beatrix Potter. 'You will not find a faded leaf or blighted blossom there,' at least in a good season. The crush of 100 tonnes represents an investment of about $1,000,000 in 1984 terms. This covers everything from elegant labels on the ends of the rows through cool storage for customers' wine to a little holiday house, Squire Cottage, set among trees in the middle of the vineyard. Customers of the vineyard can rent it with great pleasure but no threat to the local motel industry.

Robson's Cabernet-Merlot is a most unHunter-like wine, of great elegance and depth of flavour, yet his Hermitage, though cleaner than most, is a true Hunter Shiraz wine, brick-red, complex and soft. His Sémillon, at its best, is quite hard when young, but softens and develops the overtones of honey and gum blossom which so distinguish the best old Hunter whites. His Chardonnay is even better, but with much more striking varietal characteristics.

The Rothbury Estate was launched with considerable fanfare in 1968, as a new kind of winery. Not only was the building, a complex and attractive assemblage of shapes, built for its purpose rather than a collection of tin sheds or one giant shed, but also the winery was aimed at involving wine buyers as members of the Rothbury Society. The aim of this Society was to educate its members in wine, as well as simply to have them buy it and drink it. Len Evans, an ebullient Welsh publicist, who had been a very successful wine writer for the Sydney weekly, *The Bulletin*, and a number of colleagues, had seen the possibilities of the wine boom then gathering pace and determined not only to share in it but to shape it.

Initially, the vineyard was planted with Sémillon and Shiraz, the traditional Hunter varieties, in equal quantities, and from the start exceptionally good Hunter Sémillons were made, 1974 being outstanding. Not all members of the Society realized this, however, since these wines were not very attractive when young, and were at their best a decade old, when many members had consumed them at barbecues or given them away at successive Christmases. The reds were less good, the 1972 Hermitage (Shiraz) being unstable, the 1973 slowly improving over about eight years but thinning as it softened.

In the mid-1970s, Rothbury was crushing as much as 3,000 tonnes from over 300 hectares, but later cut back, accepting the fact that the red-wine boom was over almost before it had begun. The carbonic maceration technique is now used by Rothbury to make its red wines available earlier. Its Sémillons, however, remain among the best in the Hunter.

The best Hunter white wines are indisputably very fine, with a honeyed nose, a deep flavour and a lingering aftertaste, developing much complexity with age. They are difficult to describe more precisely than this. For example, in a book published in 1964 the surgeon, wine writer and wine-maker Max Lake described how 'the soft delight of the nose of the gracefully aged Hunter white more than favourably compared to the Montrachets of Burgundy. Those prepared to dispute this had better make the comparison first, as I have.' As a matter of some interest, I conducted a masked tasting of this kind. The wines chosen were the 1971 and 1973 Aucerot-Sémillon blend from Tulloch, 1967 and 1970 Sémillons from Lindeman, a 1973 Pinot Blanc-Sémillon from Penfold, as the Hunter wines, and a 1969 Puligny-Montrachet Les Pucelles

(Sichel) and a 1971 Chassagne-Montrachet (A. Lichine). All the wines except the Puligny-Montrachet had been in my cellar for at least five years, and in addition an Orlando 1968 Chenin Blanc-Madeira blend from the Barossa and a 1976 Crozes-Hermitage from Berry Brothers were included because they happened to be in the cellar.

Twelve interested people tasted these wines, and in virtually every case were able to distinguish the French wines from the Australian. Obviously, this would not be a difficult exercise for any expert, but the group had been deliberately chosen to include some who, while knowing a considerable amount about Australian wine, knew much less about French wine, and their grounds for distinguishing the French wines were not just that these were unfamiliar, but that they had much greater intensity and depth of flavour, even though they were well below the level of le Montrachet, by which, of course, all white Burgundies are judged.

None of these Hunter wines contained Chardonnay. The best Hunter Chardonnays would undoubtedly have made the exercise more difficult, but then so would the best Chardonnays from elsewhere. For example, the 1981 and 1982 Mount Mary and 1982 Yarra Yering Chardonnays will certainly be quite exceptional wines in a decade, and I would happily consent to be tricked at a masked tasting of these wines and some Montrachets in the early 1990s. The best old Hunter Sémillons have their own style and are best compared with each other. They are one of Australia's two or three significant contributions to the wines of the world.

When Max Lake made those comments, he was just establishing Lake's Folly, the first new vineyard in the Lower Hunter for some forty years. No Chardonnay was grown in the Hunter at that time and almost no Cabernet Sauvignon. It was the influence of the forceful, confident surgeon Lake as much as of any other one person which led to the upsurge of experimentation in the Hunter. In fact, Lake's wines and views have been very widely influential, for he is a vivid writer and his wines are indeed good. At their best, they have been compared cheerfully with very fine French wines: Lake has listed for me his 1969 Cabernet Sauvignon, compared by Harry Waugh in 1976 with the best Paulliac and the 1968, compared with the best St Julien by Ian Hickinbotham, among others, and with very good Pomerol by Robin Bradley.

The Chardonnay is said by Lake to stand 'well between Puligny and Corton-Charlemagne, depending on the year's influence on wine size'.

Besides Lake's, the other major recent influence on Hunter wines and wine-making has been that of Murray Tyrrell, who succeeded Dan Tyrrell, a man who had seen more vintages even than Sydney Hamilton, in the late 1950s. The Tyrrell family had settled at Rothbury on reddish volcanic soil about 1860, one family member marrying a McDonald, then of Ben Ean. Dan Tyrrell began his wine-making at the end of the century, and used very traditional methods, but very carefully, until his retirement, so that little sulphur was needed and the wines were no more earthy than the grapes allowed. He was also a firm believer in the proper use of oak for maturation of all wines, so that what Murray Tyrrell brought to the enterprise were some newer methods, some different varieties, and considerable marketing flair. His Chardonnay and Pinot Noir perhaps did even more than the Lake's Folly wines to alert the Hunter wine-makers and their customers to the Burgundian possibilities of an area which had always made soft wines, big when the summer did not have too much rain, the spring too many storms. Tyrrell is an outspoken wine-maker who has always bought in much fruit and some wine, and made no pretence to do otherwise. His true Hunter wines are outstanding examples of the area's possibilities. The whites turn gold and soften in only a few years, whether Chardonnay or Sémillon, and then for years are big, fleshy wines which somehow also possess balance and restraint. The 1973 Vat 47 Chardonnay was very fine and if I had any left would be magnificent as I write. The Vat 1 Sémillon is also one of the best of its kind, as is the Pinot Noir, and all these are still made fairly traditionally, the big, open, concrete fermenters being traps for young players. A former student who worked a vintage there told me how it was almost obligatory for new chums to be assisted to fall in, a long, thin friend of hers emerging from fermenting Shiraz looking like a new-born foal.

Crushing less than twenty-five tonnes are Château François (1970), Millstone (1973), Mount View (1970) and Tamburlaine (1966). Mount View is run by a Tulloch, so that even though the long-established Tulloch name is owned by Gilbey and Allied Vintners, Tullochs are still making their own wine.

Crushing between twenty-five and fifty tonnes are

Honeytree (1973), Lake's Folly (1963) and Oakdale (1866).

Oakdale is one of a number of vineyards owned by the Stephen family last century. It came later into the hands of the Wilkinsons and virtually went out of production about 1960 in the hands of a man called Audrey Wilkinson, a sad figure in the long decline of the Hunter. Revived, it makes traditional soft Hunter wines.

In the 50–100-tonne class are Allandale (1978), Belbourie (1964), Brokenwood (1970), Elliott's Belford (1893), Marsh Estate (1971), Mistletoe (1967), Robson (1972) and Wollundry (1971). Allandale's Ed Jouault is one of the few small makers who grow almost none of their crush. Jouault buys in all his fruit from a small number of growers, their names to be found on his labels. Particularly good are the Leonard Sémillon and Cabernet Sauvignon, the former fresher and crisper than the traditional Hunter style, the latter clean and firm, almost stalky, like a cool-area Cabernet.

Brokenwood is owned by a small group which used to include James Halliday, a lawyer who is also Australia's most industrious and prolific wine writer. He has written valuable guides to almost every Australian wine-growing area and is indefatigable in his pursuit of even the smallest, most recent grower for information. Brokenwood in a sense reflects this wide-ranging search, since it makes blends of Cabernet Sauvignon and Shiraz from its Brokenwood vineyard and its vineyard at Coonawarra. They are wines of good flavour and balance, with, at their best, almost unlimited cellaring potential. I look forward, for example, to drinking the 1981s between 1991 and 2001. Given their mixed origin, these wines are hard to identify, but worth seeking out.

The Elliotts are among the makers who kept going through all the vicissitudes the Hunter suffered, making good Shiraz and Sémillon wines and selling them identifiably in bottle rather than in bulk. They expanded as others contracted and have a number of good vineyards, Oakdale the first, Belford having been acquired when the firm was almost forty years old. Their Hunter Sémillons typify the traditional style when old. They are almost luscious, despite being bone-dry and hard when young. The 1965 was outstanding. Their Shiraz wines are also of the traditional form, earthy and soft and rich when young, but as they age they become brick-red and gain in delicacy.

In the 100–500-tonne class are Maxwell's Maluna (1971) and Terrace Vale. Terrace Vale was the name of a successful vineyard in the middle of the last century and has not been disgraced in its new incarnation, for both its Chardonnay and its Sémillon are among the best the Hunter has to offer.

Crushing between 500 and 1,000 tonnes are Drayton's Bellevue (1860), McPherson (1968), Tulloch (1893) and Tyrrell (1858).

Bellevue was first planted at the foot of the Broken Back Range, near Mount View, just north of Mount Pleasant. The Draytons thus chose some of the best possible vineyard land in the Hunter, and the wines reflect this happy choice, though between the two world wars the enterprise was divided up for financial reasons, one branch of the family taking Bellevue, the other the Happy Valley property.

Tulloch was established somewhat later, buying Glen Elgin from a member of the Hungerford family in the 1890s, and stayed in the family for almost seventy years, gradually growing through purchase to over 100 hectares of mainly alluvial soil suitable for whites. These were rather hard wines which repaid a great deal of patience when eventually they softened. The Aucerot Rieslings already mentioned have taken a good four years to become drinkable after their purchase when a year old, for example. After the takeover by Reed, the paper company, the style did not alter, but Reed was followed by Gilbey, and much wine was bought in for sale, so that, for example, a Tulloch 'Valley Selection' Shiraz 1978 did not say on the label whence it came, but did not taste of the Hunter, lacking earthiness and a firm finish to complement the softness on the palate. The wines clearly stating their Hunter origin remained good. The marketing side of Tulloch was bought in 1983 by Allied Vintners, the then Castlemaine Toohey subsidiary which owns Seaview and Wynn, and which now belongs to Penfold-Kaiserstuhl. It is not yet clear what this means for Tulloch's Hunter wines.

Wyndham Estate can claim to have been established as early as 1828, because it is Penfold's Dalwood, previously Wyndham's Dalwood, established by the Hunter pioneer George Wyndham and sold by Penfold when it made its ill-judged move to Wybong, in the upper Hunter, in the 1960s. Penfold kept the name Dalwood for its line of reliable, undefined area house-style branded wines, so that a new name was necessary. With backing from Anglo-Thai of the UK and a finance company belonging to what used to be the Bank of New South Wales, and the skills of the wine-maker and part-owner Brian McGuigan, Wyndham Estate has made a range of very sound wines, the reds usually better than the whites. It is expanding, crushing over 5,000 tonnes.

Crushing between 1,000 and 5,000 tonnes are Hungerford Hill (1967), Lindeman (1870), McWilliam (1880), Rothbury (1968) and Saxonvale (1971). Hermitage Estate (1967) was also in this category, but in the late 1970s financial difficulties led to its fragmentation, and acquisition of the largest fragment by Wyndham Estate. Mistletoe vineyard, originally in production in the early part of this century, was also part of Hermitage Estate.

Hungerford Hill has also recently been taken over, so its future is uncertain. Its lack of a clear market image has made its Hunter wines relatively cheap for their reliably high quality, as I have already mentioned for its Coonawarra wines.

Saxonvale was established very rapidly, with black grapes at Pokolbin and white at Fordwich, and its production surged rapidly to 4,000 tonnes a year. In consequence it made and sold some dreadful wines, the 1975 Cabernet Sauvignon, for example, being unattractive when young and undrinkable by 1983. Saxonvale was also involved in the financial difficulties of a large trading company which took it over, and this did not help the manager's struggle to improve quality. Now, however, it has improved, and vintages since about 1980 have been clean and well made.

The Upper Hunter

The upper Hunter area is very new, but this does not mean that it has no history: like many other currently successful areas, it had an era in the nineteenth century when it made fine wines. More than a century ago, Rosemount, the vineyard of a German, Carl Brecht, was producing good red wine.

The recent development of the upper Hunter followed Penfold's. Their old vineyard, Dalwood, first planted by George Wyndham more than a century before, was one of the last lower Hunter vineyards left on the river flats, for floods and erosion had destroyed many of the others over the years, particularly when the cost of labour and loss of markets made vineyard management an expensive luxury. The alluvial soils along the Hunter, Patterson and William rivers had made the

Upper Hunter

name of the Hunter in the middle of the nineteenth century, but in the late 1950s Penfolds found they were no longer profitable.

Accordingly, after an extensive search, Penfold planted over 200 hectares at Wybong Park, their new 'Dalwood Estate'. The move was not a success. On the lighter soils of the higher slopes, some of the plantings of Sémillon, Blanquette, Chardonnay and Traminer were suitable for the better Penfold whites, but few of the Wybong Park reds were successful. Many, in fact, began dirty and stayed dirty, the 1968 to 1971 Shirazes and Cabernets remaining in the memory for this reason.

It was an imaginative move for Penfold, the kind of move that was likely for a family-run company, in that they could take a very long view, but in 1976 the family sold out to the Sydney brewers, Tooth & Company, and Wybong Park was sold to Rosemount.

Rosemount is making a success of the old Penfold vineyards, just as the McGuigan family has made a success of the old Dalwood, in the lower Hunter, now called Wyndham Estate.

During the white-wine boom of the mid-1970s, Rosemount was very successful and later expanded, buying part of Denman Estate as well as Wybong Park. Other relatively large wineries of the area, such as Richmond Grove and Arrowfield, have had varied success, but currently it seems that, by staying with the white wines which the area certainly makes very well, both will be successful.

Arrowfield, established by the Pacific Island trading firm, W. R. Carpenter, which has recently been bought by a Western Australian coal-mining company, such is the instability in Australian company life, almost collapsed soon after its first sales began, some six years after it was started in 1969; but, by concentrating on white grapes, the winery has to some extent re-established itself. What the coal miners will do with it remains to be seen.

Mount Dangar Vineyards was one of the first vineyards in the upper Hunter to be set up with the aim of having complete supplementary irrigation. In this, as in other ways, it suffered for pioneering the area. In the 1960s, when the Adelaide Steamship Company was seeking to diversify away from its historic involvement with shipping, a former lord mayor of

Adelaide, Jim Bowen, and Robert Hamilton, of Hamilton's Ewell Vineyards, approached Adelaide Steamship with the proposal that they jointly develop a 200-hectare vineyard at Sandy Hollow. It was established in 1967–8, initially with underground piping, wherever possible, for the irrigation. This proved unsatisfactory, because the pipes were always blocking, so that the irrigation had to be re-done above ground. In addition the property suffered from early frosts – damaging the flowers and diminishing fruit set; from rain at harvest; from lack of rain; and from bird damage, not unexpectedly, as there were few other vineyards nearby. However, very good fruit was produced in a number of years, even from quite young vines. The vineyard was very fortunate in its manager, Richard Hilder, a nephew of J. J. Hilder, the noted Australian artist of the turn of the century.

When the vineyard was planted, the red-wine boom was almost at its peak and the 200 hectares were about equally given to black and white grapes, Cabernet Sauvignon, Shiraz, Sémillon, Traminer and Chardonnay being the main varieties. Since then, after a reappraisal, the vineyard has been reduced to less than eighty hectares, mostly made up of white varieties.

Initially, it seemed that the white wines were much better than the reds; the 1974 Cabernet Sauvignon, for example, was most unattractive when young, a thick acid wine, but it softened into a drinkable, slightly porty wine over about eight years, Cabernet character never having appeared at any stage. In fact, when a trial parcel of wine was sent to England, the red proved more popular than the white. However, of recent vintages, the whites, many of them made by Rosemount, have been typical of the area, fairly light and relatively attractive when young, unlike the earlier Sémillons, which took four or five years to open out, like many lower Hunter wines.

Recently, the Adelaide Steamship Company divested itself of this small operation which, while it had never been an unmitigated disaster like its Shark Bay salt venture (to quote one of the directors), had required an inordinate amount of managerial attention for a very modest return. Thus, though the Adelaide Steamship Company is indirectly the largest or second largest wine seller in Australia, through Penfold-Kaiserstuhl, it is no longer directly involved in the upper

Hunter. Mount Dangar now belongs to Rosemount, further evidence of the remarkable success of Bob Oatley, who also owns Wybong Park, which originally belonged to Penfold.

The upper Hunter is mainly the preserve of medium-to-large companies, and so the wineries are relatively large. Hordern's Wybong Estate (1965), Queldinburg (1972) and Verona (1971) all crush between 100 and 500 tonnes. Queldinburg is run by Kevin Sobels, of the family which founded Quelltaler in the Clare area. He buys in virtually all his fruit and has made some very good wines from the start. The 1974 Sémillon was a fine example of the aged Hunter style in 1983, for example, golden in colour, soft on the palate with a dusty, honeyed finish. When young, it had been very fruity, yet with sufficient hidden acid to survive.

Verona has planted Valdepeñas as well as all the expected white varieties: Chardonnay, Riesling, Sémillon and Traminer. It will be of great interest to see whether such an unusual cultivar has a future.

Six wineries crush betwen 1,000 and 5,000 tonnes a year: Arrowfield (1969), Denman Estate (1969), Hollydene (1967), Mount Dangar (1968), Richmond Grove (1977), Rosemount Estate (1969) and Segenhoe (1970). As I have already described, some of these are connected with each other or with other groups, so that they are effectively parts of larger organizations, which should make for more consistency than some upper Hunter makers have achieved in the past, though perhaps for less distinctiveness. Segenhoe was begun as a kind of consumers' cooperative, but is now run by Tyrrell from the Hunter proper. Richmond Grove is associated through the wine merchant Rhinecastle Wines of Sydney with Thomas Hardy, which gives it a national presence which even its original labels (such as 'Hunter River White Bordeaux') would not otherwise have achieved.

Mudgee

Mudgee was first settled in 1822. At an altitude of almost 500 metres, it lies in the valley of a tributary of the Macquarie River, a little more than 250 kilometres north-west of Sydney. The name is an aboriginal word for 'nest in the Hills' and that is how the town sits. Vines were planted very early and one of the wineries, Craigmoor, was established in 1858; none of the others of the time have survived. The altitude makes the nights cool, and vintage is a month later than in the Hunter, which helps wine quality.

Most of the early viticulturists were Germans, brought out because the mainly British settlers knew so little about vines. During the First World War, when many of the sons and grandsons of the German settlers were being killed fighting for English King and British Empire at Gallipoli and elsewhere, anti-German feeling resulted in one of the more notable German vineyards, Fredericksburg, being renamed Westcourt, after the winner of the 1917 Melbourne Cup. This vineyard no longer exists, so one does not know whether the name would have been changed back, as has rightly happened with many of the place-names which were xenophobically changed.

The appropriately named Dr Thomas Henry Fiaschi established a winery somewhat later than the Germans, and it lasted almost until the Second World War, by which time the only survivor was Craigmoor, once named Rothview by the Roth family who had established it.

Learning of Botobolar's existence from a student daughter of the proprietors, Gil and Vincie Wahlquist, I was not surprised by the intelligent yet unconventional atmosphere of the winery and its remarkable publicity machine, the *Botobolar Bugle*, published from the vineyard to advertise both it and the Mudgee area. It is quite different from most wine journals: the lead story may tell how Botobolar in 1983 harvested ten tonnes instead of the normal 120, on account of the drought, or it may simply announce new wines, but inside the *Bugle* can tell you how to run an ecologically sound vineyard, where the native birds keep out not only introduced pests like starlings but insect pests as well, and the sheep keep the weeds down in winter, or how to prune and what the cost should be (24 cents a vine in 1982), or how to build a stone-walled winery with none of the stonemason's art.

The wines are equally individual, apart from the Shiraz, which can be surprisingly thin from such a 'big' area. A straight Mataro of limited charm has sensibly been eliminated from the range. The Cabernet Sauvignon is extremely fruity when young, and quite forward, yet ages very gracefully. But the oddities are the most interesting. 'Vincentia' was named after one of the proprietors and was a successful

full-bodied dry white, yet in 1981 it was changed to a dessert wine aimed at the Sauternes style, very high in alcohol, flavour and sugars. 'Budgee Budgee', called after a township near Mudgee, is a pink wine made from muscat and Shiraz, low in alcohol, high in acid and sugar. Add to these the only Marsanne in the Mudgee area and a surprisingly intense and yet well-balanced Riesling, and one can see why so few Australian vignerons are quite sure what to make: they can enjoy making so many different wines.

In the Mudgee district proper, the only winery crushing less than fifty tonnes is Mudgee Wines. However, it carries the name of the area, suitably enough since it was set up in 1964 by Alf Kurtz, a descendant of Andreas Kurtz, one of the area's first wine-makers.

There is also a very small winery, Glenfinlass, which crushes less than twenty-five tonnes at Wellington, near Mudgee; and another, Markita, at Neurea, near Wellington.

There is one winery which crushes between fifty and 100 tonnes: Burnbrae (1971). Most crush between 100 and 500 tonnes: Amberton (1975), Augustine (Dr Fiaschi's winery, established in 1918 and re-established in the 1960s after a lapse of some twenty years), Botobolar (1970), De Windmolen (1979), Huntington Estate (1969), Mansfield (1975, also established by a member of the Kurtz family), Miramar (1977) and Montrose (1974).

Amberton has made many good, full-bodied whites, including a blend of Sémillon, Chardonnay and Sauvignon Blanc. Its Dutch wine-maker, Pieter van Gent, now has his own winery, De Windmolen.

While a number of wineries, such as Botobolar, Huntington Estate, Montrose and Craigmoor, make good wines, usually better whites than reds, probably the best whites have come from Miramar. The wine-maker, Ian Macrae, who taught at Roseworthy as well as taking the course there, has wide experience of wine-making and winery design and made exceptional wines at Mudgee before having his own winery. His Chardonnay has been particularly good, his rosé one of the best in the country. Huntington's reds are very good.

Craigmoor (1858) is the largest and oldest winery in Mudgee, crushing over 500 tonnes. Its Shiraz, a rich, earthy wine, is usually good value for money. It develops rather fast, so that it is best drunk fairly young. The 1980s have been disappointing years for Craigmoor, so the very recent association with Montrose will probably aid in yet another restoration of this very old winery.

The Murrumbidgee Irrigation Area

The Murrumbidgee Irrigation Area was established in the first decade of this century, following the earlier ones on the Murray. The McWilliam brothers arrived at Hanwood in 1912, built their first winery there during the First World War and expanded to Yenda just after the war, as soldier-settlers took up irrigation blocks and needed an outlet for their fruit. Italian wine-makers followed, and this area is still the major one in which Italian names predominate, though there are many families of Italian settlers along the river in South Australia and at Stanthorpe, in Queensland.

Griffith has the reputation of being the marijuana capital of Australia, though much of the production is said to be subcontracted to growers in South Australia. This recent perception of the region's character has not aided in the national acceptance of its wines.

McWilliam has overcome the problems of production essentially based on low-quality, irrigated fruit, firstly by its identification with the Hunter through its Mount Pleasant vineyard, secondly by marketing skill, and thirdly by great attention to prevention of faults in its wines from Hanwood and elsewhere. Other Griffith wine-makers have not been so successful. San Bernadino wines, a winery which on the basis of its 1981 crush of 18,000 tonnes is as large as Hardy or Mildara, does not have national marketing arrangements or identification as a high-quality producer. The wines are generally clean and fresh, but I can recall a 1977 Traminer which, though true to variety on the nose, had a taste reminiscent of mixed essential oils. While it seems that it may well trade out of its current difficulties, San Bernadino is the kind of medium-sized winery which will be in increasing difficulty as the wine glut persists.

Whatever its financial troubles, San Bernadino has certainly shared in the training of one of the best Griffith wine-makers, John Swanston, of Jolimont. At Jolimont, light, fresh, fruity wines of great charm and immediate appeal are being made. Furthermore the wine-maker has, in his

Murrumbidgee Irrigation Area

Cabernet-Merlot, overcome the problem of using lightweight fruit of good variety to produce balanced wine. Available for drinking within six months of vintage, this Cabernet-Merlot is a bright red wine showing strong Cabernet character and delicious fruit on the palate. It is the kind of wine for which one hopes from the irrigated areas but so rarely finds.

De Bortoli is a growing company, which recently bought Seppelt's vineyard as Seppelt withdrew from the area. It has moved away from being solely a mass producer of sparkling and fortified wines, to make botrytis-affected white wines of surprising complexity and balance. These are not wines to replace the 40 per cent of sales which came from fortified wines, sales so severely affected by the fortifying-spirit tax briefly imposed in 1983. They are simply very good. Tasted in 1984, the 1983 Sémillon showed considerable development: bright gold in colour, the varietal character almost swamped by the botrytis smell, the palate broad and creamy with vegetable overtones. Carrying 12½ per cent alcohol and a great deal of residual sugar, the wine held not quite enough acid, and the 1983 Sémillon, still greenish in colour and much more closed in flavour, held promise of being outstanding in a few years' time. The 1982 Pedro was a much more grapey wine of rather less interest.

For any winery's first attempts at a style, these wines are remarkable. The problem will be to justify making them. De Bortoli has only sixty hectares of its own grapes, on account of the restrictions of ownership in the irrigation area. It therefore, has to buy botrytis-affected fruit and it must pay growers not to spray with fungicides and to deliver one to two tonnes of grey, crumpled berries per hectare rather than fifteen tonnes of gleaming, bulging bunches. That means, the fruit is twelve times the usual irrigated price. With so many makers producing these rich wines, the market may be over-supplied even without the import competition which I mentioned in connection with Primo Estate (see p.88).

There are two very small wineries at Griffith, each crushing less than fifty tonnes: McManus (1969) and Stanbridge (1977). Despite their size, both make a large range of wines from most of the high-quality varieties, one of the advantages of buying in one's crush from a large number of growers.

In the 100–500-tonne class there is only the West End Winery (1948) – despite its name, run by a family hailing from Italy. Its port is most enjoyable when young.

In the 500–1,000-tonne class are Jolimont (1980) and St Peter's Distillery (1978). The latter was established very courageously, given the glut of brandy which followed the removal of its tax advantage in about 1970, and it is not clear what the future of such a distillery can be, unless it can achieve a large share of the market for fortifying spirit, which seems unlikely.

In the 1,000–5,000-tonne class are Franco's (1959), Sergi (1971) and Toorak (1963). Franco's, like many more recently established wineries elsewhere in the country, began on a well-established farm which the family had taken up in the 1930s. Its reds are surprisingly drinkable, with only a little of the hot-fruit taste one expects.

Crushing between 5,000 and 10,000 tonnes a year are Wynn, which came to the area in 1930, Miranda (1939) and De Bortoli (1923). Miranda is notable for having had as its wine-maker Ron Potter, inventor of one of the more successful cold fermenters; Potter now has his own manufacturing company. Wynn's Yenda operation is not one of its more widely publicized activities but provides fruit for its bulk and soft-packed wines.

San Bernadino (1973) crushes between 10,000 and 20,000 tonnes a year, and McWilliam dwarfs the others with its crush of more than 30,000 tonnes. McWilliam's Hanwood wines are extremely well made, and the Cabernet Sauvignon and Chardonnay frequently belie their irrigated origin in their balance and depth of flavour. The Cabernet can be most enjoyable when a decade or more old, despite having gained a slightly cooked flavour during this time in bottle.

The Australian Capital Territory

Grapes grow satisfactorily in the Australian Capital Territory but the vineyards, as yet, have not established themselves otherwise than in their captive market, the out-of-this-world world that is Canberra. Visitors gawp at the War Museum, the National Library, the National Gallery or the High Court, but they are unlikely to drive out to the north past Hall and sample the local product, from the Murrumbateman Winery. Customers are mainly local, as they are for the other, smaller, less actively promoted wines. (Some, like Lark Hill, at very high altitude near Lake George, show real promise but are not widely available.) There are other signs of the wine industry, however: the Embassy Hotel, for example, is owned by Denman Estate Wines, an upper Hunter winery, and these one can buy in the dining room.

Other minor areas

George Wyndham was a well-educated, well-travelled Englishman of the gentleman farmer type. He came to Australia in 1827, when almost twenty-seven, and at his property, Dalwood, near Branxton, he tried growing almost everything. What was successful was the grape vine. However, although it was a very successful property during the mid-nineteenth century, Wyndham himself had to leave the Hunter during the rural depression of the 1840s, so he moved north to Inverell, establishing vines there also. Today there is only one commercial vineyard, Gilgai, at Inverell but, should the current wine industry depression pass, it is one of the many areas in Australia which holds promise for the future.

A number of other areas have single pioneering vineyards. For example, near Shoalhaven, inland from the heavy-industrial city of Wollongong, is Jasper Valley Wines (1976). Although it is over 100 kilometres from Sydney, in the opposite direction to the Hunter and Mudgee, it has every chance of success because of its proximity to Wollongong and Port Kembla. With a wine-maker trained at Roseworthy and a climate not unlike Mudgee, its early vintages have been well received in the local market (and are unobtainable elsewhere). In the opposite direction, north of the Hunter, is Cassegrain Wines (1980), near Port Macquarie, where a century ago there were scores of small wineries.

Other wineries are also mostly very small: Barwang (1975), near Young, and Chislett's Wines, near Forbes in the Lachlan Valley, both grow and crush less than fifty tonnes, for example. These areas may be successful but, given the increases in production from established and successful areas, one must predict little market impact in the near future.

At Tumbarumba, in the Australian Alps, the very small Tumbarumba Champagne Estates makes a promising sparkling wine, Beaumont Brut, by the *méthode champenoise* from Chardonnay and Crouchen. It does not yet have the small bead of a good champagne or the strong fruit character of the best from Château Remy or Yellowglen, but it is good enough to be a wine to watch.

An exception to the rule that unrecognized areas will have small wineries is Cubbaroo Wines (1970), which crushes over 500 tonnes from twenty hectares of vines in the Namoi Valley, Australia's main cotton-growing area. Despite the unpropitious climate and the irrigated vines, this hot-area vineyard produced quite drinkable red wines, though of the thick, inky type which is not to everyone's taste. Much of the credit for the wines' quality must go to Brian McGuigan of Wyndham Estate, in the Hunter, who has made them.

7

Western Australia

Grape growing in Western Australia began almost as early as in Tasmania and earlier than in Victoria or South Australia. The cool, wet winters and long, dry summers made for reliable high yields and few disease problems. Only much later was it realized that these same advantages made fine wines harder to achieve, and by then the Swan Valley was established as the centre of the industry.

Change has come recently but rapidly, just as it has come to other aspects of Western Australian life, so that this very separate part of Australia, which voted – without success – to secede from the Commonwealth in 1933, is now richer and growing in population faster than most other parts of Australia, rather like California, in the United States, a generation ago.

The Swan Valley

The most notable of all the Western Australian vineyards is Houghton. It was established quite early. The name came from Colonel Houghton, one of three proprietors who jointly planted vines on the Swan, but it was a Scottish medical man, John Ferguson, who established the vineyard properly after buying it in 1859.

His son, Charles Ferguson, who was born in Perth in 1847 and died there in 1940, was the first cellar-hand, writing of the first vintage of 100 litres in 1859: 'It was my job to drop in more pebbles as evaporation went on, until fermentation ceased. This was tested by a match at the bung hole and when

Western Australia regions

half a dozen burned one's finger before going out, fermentation was deemed to have run its course.' Despite being associated with wine for most of his very long life, Charles Ferguson went pearling in the north-west of Western Australia in the 1870s, and before this had caught a notorious bushranger, 'Moondyne Joe', in the Houghton cellars. By the time Ferguson retired in 1911, there were over fifty hectares of vines at the property on the middle Swan, together with a cricket pitch which was for many years the home ground of the Swan Cricket Club.

For over a half a century, through various changes of ownership, Houghton had a constant factor: the Mann family as viticulturists and wine-makers. They came in 1910, to make the Ferguson family's wine. It was a vineyard aimed at making the best wines, with yields kept down below five tonnes per hectare, and grapes bought in when their own were not good enough.

In 1922 Jack Mann had his first vintage and remained in charge of fifty-one. His son, Dorham Mann, was also a leading wine-maker, with Houghtons and elsewhere, but it was Jack Mann who set the company on the path to success. In the 1930s he used Chenin Blanc to make what was called a 'Chablis' in small quantities, most of the fruit being used for sherry, for from Western Australia, as elsewhere, sherry was what was wanted by the English market.

In 1937, Mann had made his first 'White Burgundy', also mainly from Chenin Blanc grapes, but picked riper and left on the skins for twenty-four hours, with extra acid added if the wine was too soft. As a result, a wine of tremendous flavour yet with good balance was produced, quite different from the Hunter Sémillon and yet appealing to the same kind of drinker. For many Australians, in fact, 'White Burgundy' meant Houghton's, not Hunter Riesling.

The isolation of Western Australia perhaps also encouraged Mann to experiment in other ways, for example with a Verdielho and Tokay (Muscadelle) blend, sold simply as 'Verdell'. Another experiment was a red wine called 'Strelley', light in character but very similar to the Cabernet and Shiraz which were made at the same time. Typical hot-area wines with considerable amounts of butter (diacetyl) and burnt jam on both nose and palate, they were nonetheless cheap and enjoyable drinking in South Australia from the early 1960s to the early 1970s, remaining tolerable until a bitter finish began to develop. Changes in markets made them less cheap after this, and the acquisition of the company by Hardy led to changes in wine-making, so that they are less distinctive but better wines.

Sandalford was another vineyard established very early in Western Australia which is still in production. It was started by the explorer and surveyor, John Septimus Roe. It too was on the Swan, and indeed most of the early vineyards were on the river flats or banks, where clearing the timber was easier, the soil better and the water more reliable. Roe made sixteen journeys of exploration, seeing himself as finishing the work of Matthew Flinders and then surveying the hinterland of the new colonies in Western Australia. Thus, it was his descendants who established the vineyard, initially for table fruit and dried fruit and later, especially this century, for wine grape production. Hence, while Sandalford is a very old vineyard, it has not made as great a contribution to wine development as Houghton.

Swan Valley

The same applies to Olive Farm, the other very old vineyard, indeed perhaps the oldest surviving in Australia. Thomas Waters, an Englishman who had worked in the South African wine industry, arrived, unlike most vignerons, with the declared aim of establishing a vineyard. He planted it in 1829 and 1830. Waters' cellar is still in use, though the vineyard has been in the hands of one of the many Yugoslav wine-making families for about fifty years. The current Yurisich wine-maker is Roseworthy-trained, however, not European-trained. Olive Farm's White Burgundy, similar in character to Houghton's, has been reliable for many years, always enjoyable by those who like their dry whites fruity.

Bassendean Estate is one of the best small wineries on the Swan, and very easy to reach, as it is less than twenty minutes' drive from the centre of Perth. Established by an Italian family in 1951, it still only crushes about fifty tonnes a year, of which less than half is grown on the property. Despite its small size, it makes good wines of the slightly more old-fashioned style: the reds, mainly made from Shiraz, are soft, rich wines showing a little of their warm-climate ancestry, altogether delicious, and the Chenin Blanc is reminiscent of the earlier Houghton White Burgundies in its abundance of fruit flavour and in the way it develops an attractive slightly oxidized flavour fairly young.

Just as there is a Côtes de la Vallée on some of the flattest land at McLaren Vale (established by a retired French teacher, D. L. Noon), there is a Côte de Boulanger in the Swan. The proprietors of the latter, Evans & Tate, are making some of the best wines of the area.

They seem to have done everything right since buying Gnangara Wines, on the river. With the aid of refrigeration and air-conditioning, they have been making elegant Swan wines and from their property, Redbrook, at Willyabrup, in the Margaret River region, they have been producing even better wines. In the future one feels that their Swan wines will become much less important, since there are only four hectares at Gnangara and even less at Bakers Hill, the farm of one of the proprietors. Accordingly, their wines should improve further, from a current very high standard.

In the smallest category, that is less than twenty-five tonnes, the wineries are all relatively new: Baskerville (1951), Lakeville (1978), Lamont (1978) and Vindara (1978). It is therefore pleasing to note that, as well as aiming at the premium table-wine market, these vineyards are still growing varieties like Muscat to make rich dessert wines of the type which the area has always made so well, though in such small quantities that they are little known outside Perth. Baskerville is one of the few vineyards in the Swan Valley to plant Malbec, making a fine, rich, soft red of good reliable quality. The proprietor of Lamont is the son-in-law of Jack Mann, formerly of Houghton, and the wines are as one would expect: made with great care and affection, and full of flavour.

Making between twenty-five and fifty tonnes are Bassendean (1951), Glenalwyn (1933), Henley Park (1935), Highway Wines (1953), Revelry (1930) and Westfield (1922). Glenalwyn and Henley Park are among the many wineries in the Swan whose proprietors originate from Yugoslavia. Probably the most notable of these wineries is Westfield, which has a vineyard of less than eight hectares on which the aim is to limit production and raise quality, with modest quantities of very good fruit bought in to complement what is grown. The usual Swan full-bodied whites are made, from Verdielho, Sémillon and Chenin Blanc, but clean yet very fruity reds are also made, from Cabernet Sauvignon, Shiraz and Malbec.

There are only two wineries in the next largest category, 50–100 tonnes: Peters (1955) and Twin Hills (1937).

The 100–500-tonne class includes two already discussed, Olive Farm and Evans & Tate, notable for introducing modern wine-making techniques to the Swan. The wineries are Ellendale (formerly Sveta Maria) (1904), Evans & Tate (1971), Jadran (1927), Olive Farm and Vignacourt (1955). Vignacourt makes a good vintage port of the older style, much rich blackberry fruit and a rather soft finish.

Crushing between 500 and 1,000 tonnes is Sandalford (1840). Valencia was once in this category, or larger, when it was part of Emu Wines, of the United Kingdom, but now the name is no longer used by Hardy, the present proprietor, and the twenty hectares of black grapes which recently remained no longer have a separate identity.

Houghton crushes several thousand tonnes, much of it from Moondah Brook, over 100 kilometres north, and Frankland River Vineyard, in the Mount Barker area of the far south. Thus, as at McLaren Vale, Hardy is the dominant producer.

About thirty kilometres south-east of Perth, at Bickley, is Woodhenge Wines, where Brian Murphy, a jovial computer software entrepreneur, makes rich Cabernet-Shiraz wines with something of the Swan's character. The cooler climate may lead to even better things.

South-western Western Australia

In most cases, the surroundings of vineyards are boringly gentle slopes or even completely flat land susceptible to frosts, together with towns and villages, for vineyards are often planted on the land where life is less real and earnest than usual, and there people want to live as well. Only in a land of vast space, developed recently, are houses rare in vineyard land.

Travelling south from Kojonup towards Albany, one drops gently a few hundred metres in altitude over 200 kilometres into what is, though there is still considerable karri and jarrah forest remaining, for the most part relatively intensive mixed farming country, the houses closer together than in the sheep country further inland; as one nears Mount Barker much of it remains relatively green all the year round. Western Australia is huge, but only a little of it is really suitable for vines: impose the fifty-centimetre rainfall isohyet and the 18°C January mean temperature isotherm on the map, seek out suitable soils and the area is tiny.

However, around the farming towns of Mount Barker and Franklin River about twenty vineyards have been established, and a couple of hundred kilometres west, around Margaret River, rather more. And they have all been established since the Western Australian Department of Agriculture, led by John Gladstones, identified some twenty years ago the combination of long, cool, dry summers, cool winters and adequate soils necessary for production of really high-quality fruit.

Wine people are friendly everywhere, and Western Australians of all kinds are renowned throughout the Commonwealth for the warmth of their hospitality. Naturally the Western Australian wine districts are particularly friendly. When an elderly relation of mine was headed in that direction, I commented to her, on one vigneron, that I did not know him, though the name was familiar. As she is a little hard of

Western Australia climate

hearing, when she and her sister arrived in the district, she said, 'These people are friends of Oliver's: we must visit them.'

At the vineyard, the proprietor, they found, was away and the shop shut because the new season's wines were still in wood. However, armed with my name, the intrepid ladies were welcomed in, shown the wines from the wood and the delightful holiday house and sped on their way much cheered. I have never had the courage to visit my unknown friends.

Lower Great Southern Area

There are at least eight very small vineyards in the Mount Barker region, all crushing less than twenty-five tonnes: Hay River (1974), Mount Shadforth (1975), Narrikup (1977), Perillup (1976), Redmond (1975), Tinglewood (1976), Waterman (1976) and Yannup (1980). Because they are so small – Narrikup and Perillup, for example, each crushing less than five tonnes – they can be eccentric, or at least different. Tinglewood is the only vineyard actually located in the karri forest, not quite like the witch's cottage in Hansel and Gretel, but with fifty-metre-tall timber not far away. It makes 'Red

195

Perth 250 km

0 20 km

Katanning
◆ Pinwernying

Kojonup

Cranbrook

Alkoomi ◆

◆ Frankland River

Château
◆ Barker   Jingalla ◆

Rocky Gully   ◆ Perillup

Conti Forest Hill   Mount Barker

Plantagenet   Goundrey   Narang ◆

Genesta Estate   Waterman

Hay River   Narrikup   ◆ Narrikup Wines

Tinglewood ◆   Redmond   Redmond

Denmark

Albany

Lower Great Southern Area

Tingle' and 'White Tingle' from Cabernet Sauvignon, Shiraz and Riesling. I have not tried them. Hay River, with a Roseworthy-trained wine-maker, planted only Cabernet Sauvignon, and Narrikup Riesling only. Narang (1980), somewhat larger than Narrikup, has also planted nothing but Riesling.

Alkoomi (1971), Conti Forest Hill (1966), Galafrey (1975), Genesta (1975) and Goundrey (1971) crush between fifty and 100 tonnes. Alkoomi grows Merlot, Malbec, Sémillon and Sauvignon Blanc as well as the expected Cabernet Sauvignon, Shiraz and Riesling, and all are clean, fresh, fruity, well-balanced wines when young, suggesting that they will develop well. Conti Forest Hill, which had Dorham Mann as wine-maker initially, is in orchard country, for the Denmark-Mount Barker area has long been notable for the quality of its apples, codlin-moth free, unlike those of the eastern states'. Goundrey has its winery in the town of Denmark in a former butter factory, like Grosset at Auburn, in South Australia. The rise of the wine industry has helped ease the decline of other primary industries in a number of high-rainfall areas of Australia, though wine remains relatively small as an industry.

Plantagenet began crushing what has now risen to more than 100 tonnes a year in a converted apple-packing shed in 1968 and its wine-makers have helped Goundrey, Waterman and others with their early vintage. As the largest local wine-maker, Plantagenet has very happily determined much of the style of the area. Its Riesling is reliably good, its Shiraz much better.

Frankland River is, of course, much larger than Plantagenet, its 100 hectares of vines putting it into the 500–1,000-tonne class, but as the wines are made in the Swan by Houghton, its influence has not been as great as one might have expected from the fact that it has almost half of the vines in the area.

Margaret River

Most birds look awkward in palm trees, but it was not to keep them away that Seppelt planted its extraordinary avenues of palm trees half a century ago: it was to keep workers employed in the Depression. Bird damage is in any case a particular problem with small, isolated or fringe vineyards.

When Vasse Felix was established eight kilometres west of the small town of Cowaramup in 1967, it had marri, *Eucalyptus calophylla*, very close to the vines, and virtually no other vineyards in the area. The marri is a handsome, slow-growing tree, similar in appearance to the red-flowering gum, *Eucalyptus ficifolia*, with pale, fissured, fibrous bark and gum-nuts about three centimetres in diameter. In January, when it flowers, large flocks of silvereyes, *Zosterops lateralis*, congregate to feed on the nectar. For Vasse Felix, the bird attacks on the small initial crops were disastrous and could have been so for later, larger crops. Not only are berries eaten by birds, but damaged berries are splendid hosts for fungi of all kinds.

Vasse Felix's proprietor, medical practitioner Tom Cullity, tried everything possible, including the falcon which now decorates the label, but the only real solution to bird damage comes with much more extensive contiguous vineyards. Temporary aid has come from amplifying confusing sounds which interfere with the birds' contact calls, which they use in dense woodland to keep the flock together.

Fortunately, good wines have been made despite this problem. The reds tends to be lighter in style than others in the area, but clean, fruity and attractive, especially when young.

Margaret River has a maritime climate: the vineyards all lie on the coastal strip between Cape Leeuwin and Cape Naturaliste. Such a climate should protect against frosts, but in fact these have on occasion been very severe. Moss Wood, for example, lost three of its first five possible Chardonnay crops to frost. For later-flowering varieties, however, such as Cabernet Sauvignon, the very cold spring in years like 1981 seems to have been helpful. In that year, Moss Wood, Cullen's Willyabrup and Cape Mentelle all produced exceptionally fine Cabernet wines, deep reddish-purple, with strong berry overtones to smell and rich, strong, fruity taste. One remarkable characteristic which the red wines of this area seem to share is balance when young, so that even though the wines give promise of staying at their best for a decade or more, they are very drinkable when only one, two or three years old. In this, they differ from the colder-climate wines of Geelong or the Yarra Valley, and are closer to Coonawarra, though they are usually more intense than the Coonawarra wines.

A friend who has some land in south-western Western Australia gave us in the winter of 1982, for reasons best known to

CAPE NATURALISTE

GEOGRAPHE BAY

Perth 170 km

Stratham

Capel Vale ◆ Capel

Kirup

Ludlow

Albert Vinci ◆

Happ ◆

Busselton

Vasse

Clairault

Woodlands ◆

Moss Wood ◆

Woodlands

Willyabrup

Margaret River

1 2 3 4
5 6 7
8 9

Cullen's Willyabrup

Wright

Margaret River

T & G Merchant

Cape Mentelle

Château Xanadu

Gherardi

Redgate ◆

Witchcliff

Leeuwin Estate

Gillespie ◆

1 ◆ Redbrook
2 ◆ Sandalford
3 ◆ Willespie
4 ◆ Sussex Vale
5 ◆ Ribbon Vale
6 ◆ La Taj
7 ◆ Ashbrook Estate
8 ◆ Graylin
9 ◆ Vasse Felix

Blackwood River

Karridale

0   20
        km

Augusta

CAPE LEEUWIN

Margaret River

himself, a 1962 Léoville Poyferré, a 1977 Vasse Felix Cabernet Sauvignon and a 1977 Moss Wood Cabernet Sauvignon. They were quite distinguishable. The French wine was in beautiful condition, light, soft, clean, balanced and elegant, with an indescribable nose and flavour. The Vasse Felix seemed to be nearing the end of its run, since it had a slightly bitter finish. The Moss Wood, on the other hand, was in splendid condition, showed fine chocolate caramel fruit and offered the possibility of further development. The comparison was most unfair: in twenty years' time, some of the current wines from both Vasse Felix and Moss Wood should be compared with some of the current third- or fourth-growth clarets, to the great satisfaction and edification of all.

At Cape Mentelle, David Hohnen, who worked previously at Stonyfell, in South Australia, and Taltarni, in Victoria, is making really big wines, influenced a little, perhaps, by the styles with which he has previously worked but more by the remarkable fruit which Margaret River produces. The wines have richness and complexity in their fruit, great depth of tannin and strong acid, so that they can cope with quite a bit of oak treatment, yet they are enjoyable when only two or three years old, with the certainty of five or ten years' improvement ahead. Merlot is not needed to soften the Cabernet Sauvignon, but Hohnen uses it to add further complexity to his wines. He has won the Jimmy Watson Trophy for the best one-year-old red at the Melbourne Show twice in succession (1983 and 1984), showing how the richness of his wines attracts when young.

With about ninety hectares under vines, and a crush of up to 500 tonnes per annum, Leeuwin Estate is much larger than the other wineries in the Margaret River area. It is unusual in other ways, too: the proprietors have aimed very deliberately at the top of the market, in quality and in price, the aim at one time, according to press reports, being to have 'the highest priced Chardonnay on the shelves of New York bottleshops in 1984' (*Australian Financial Review*, 8 July 1983).

The winery is also unusual in that it aims to make all of its grapes into first-grade wines, as do the French Châteaux, but unlike, say, Château Lafite-Rothschild, with its eighty hectares of three varieties, yielding approximately 200,000 litres of one wine, Leeuwin Estate grows Cabernet Sauvignon, Chardonnay, Gewürztraminer, Riesling, Pinot Noir and Sauvignon Blanc.

The winery has simple, wooden-posted verandahs around a building where form suggests function, and function, as so often in Australia, suggests pressed sheetmetal. However, it is not the corrugated galvanized iron which is such an important part of the Australian landscape; at Leeuwin Estate the metal is Lysaght 'Colorbond' or some similar product in army green. Ducks flying by moonlight are most unlikely to plunge into the roof under the impression that it is a pond, as happens with new galvanized iron.

Whether the wines justify their remarkable prices ($15–$17 a bottle for 1980 Chardonnay in 1982, and $23–$25 a bottle for 1981 Chardonnay in 1983) is a matter for time and the market to tell, but the wines are very fine. The Chardonnay smells of ripe peaches and tastes much, much better, and the Cabernet, intense and powerful, with very big berry fruit, is a wine which will last for years, and yet has some finesse.

Only two vineyards in the Margaret River area crush less than twenty-five tonnes: Redgate (1977) and Thomas (1976). Redgate has planted most of the Bordeaux varieties, black and white, but Thomas grows only Pinot Noir, with already most impressive results from young fruit, soft wines with plenty of depth of flavour.

Most of the area's wineries crush between twenty-five and fifty tonnes: Ashbrook Estate (1976), Clairault (1976), Gherardi (1979), Graylin (1975), Happ (1978), La Taj (1980), T. & G. Merchant (1982), Ribbon Vale (1978), Willespie (1976), Woodlands (1974) and Wright (1974). Most have planted Bordeaux varieties, but too few vintages have passed for many to make a major impression, given the eagerness with which their wines are snapped up in Western Australia, a problem shared with the very small wineries of Tasmania. Graylin is notable for taking its name from the given names of its proprietors, Graham and Merylin Hutton. They are primarily graziers, so that they have been able to experiment and make the area's first fortified sweet red wine from their Cabernet Sauvignon and Shiraz fruit. It is said to be a wine of considerable promise, though one feels that the strength of the region should lie in table wines.

It is in the next category, 50–100 tonnes crushed, that the rather older wineries have made a great contribution to Australian wine quality in the last decade. There are five: Château Xanadu (1979), Cullen's Willyabrup (1971),

Gillespie (1976), Moss Wood (1969) and Vasse Felix (1967). Cullen's wines vary from very good to excellent. The Chardonnay is a fine example of the Australian style: big, rich, generous, so delicious at one, two or three years old that no one waits to see how it will develop.

The three largest wineries have also established themselves in the same way, Cape Mentelle (1969) and Redbrook (established by Evans & Tate of Gnangara, in the Swan, in 1974) making 100–500 tonnes and Leeuwin Estate (1974) crushing almost 1,000 tonnes.

South-west Coastal Plain

The coastal plain has a small number of vineyards stretched out over a long distance south from Perth. The Tuart sands, on which most of the vines are planted, are well drained acid sands over limestone, the maritime climate providing adequate rainfall in most cases, though some have drip irrigation. Yields range from moderate to very high: Capel Vale, for example, averages over nine tonnes a hectare. Some of the wineries are relatively long established. Luisini, for instance, began in 1929 and uses relatively traditional methods to make big Chenin Blanc wines in the Houghton manner.

Contiville is one of the most interesting, since it also has vineyards in the Lower Great Southern area and at Yanchep, to the north of Perth. It was established in 1948 and so its expertise has helped others, such as Peel Estate.

Because these wineries are closer to Perth and longer established, they can more readily sell larger quantities of reasonable but unremarkable wine than the more southerly areas can. For the most part, their wines are less good.

Hartridge (1970) is the smallest in the area, crushing only about twenty tonnes a year. Capel Vale (1975) and Leschenault (1973) crush between fifty and 100 tonnes, Leschenault being among the few growers of Zinfandel in Australia. Contiville and Luisini fall into the 100–500-tonne category.

All of the wines from the south-west of the state show great promise, and they show it young. These wines may be distinguished from those of the colder parts of Victoria by their early attractiveness, the forwardness of their fruit. Yet many of them last and develop very well.

8

Tasmania, Queensland and the Northern Territory

Viticulture has been economically significant in only four states, those already considered, and only in South Australia has it been of real importance (see Table 5 in the Appendix). In South Australia, this has largely been because other industries have failed to develop. In the other states, wine has been of even less moment. Despite this, these smaller wine industries are of great interest, and Tasmania's at least will in due course be widely recognized for its outstanding wines.

Queensland and the Northern Territory are, by and large, too hot to make good wine and Tasmania too wet and cold to make it in quantity. They represent the extremes offered by an island continent and its largest non-tropical offshore island.

Tasmania

Tasmania, or Van Diemen's Land, as it was known at the time, was the second British penal colony to be established in Australia, so it is not surprising that grapes were planted there more than a decade before the establishment of Victoria, Western Australia or South Australia. The first vineyard was planted by Bartholomew Broughton in the mid-1820s at Newtown, near Hobart, or Hobart Town as it was called then. However, he did not long survive and his vineyard was bought by Charles Swanston, a pensioned-off captain in the East India Company's army, who had arrived at Hobart Town early in 1829. Swanston had been a successful military paymaster for six years in India, so that he was able to buy Fenton

Forest, a property on the River Styx, other properties further from Hobart, and Newtown Park at Newtown, which was Broughton's property. By the late 1840s, the vintage was almost 10,000 litres a year and plans were in hand for further expansion, but Swanston's Derwent Bank ran into great difficulty in the depression of the 1840s and, when two major banks withdrew their support in 1849, Swanston was forced to resign, his creditors receiving ten shillings in the pound. While returning from a brief trip to America to raise funds, he died at sea in 1850.

While Swanston's vineyard was unsuccessful and his bank collapsed, he is remembered as being one of the two major supporters of John Batman's colonization of Port Phillip, which led to the establishment of Melbourne and the colony of Victoria.

Many attempts were made to grow wine grapes in Tasmania over the next hundred years, the obvious attraction being that the major European wine regions lie at latitudes more than 40° North, and none of the mainland of Australia is as much as 40° South, whereas as the 41st Parallel runs through the north of Tasmania, and Hobart lies almost at 43° South.

The map shows some of the places where grapes have been grown in the past or are being grown now, all in the eastern two-thirds of the island, for the western third is too wet.

It is very hard for mainlanders to obtain Tasmanian wines, for the quantities produced are tiny: at the moment, less than 500 hectares are planted to vines in the entire island.

In the mid-1950s, a Frenchman, Jean Miguet, made wines at La Provence, near Launceston, from Cabernet Sauvignon, Pinot Noir, Gamay, Chardonnay and Grenache, and those who tasted them, myself not among them, have suggested that, had Miguet stayed in Australia rather than returning to France in the mid-1970s, he might have made very fine wines indeed.

A little later, Claudio Alcorso, an Italian-born businessman and opera patron, started a vineyard – Moorilla – at Berriedale, just north of Hobart. Like most new vineyards, his suffered great bird damage for the first few years, and the tiny vineyard, which grows Pinot Noir, Cabernet Sauvignon and a few other fine varieties, was entirely netted to keep the birds out. Both as a result of this kind of problem and of the much

100

75

41°S

75

75

75

Devonport

Spreyton

Legana

Heemskerk &
Piper's Brook

**Tamar Valley
Vineyards**

Lilydale

Scottsdale

125

△ *Mount Arthur* 1200 m

St Helens

—125

Launceston

South Esk River

100

St Marys

100

75

Great Lake

Lake St Clair

75

50

◆ **Freycinet**

Swansea

OYSTER
BAY

Derwent River

Melton
Mowbray

Campania

75

50

Meadowbank Lake

Meadowbank ◆

New Norfolk

Moorilla ◆

Berriedale

Richmond

◆ Bream Creek

Hobart

Mount Wellington 1270 m △

75

75

100

Koonya

Port Arthur

100

Tasmania

colder climate, costs are extremely high, and so are prices. In Adelaide, his 1981 Cabernet Sauvignon, when first on sale, was almost twice as expensive as the best of Balgownie, Brokenwood, Petaluma or Cape Mentelle. It is a very firm, dark wine, with a strong, herbaceous nose and an almost stalky palate, so strong is the tannin. While its quality is very high, it will not be sought out by everyone, simply on account of price.

To the north-east of Hobart, on the east coast, near Marion Bay, Alcorso and a number of others have established another vineyard, Bream Creek, encouraged by the quality of the Moorilla wine.

While the wines from the south of Tasmania are of great interest, not far inland from the north coast, at Piper's Brook on the Piper River, are two already successful vineyards. One, called Heemskerk (after the ship in which Abel Janszoon Tasman discovered Van Diemen's Land, New Zealand and the Tonga Islands in 1642) was established by a group involving a member of the Haselgrove family of Mildara, and the Sydney wine and spirit merchant, Bill Fesq. To the south are mountains 1,000 metres high, to the north is Bass Strait, and on the far slope is Piper's Brook, established by the Pirie family in 1973. Like Petaluma, in the Adelaide Hills, Piper's Brook has very closely-spaced vines, and the wines from this vineyard are also of quite remarkable quality.

Piper's Brook vineyard has almost exactly the same number of degree days – that is, essentially, fruit development time – as Burgundy. All its wines seem to be very good. It will be some time before it is known just what grapes should be grown there. Meanwhile, when the wines can be found and afforded, they can certainly be enjoyed. The Rieslings are quite exceptional. The 1980 Riesling showed great depth of fruit at three years old, with fruit sweetness, rather than sugar. The nose was floral, like a Moselle, the finish firm, with a pH well below three, the wine light and graceful yet promising long life. Subsequent wines have shown richer flavour, and it is very difficult to see how these wines can change except by getting better and better. The 1983 'Northern Slopes', for example, is a wine of extraordinary complexity of flavour, partly reflecting a moderate degree of noble rot infection. Fermented to dryness, it is difficult to compare with other Rieslings, except some of Hickinbotham's. The cellar, however, seems to be seeking a more elegant style, as in its 1982 wine.

Not every Tasmanian wine is outstanding. Some are merely drinkable. The Heemskerk Traminer Sylvaner 1981, for example, though quite attractive, with a firm, acid finish, was so light that I could detect in it virtually no fruit character.

The other vineyards shown on the map – Tamar Valley (1980), Meadowbank (1979) and Freycinet (1980) – are as small as Moorilla (less than twenty-five tonnes crushed); Piper's Brook and Heemskerk are the only two vineyards whose wines are widely available.

Frosts, birds and cold will certainly keep yields low but, for those who can find them, Tasmanian wines are very fine. Because the Tasmanian industry has inherently high costs, problems will arise if the industry grows so large that the tourist market, the parochial island market and the highest-quality end of the mainland market all become saturated. As one of the Tasmanian growers put it to me, 'I rarely drink Australian wine when I can buy French anywhere near the price.' The higher the Tasmanian (or indeed any Australian) prices, the more competitive French wines become.

Queensland

In 1873, Anthony Trollope wrote:

... vineyards have been made, the owners of which make wine, and think that in a little time they will make good wine. I have drunk fairly good wine in Australia, but none made in Queensland. If on this head any wine-growing Queensland squatter should accuse me of falsehood, – remembering the assenting smile with which I have seemed to acknowledge that his vintage was excellent – let him reflect how impossible it is for the guest to repudiate the praises with which the host speaks of his own cellar. All the world over it is allowed to the giver to praise his own wine, – a privilege of which Australians avail themselves; but it is not allowed to the receiver to deny the justness of such encomium, except under circumstances of peculiar intimacy. Here, in these pages, truth must prevail; and I am bound to say that Queensland wine was not to my taste. I am delighted to acknowledge that their pineapples are perfect.

A century later, other Australians tend to make similar comments, perhaps rather less well expressed, about Queensland's wines. However, around Stanthorpe, 220 kilometres from Brisbane, at relatively high altitudes, a number of small wine-makers are bent on using the best techniques available to prove everyone else wrong.

Trollope tried wines made in the same general area, but where they were grown is not clear, since most authorities seem to trace wine growing to Father Jerome Davadi, who planted his first vineyard at about the time of Trollope's visit. Davadi had learnt about horticulture and wine-making in his native Italy, and is called the 'Father of the Fruit Industry', as he saw that it would outlast the tin mines which had brought substantial numbers of settlers to the area. His first vineyard was the horse paddock of his presbytery, and later he planted one at the foot of Mount Marlay, on the outskirts of Stanthorpe, a town originally called 'Quart Pot'.

Ballandean Station, where Angelo Puglisi's Sundown Valley vineyard is now established, is regarded as having had the first planting of vines. In fact, a White Syrian vine planted in 1859 is still growing. However, the first Queensland wine industry collapsed in the 1880s, and was not re-established until Italian immigrants began making wine in the late 1920s, the period of the Imperial Preference and export bounties.

The first of these wineries was Zanatta's Biltmore, which has suffered financial problems since the Zanattas sold out in 1981.

Until the early 1970s, all wines were made from table grapes, but in 1970 Angelo Puglisi saw the need to grow wine grapes, and planted Shiraz, Cabernet Sauvignon, Riesling, Sémillon, Chenin Blanc and Sylvaner, and since 1972 has been producing a range of table wines from these varieties. They are made with great care. Recently, after tasting a six-month-old Riesling, a very floral wine with considerable residual sugar and little acid, I put the bottle to one side for an hour or so. On re-examination, the wine had turned from a fresh greenish yellow to a clear, bright pale pink.

As wine-makers and vineyard managers have paid greater and greater attention to prevention of oxidation in grapes – by harvesting at night, cooling the must, fermenting at low temperatures, storing juice at low temperatures, and blanketing

Granite Belt (Queensland)

harvested grapes and fermenting must with inert gas – they have protected some of the phenolic compounds which, when they oxidize, form pink coloration in a wine without affecting aroma or taste. In the past, sufficient oxidation normally occurred between harvest and the end of fermentation for pinking to be a relatively unusual problem. Now, however, it can be the most carefully-made wines which are most susceptible to pinking. Furthermore, because it is a problem of slight instability in the wine, it is not predictable, and indeed a wine which has become pink in the bottle may lose this colour with time. Accordingly, wineries which have found this problem have sought aid from the Australian Wine Research Institute and elsewhere.

Because the compounds which cause pinking are phenolics, they can be removed with fining agents such as casein and polyvinylpolypyrrholidone (PVPP). However, this can lead to problems in itself, since it has now been shown that many fining agents remove not just unwanted components but also some of the minor compounds which are very important in flavour.

Angelo's red wines are also well made, the 1982 Cabernet being a bright purple when a year old, with rather too much oak for the fruit but with sufficient acid to improve for a number of years.

Bungawarra, one of whose proprietors is a dentist, rather than the usual medical practitioner, and which had its first crushing in 1979, is the winery which so far has produced the most notable Granite Belt wine, a 1981 Cabernet Sauvignon, deep crimson, with a strong stalky blackcurrant nose, reminiscent of young Penfold reds to some: deep fruit flavour, fine balance, enormous body, a compact and powerful wine with tremendous possibility of development. It recalls the best of the older style of Clare wine, and is a great portent to the future of the Granite Belt, which has as yet only intimations of an area character.

The Robinson family winery at Lyra, slightly south of Stanthorpe, is another winery already making wines with considerable potential. The proprietors are John and Heather Robinson, and Heather Robinson was a Salter, of the family which established Saltram at Angaston, in the Barossa Valley. The label has a strange, almost Pre-Raphaelite family group on it, but the wines are well made, with a hint of the hot-climate flavour about the reds.

A winery with a peculiarly Queensland flavour to it is Old Caves, on the New England Highway, just to the north of Stanthorpe. It was started by two members of the Zanatta family, and is distinguished by a grotesque mural with spaces for tourists' heads to be pushed through and photographed by other tourists.

Though they are evidently from single vintages, not all the

Old Caves wines have the year of vintage indicated on the bottle. For example, wines labelled 'Riesling' and 'Cervante' consumed in late 1983 both showed considerable development, but probably this mainly resulted from the making. Drinking them with pork chops, we found that the Riesling had good colour, a Sémillon flavour, and some bottle stink, showing considerable development, whereas the Cervante was slightly sweet, with a hint of lime juice, rather an Italian wine, and much more drinkable, yet it too tasted old. In Australia, Riesling, as I have already mentioned, does not simply mean (as it should) the noble grape of the Rhine, the Mosel and Alsace, so that the Sémillon flavour was not surprising. Cervante, a table grape, carried with it no expectations.

At present, the total production of the area is less than 1,000 tonnes of wine grapes, compared with about 4,000 tonnes of table grapes. If the enthusiasm of the proprietors is matched by success in the market-place, no doubt this crush will increase substantially. With the New England Highway passing through the area, these vineyards have the opportunity to capture a part of Queensland's enormous tourist industry. They have yet to gain a significant part of the Australian wine market, and have won few prizes at shows other than Brisbane's.

More than 1,000 kilometres north, near Herberton, not far from Cairns, is Foster's Wines. It makes a rich wine of the port type, smelling of stewed plums.

Northern Territory

Table grapes are successfully grown 200 kilometres north of Alice Springs, in unpromising mulga country. Mulga is *Acacia aneura*, a nondescript, small, grey-green tree which with other related species and a range of tussocky grasses makes up the sparse shrubby cover of the infertile red soils of much of central Australia. Wine could be made from these table grapes, since the varieties grown include Muscat Gordo Blanco and Sultana. However, what is in some ways the most remarkable vineyard in Australia is closer to Alice Springs, on the Racecourse Estate, just south of Heavitree Gap. Here a pharmacist, David Hornsby, has established Château Hornsby, the 'Château' being a converted orange-packing shed. In 1972, planting was begun, with the aim of growing some eight hectares of Shiraz, Cabernet Sauvignon, Sémillon and Riesling, to yield, eventually, 100 tonnes. The yield is attributable to drip irrigation, without which no grapes could be grown. The first vintage was 1977, and the wines have been consistently drinkable, as would be expected from a hot area with no disease problems. The dry continental climate and altitude of 600 metres are also of some advantage. However, the major attraction of the Château is that it is so unlikely in the red heart. It is a tourist attraction with a restaurant in which the proportion of *vin du pays* consumed is very low, but to which that wine has drawn the drinkers.

9

The Future

Consumption of wine per head in Australia has doubled in ten years from about ten litres to its current level of about twenty litres. Part of this increase has been at the expense of beer, since bottled beer provides alcohol at about twice the price of wine in casks, as these modern bag-in-the-box devices are usually called, but part has reflected an increase in alcohol consumption. Firmly ensconced in the folklore of the Geelong area is the story that rabid temperance advocates would sneak into wine cellars and add salt to the wine, or even smash the casks. Whether this happened or not, the temperance movement was certainly one of the factors involved in the collapse of the Victorian wine industry about the turn of the century. One of the changes that we will equally certainly see in the future is an increase in health-related criticism of all the alcohol industries. Advertising will be curtailed, labelling of the alcohol content of beverages will become mandatory, as it is in most other countries, and certain types of advertising will be restricted or banned. But it is unlikely that such changes will affect the increasing consumption of wine unless the community as a whole changes its view of alcohol. There is little sign of this happening as yet.

Meanwhile, the bag-in-the-box becomes more and more important. It was a brilliantly simple idea to make a plastic bag with a simple tap opened by deforming a handle, fill the bag with cheap wine, and enclose the whole in a cardboard carton with a carrying strap at the top. It was ideal for outdoor drinking, and has changed the face of picnics, and their detritus. The device had teething troubles, mainly with

213

leakage, but these have been mastered, and one can buy drinkable red wine for 60–90 cents a litre in bags and equivalent white for only a little more. The main drawbacks are twofold: only by counting can one assess one's consumption; and the price wars of the 1980s have made much of the increased production and sales unprofitable. Some large makers, such as Hardy, have left the cask market.

Tables 3 and 4 in the Appendix show how wine sales have changed in Australia over a recent six-year period. A number of distinct trends may be seen. First, the bag-in-the-box, which allows the drinker more control over ullage, has almost completely taken over the white-wine market. (In 1984, it had over 60 per cent of the entire retail wine market.) Secondly, sales of better red wines are slowly increasing. Thirdly, rosé consumption is actually declining.

Australia has a substantial negative balance of trade in wine, but the figures conceal some of the most interesting facts. In the case of bottle-fermented sparkling wine, the share of the market held by imported wine is well over 10 per cent. Most of this is champagne.

Exports will only grow as Australian wines' distinctive qualities are recognized, since there are no markets like the United States in 1933, under-supplied and undiscriminating, and if there were they would be supplied by the surplus of the world's two biggest producers, France and Italy. These countries have lower marginal costs of production, quite apart from the possibility of subsidized export from the European Economic Community.

North America, South-East Asia and Japan are all potentially worthwhile markets for a small producer, provided that they are continuously attended to. Japan is now Australia's largest single export market. Small producers who have made opportunistic exports to California have sometimes been successful but frequently, because of variation in the size of the vintage and increases in home sales, have failed to export continuously and have thereby lost their market.

Exporting is rarely very profitable and is usually more time-consuming than selling in the domestic market. Yet for a country with few inhabitants which is in the top ten in consumption per head but in the top twenty in total production, exports are necessary. Nevertheless, short of political intervention, an increase in the excess of imports over exports seems quite likely.

Extrapolation from these figures is very difficult; it is most unlikely that rosé will disappear completely, for example, or that no red wine will be sold in bulk in another ten years' time. There will always be home bottlers.

Turning to the other end of the scale, one finds that most secondary industries in Australia show a high degree of concentration, oligopoly being the norm. There are, for example, only six brewers: three public companies which are predominately brewers and hoteliers, two which are very successful parts of public companies, and one which is still run by the family which started it more than a century ago. However, even this one, Cooper's, which is the smallest and best, has a large minority of its shares held by one of the others, which in turn has a large minority held by the largest of all, Carlton and United, itself a subsidiary of a conglomerate, Elders IXL. In three states there is a regional monopoly, and in most other states only two brewers. What is available to the beer drinker is changing, as preservation and storage of beer are not the problems which they were when the regional monopolies were developing.

The wine industry is quite different. As the economists would say, it has low barriers to entry: while not at all profitable, it is in business terms cheap to establish a winery. Thus, it is a highly fragmented industry, dominated by less than a dozen large firms which between them sell about 90 per cent of all Australian wine. The pattern of control of these firms is, however, rather unusual. Berri-Renmano, a grower-owned cooperative, is the largest in terms of production, but Lindeman may be the largest in terms of sales, and it is controlled by an American tobacco company, Philip Morris, though a 50 per cent stake may soon be sold back to Australian investors.

Penfold Kaiserstuhl also may well be the largest following its acquisition of Wynn, and it is controlled indirectly by an acquisitive conglomerate, the Adelaide Steamship Company. (Wynn was until 1985 a part of Castlemaine Toohey, a large brewer, in which Allied Brewers of the UK had a significant minority holding.) McWilliam is a very large family company. Orlando is controlled by the locally listed offshoot of Reckitt & Colman. Seppelt is owned by a public company, the South Australian Brewing Company, but still run by the family.

Mildara is a public company, in which William Grant & Son of Glasgow has a large minority share. Hardy is a large family company. Yalumba is a large family company. Of these firms, only Berri and McWilliam were started this century, and McWilliam began before the First World War.

The personal involvement which good wine demands in its manufacture may be the reason for the persistence of family connections. So too may be the very low profitability of wine, so that while during the wine boom many large companies adventured into the wine industry, many of them have since left it. Furthermore, as fashion-following conglomerates have divested themselves of their wine interests, they have frequently sold them to the large, long-established wine firms, and when small but high-quality wine-makers have sold out to big companies, the family members most closely involved in the wine industry have in many cases started again on their own.

All these firms crush at least 15,000 tonnes a year, the largest over 50,000. They are small by world standards but, because of the nature of wine, there are only limited economies of scale in making it well, so the main reason for growth is to combat the increasing buying power of the retail chains which have come to dominate wine selling.

While a few other firms are of similar size to the smallest of these, and a few more slightly smaller, the history of the wine industry in Australia and the present state of the market together suggest that it may be much the same for the next fifty years: a mixture of foreign-controlled, market-orientated companies and long-established family concerns. The introduction of a wealth tax, or the reintroduction of estate taxes, could change all this, but it is a mixture which makes for strong competition and good value for either the discerning or the heavy drinker. What will change is the composition of the 300 very small companies. Nothing is more certain than that a high proportion of these will be out of business by the turn of the century. This is because vineyards are such poor investments. The Victorian Department of Agriculture published in 1980 a very thorough account of the establishment and development costs of a four-hectare vineyard with an attached winery designed for cellar-door sales. Excluding the price of the land, the Department found that there would be negative cash flows for at least five years, during which time

$170,000 would be spent. (The reason for not counting the purchase price of the land is that it should hold its value in the event of sale or closure of the business. The cost of the land would vary widely but would be within the range $1,000 to $10,000 per hectare, depending on region and merit within region.)

Again ignoring the cost of the land, over a twenty-year period the rate of return on capital would be between 5 and 10 per cent per annum. This is not good when one compares alternative investments, whether agricultural or otherwise. Under the most favourable conditions, the break-even point, the simplest though not necessarily the best investment decision criterion, would be thirteen years, and if there were adverse seasonal conditions and the wine market stayed over-supplied, the break-even point might not be reached for twenty years.

For these reasons, successful enterprises are likely to be ones where there is a significant cash flow from other sources to get through these early years. This means medical practitioners who begin to establish their vineyards in middle age or earlier, or farmers who can support their vineyard enterprise within their other more important farming activities.

The successful establishment of a small winery requires more than just good viticulture, wine-making and accountancy: it requires brand identification. The small grower has to gain attention for his product. Yet he is not in a position to advertise or to demand shelf space in bottle shops. He must rely on wine shows and wine writers, and is very vulnerable to early criticism and to shifts in fashion. Small wonder that he will tend to plant too many varieties and forget the less good ones on his labels.

There is much misleading labelling in the Australian wine industry. While writing this book, I was speaking with a wine-maker who had just lost his source of supply of high-quality white fruit from a non-irrigated area and had been seeking out irrigated fruit to replace it. He had made a verbal agreement with a grower on the river, who had then rung up in considerable embarrassment to say that another customer, in one of the eastern states, had increased his order for Chardonnay, and there was none available. Now the wine-maker in the eastern states does not sell Qualco Chardonnay, or Moorook Chardonnay, or even Cobdogla Chardonnay: his

Chardonnay is labelled as if it came from the region where his winery is. Just as the Tartar's home was wherever the Tartar's horse had trod, so that wine-maker's wine was from where his winery was. It is very difficult to be more specific on account of the difficulty of getting written evidence of what one knows to be the case.

Given that such problems are occurring, what is the solution? Perhaps there is no one solution. The ability to detect wines from different areas by chemical means is improving, though it is still not very satisfactory, and this, and prosecutions under the various consumer protection laws, are all that one can hope that government will do. A system of controlled appellation run by government in Australia would founder on the federal-state problem.

Tasmania and Western Australia have a system of guarantee of origin for their wines, and they are run by the Departments of Agriculture in those states. However, the Tasmanian wine industry is tiny, and the Western Australian industry is remote from the main source of anonymous fruit, the River Murray. As noted earlier, one of the characteristics of the Australian wine industry is that enormous quantities of fruit are trucked around the country, and the controls necessary to ensure that every load of fruit is made into wine identified with its origin, not with its destination, would be horrendous. They could probably also be defeated, at least for the first century or so, given the success that some wine-shippers in Bordeaux briefly had, as recently as 1970, in defeating a system which had been in existence for a considerable time.

The wine-makers of the Mudgee area have a Society for the Appellation of Mudgee wines: such a cooperative venture, based on goodwill and a recognition of the value of trustworthy labelling, seems the best way for the industry to move. However, it seems unlikely that it will unless the largest companies take the lead and they, however ethical their individual actions, have no need for the protection of guaranteed origin.

The question of how one might introduce laws of *Appellation d'origine* is, then, a vexed one. Consider the laws set down for Châteauneuf-du-Pape in 1923, and how they might apply to Australia.

First, it was suggested that grapes could only be grown on

land capable of bearing lavender and thyme, as these plants, like the vine, were regarded as preferring similar poor soil. This regulation would affect few of the vine-growing areas of Australia, but would be very difficult to enforce, should a grower be found to be currently growing grapes on other soil.

Secondly, only certain named varieties were permitted to be planted. Of the 400 wine growers and makers in Australia, less than twenty do not grow Cabernet Sauvignon. More than half grow Riesling. More than half grow Shiraz. Thus, in every area, one finds the most important grapes of the Rhine, the Rhône and the Médoc being grown together. It is difficult to see how one would start enforcing any relevant regulation.

Thirdly, only specified methods of training and pruning vines were to be permitted. Viticulture is in a poor way in Australia, traditional practices reflecting what was workable with a minimum of labour in a country where land was not scarce and where the best vineyard areas were not defined. There is no reason to suppose that the best practices for each area have been determined, and in some areas, little effort is being made to determine such practices.

Fourthly, the alcohol content of the wine had to be 12½ per cent by volume. It is usual to achieve this amount of alcohol in most Australian wine-growing areas, but not always possible in the coldest of them, and all too easy in the hottest. Given current concerns about health, this stipulation might work against the interests of wine growers, quite apart from interfering with the vignerons' decisions about when to pick, based on the balance of sugar and acid in the ripening grapes. Certainly a case could be made in the coldest areas that, when the red wines could not be made with more than, say, 10½ per cent alcohol, they should not be sold as wines of that area, but this would be about as much as one might expect to achieve.

Fifthly, the *triage*, whereby the grapes were sorted at harvest and at least 5 per cent had to be discarded as unfit for wine-making, would be impossible to introduce where there is mechanical harvesting. Where growers sell grapes to large wine-makers, such sorting occurs, but the basis is monetary rather than mandatory.

Sixthly, no rosé wine was permitted to be made in Châteauneuf-du-Pape. Wine consumers' dislike of rosé is rapidly ensuring that this happens in most Australian wine-growing areas, possibly because the appropriate areas, varieties and vinification for good rosé have not been determined.

Finally, a tasting panel was to try all wine, and only that which passed could be sold as Châteauneuf-du-Pape. This seems a good idea, but given that the industry is already well established, it might mostly lead to corruption and litigation.

Australia needs first to establish an acceptable nomenclature. The names 'Claret' and 'Burgundy' are slowly declining in favour of names related to varieties, as are some of the European white-wine names, though to a much lesser extent. Only when, for example, Australian 'champagne' is no longer called champagne can Australian nomenclature be regarded as having come of age. French nuclear tests at Mururoa Atoll seem likely to delay this day. Imports of champagne, however, continue to rise, Australians drinking more per head than any other customer nation, reflecting the limited success of Australian producers in meeting increasing demand. At Christmas in 1984, a discount war led to Australian wine made by the transfer process – i.e. fermented in bottle but then disgorged in bulk and rebottled after cleaning – being sold below $2.90 a bottle, barely covering costs, and basic champagne, such as Laurent Perrier NV, for less than $14.00 a bottle. Case prices were even lower. This kind of instability will lead to further success for the importers and financial difficulties for the Australian producers. Seppelt has been taken over by the South Australian Brewing Company, which would provide it with a breathing space, were it not for the fact that the Adelaide Steamship Company's Penfold-Kaiserstuhl has acquired the Seaview brand through its purchase of Wynn and has continued the discount war. At Christmas 1985, sparkling wine prices had not risen for twelve months, despite a weakened dollar and continuing inflation.

For many years, Seppelt has been the undisputed market leader in the Australian bottle-fermented sparkling-wine industry. At Great Western, it has, in its kilometres of tunnels through the soft gold-bearing rock, a unique resource for maturation. In addition, as a family company, it was able to pursue its own aims in a manner different from a public company or an arm of a huge overseas firm. Because of the enormous demand for its Great Western Imperial Reserve, Seppelt has tended to make this wine rather thin, light and characterless, but its better wines are often exceptional, occa-

sionally achieving the tiny bubbles, hint of aniseed and overtones of nuttiness which champagne drinkers should be able
to take for granted. Perhaps their replacement of much of
their Ondenc by Pinot Noir and Chardonnay and the fruit
from their new plantings at Mount Pleasant, in the Adelaide
Hills, will lead to better sparkling wines overall.

Because so many Australian wine-makers feel they must
offer a full line of wines, many of the smaller companies buy
sparkling wine from the Seaview Champagne Cellars in the
Adelaide suburbs, just near the Grange Vineyard, and sell it
under their own label. For this reason, Seaview and Kil-
lawarra brands are very frequently discounted, but are good,
serviceable sparkling wines, very suitable for Christmas. It is
at Château Remy and Taltarni, in the Pyrenees district of
Victoria, and Yellowglen, near Ballarat, that the most
champagne-like sparkling wines appear to be made. It is
hardly a coincidence that Château Remy is an offshoot of
Remy Martin and both Yellowglen and Taltarni have French
wine-makers, Dominic Landrigan of Yellowglen having
worked previously at Great Western. All these wines are
elegant, all show good yeast character, and some show considerable fruit, on account of varieties other than Pinot Noir
and Chardonnay having been used in some years. Given the
area's propensity to produce rich fruit character in its grapes,
even when Chardonnay and Pinot Noir are the dominant
varieties, one expects the fruitiness to persist. They will be
splendid wines, as no doubt will be Moët et Chandon's Australian sparkling wines when they appear.

In its Taché Brut, Taltarni has also both made a pink
sparkling wine of great charm and named it in a way which
will annoy very few, although the name is French.

Because of the long influence of Imperial Preference and the
English demand for fortified wines, good, sweet fortified red
wines of the port type are made in almost every wine-growing
region of Australia. In addition, the initial bias at Roseworthy
was towards wine-makers who could make good fortified
wines. Thus, it is very hard to nominate where the best ports
are to be found.

Over the years, the big companies, with their enormous
reserves of material, have been the most consistent, and Seppelt, Stonyfell, Mildara, Yalumba, Hardy and Reynella are
names which have always had substantial followings. Yet in

each area smaller companies can compete: at Clare, Wendouree and Clarevale have always made fine vintage ports, elaborations of their old heavy red wines. In north-eastern Victoria, companies like Stanton and Killeen use their irrigated fruit to great advantage, and even in the Hunter one can find a firm like Saxonvale making a surprisingly good vintage port. Overall, these wines have fine fruit and adequate balance but very rarely have the smoothness of true ports nor the scented complexity of the spirit used in Portugal.

It is very difficult to predict a future for Australian ports, given the recent absurdly designed tax on fortifying spirit and the glut of cheap fortified wines. Like the dry fortified aperitif wines, Australian port is a victim of a change in community attitudes as well as of the Common Agricultural Policy of the European Economic Community. Much adaptability is needed, and may even be forthcoming.

Wine research in Australia has been much influenced by the problems of hot areas. I asked a number of senior wine researchers for their informal views of the current major problems, and they considered that oxidation and loss of flavour during wine-making were some of the most important. Past problems have also been dominated by hot-climate difficulties, as may be seen by a brief listing of them.

The technology of pure yeast culture is now well advanced, leading to reliable fermentation properties, especially when temperature is properly controlled. Similarly, control of hazes and deposits by fining, filtering and constant low temperature is now hardly a problem. Ion exchange, for pH control and prevention of potassium bitartrate precipitation in cheap wines, is also widespread. One feels there must be a better method than ion exchange, and that it mainly relates to control of excessive vigour and prevention of moisture stress in the vineyard, as substitution of sodium for potassium is hardly healthy for the drinker. Thus, good fruit from the cooler areas does not need ion exchange, and it makes the best wine. Reliable starting and completion of the malolactic fermentation has led to more consistent red wines from both cooler and hotter areas. Temperature control in wine-making has been most vital in making good wine for cool areas and tolerable wine from hot areas, but it had hardly been a scientific advance, more an acceptance of technology developed in California and elsewhere, despite the pioneering attempts of Sydney Hamilton and others in the 1930s.

This emphasis on the correction of faults in wine-making carries over to consumer education. French and North American organizations have prepared kits which allow drinkers to detect the different fruits and flowers which contribute to the bouquet of wine, including lemon in Riesling and Muscat, pepper in Shiraz and Cabernet Sauvignon, green pepper in Cabernet, rose and orange blossom in Gewürztraminer and violet in Pinot Noir. Roseworthy, on the other hand, has an excellent tasting pack which allows one to detect faults such as excessive sulphur dioxide.

There has been considerable recent work at the Wine Research Institute on the retention during wine-making of flavour compounds, mainly highly volatile esters and higher alcohols which contribute floral and fruity attributes to the wine. Such activities are moves in the right direction. In sum, however, little has been done directly for the cool climates, and few innovations in vineyard practice have arisen in Australia, despite their different appearance from those of the traditional European areas. Cool-climate wine-making and viticulture are the areas of concern to the makers and lovers of fine wines, but to the major companies and the actual dominant wine consumers, the problem is the shelf life of the bag-in-the-box. The plastic bag is permeable to oxygen despite the best efforts of the plastic makers, and air also creeps in through the tap as the box sits on the supermarket shelf. Something must be done about this. Wine coolers, mixtures of soda water, fruit syrups and cheap white wines, will also produce interesting technical problems as their popularity reaches a plateau and they move more slowly off the shelves. (I recall the designer of a blue, carbonated wine product, now happily off the market, saying to me: 'As it's a flavoured wine, we can't use artificial colouring, but who's to know what the blueberry syrup suppliers have put in that?') But the cheap wines are reliable and good value as they are and the best wines are already very good. Grange Hermitage, Petaluma Riesling, Moss Wood Cabernet, Bailey's Muscat, Robson's Shiraz, Mount Mary Pinot Noir: one could add a score of names of wines which can be sought out with confidence of delight, showing the trait of disappearing from the market as soon as they are released.

In September 1983, some friends gave us the following dinner:

Sesame Asparagus with Avocado	Lindeman, Hunter River White Burgundy, 1967.
Veal Goulash and Vegetables (green beans, new potatoes)	Lake's Folly, 1973. Mildara Coonawarra Cabernet Sauvignon, 1963
Exotic Fruits with Honey Rum Cream	Orlando Auslese Rhine Riesling, 1974.

Coffee.

Two Hunter wines, one traditional, one not, one Coonawarra wine, one Barossa wine: in another twenty years, will the best Australian wines come from these areas in these proportions? It seems unlikely, given the revival of the old Victorian areas and the promise of Tasmania and south-western Western Australia. Yet the big areas, the big companies and traditions have much to offer still. 'When we know our own strength, we shall then better know what to undertake with hopes of success,' as John Locke said; and the strengths are considerable: reliable climate, high average standards of production, and fruit with a superabundance of flavour. Carefully used, these strengths will mean better and better wines, distinctive in their generosity and intensity of flavour.

Appendix

TABLE 1. Area of vines and production of grapes in SA, WA, NSW and Victoria, 1982–3.
(Australian Bureau of Statistics)

| | Areas of vines at harvest | | | Grubbings (actual and/or) intended | Grapes used for: | | | |
	Bearing	Not yet bearing	Total		Wine-making	Drying	Table	Total
	hectares			hectares	tonnes (fresh weight)			
RED GRAPES								
Cabernet Sauvignon	3,462	302	3,764	109	19,842	—	115	19,957
Currant (incl. Carina)	1,703	121	1,824	53	260	15,915	41	16,216
Grenache	4,001	33	4,034	308	35,535	—	276	35,811
Mataro	1,159	13	1,173	65	11,980	—	157	12,137
Pinot Noir	252	105	357	1	1,121	—	1	1,122
Shiraz	6,958	84	7,042	324	45,787	1	294	46,082
Other red grapes	1,777	322	2,099	109	8,222	55	4,278	12,560
Total red grapes	19,312	980	20,293	968	122,752	15,971	5,162	143,885

WHITE GRAPES

Chardonnay	881	724	1,605	5	4,627	—	17	4,644
Chenin Blanc	157	32	190	—	1,866	—	21	1,886
Colombard	275	145	420	2	4,230	—	—	4,230
Crouchen	1,018	18	1,037	76	10,754	—	—	10,754
Doradillo	1,597	13	1,610	90	31,026	102	171	31,299
Muscat Blanc	589	94	681	14	5,203	—	81	5,284
Muscat Gordo Blanco	4,203	280	4,484	114	67,625	6,917	581	75,123
Palomino and Pedro Ximenes	2,267	63	2,330	132	26,711	—	16	26,726
Rhine Riesling	4,282	515	4,796	76	28,867	—	67	28,934
Sémillon	2,697	172	2,869	60	28,447	—	87	28,533
Sultana	17,311	776	18,084	232	50,804	280,676	7,955	339,436
Traminer	588	125	713	1	4,195	—	1	4,196
Waltham Cross	1,434	49	1,483	55	6,694	6,501	3,911	17,106
Other white grapes	3,793	432	4,228	100	36,877	109	3,151	40,138
Total white grapes	41,092	3,438	44,530	957	307,926	294,305	16,059	618,289
TOTAL GRAPES	60,404	4,418	64,823	1,924	430,678	310,275	21,221	762,174

TABLE 2. Vintage Chart (combined assessment of red and white wines)
(scale 1–11: worst–best)

Year	Swan Valley	SW WA	Clare	Barossa	Southern Vales	SE SA	SW Vic	Yarra	Geelong	Central Vic	NE Vic	Hunter	Mudgee	Tas-mania
1962	9		9	10	9	10	6			9*	6	6		
1963	8		7	6	6	10	6			6	6	7		
1964	6		7	8	7	4	8			7	8	9		
1965	7		5	4	6	4	4			8	7	10*		
1966	8		7	7	4	8	8			7	8	7		
1967	7		9	8	10	8	8			7	9	9†		
1968	10		6	6	5	6	7			6	5	6		
1969	7		5	4	2†	6	6			5	7	9		
1970	7		8	8	7	7	7			7	7	8		
1971	9		5	5	7	6	10		5	8	8	4	4	
1972	7		9	10	6†	6	8	5†	5	6	6	7†	9	
1973	6		4†	3†	7	8	5	4	5	7	7	8*	6	
1974	7	5	7	5	2†	6	10	8	5	6	6	7†	9	
1975	8	7	7	9	7	8	7	6	6	4	8	6*	8	
1976	6	6	9	7	9	6	4	6	7	7	7	6†	8	
1977	7	9	7	7	8	8	4	6	5	8	9	7*	5	
1978	6	6	7	6	7	7	8	9	6	9	7	6†	8*	
1979	8	7	8	7	7	8	9	8	6	9	8	9	10	
1980	9	8	9	8	6	10	7	9	7	10	7	7	9	8
1981	7	9	7	9	7	7	7	10	9	8	6	9	5	8
1982	8	9	9	9	8	9	6	7	6	8	7	6	7	9
1983	8	10	4	4	4	5	9	6	9	5	5	7	5	8
1984	8	8	9	7	8	7	9	9	9	8	7	8	9	7
1985	9	9	8	9	9	9	9	9	9	9	9	9	8	8

*red better than white   †white better than red

228

TABLE 3. Sales of wine in Australia and exports (in million litres; from the Australian Bureau of Statistics).

	Table wine			Sparkling wine			Others*			Total			Exports
	Domestic	Foreign	Total	Domestic	Foreign	Total	Domestic	Foreign	Total	Domestic	Foreign	Total	
1977–8	116.6	5.2	121.9	23.7	1.8	25.5	54.3	0.8	55.1	194.7	7.8	202.5	4.6
1978–9	143.2	5.6	148.8	27.1	2.2	29.3	57.4	0.7	58.1	228.4	8.5	236.8	5.2
1979–80	160.9	5.1	165.9	29.9	1.4	31.3	54.3	0.4	54.7	245.0	6.9	251.9	6.9
1980–1	179.3	5.6	184.9	29.6	1.5	31.1	54.0	0.4	54.4	262.9	7.5	270.4	7.5
1981–2	197.9	6.7	204.6	27.7	1.7	29.5	52.9	0.5	53.5	278.6	9.0	287.6	8.6
1982–3	216.9	5.4	222.4	27.0	1.6	28.7	49.6	0.4	50.0	293.6	7.5	301.0	7.9
1983–4	227.8	6.8	234.5	29.0	2.5	31.5	49.0	0.4	49.4	305.8	9.7	315.5	8.9

*fortified wine, flavoured wine, etc.

TABLE 4. Composition of table wine sales (in million litres; from the Australian Bureau of Statistics).

	RED				ROSÉ				WHITE			
	Glass		Plastic Bulk		Glass		Plastic Bulk		Glass		Plastic Bulk	
	1 litre or less	over 1 litre			1 litre or less	over 1 litre			1 litre or less	over 1 litre		
1977–8	10.3	6.4	7.1	4.5	2.2	3.4	2.4	0.6	29.5	21.4	22.7	5.5
1978–9	10.3	6.7	7.5	3.8	1.9	3.4	3.1	0.7	31.5	28.0	37.9	8.4
1979–80	11.5	5.5	7.5	3.2	1.8	3.1	3.2	0.6	34.3	30.2	51.1	9.0
1980–1	12.5	5.4	8.9	2.5	1.7	2.5	3.6	0.4	36.7	28.7	69.5	7.0
1981–2	12.3	5.1	11.3	1.8	1.7	2.0	3.8	0.3	39.4	28.1	84.7	7.7
1982–3	12.7	4.9	12.7	1.5	1.3	1.9	4.3	0.2	38.6	28.3	103.6	6.8

TABLE 5. Total Australian wine production in megalitres, including wine for distillation; from Australian Bureau of Statistics.

Year	South Australia	New South Wales	Other states	Total
1980–1	225	92	58	375
1981–2	274	74	55	403
1982–3	203	76	61	340
1983–4	234	85	77	396

References

Antcliffe, A. J., 'Four new grape varieties released for testing', *J. Aust. Inst. Agric. Sci.*, 41, (1975) 262–4.

— 'New CSIRO grape variety for irrigated regions', *Aust. Wine Brewing & Spirit Rev.*, 99 (1979), 161–99.

Australian Bureau of Statistics, *Sales and Stocks of Australian Wine and Brandy by Winemakers*, Pub. No. 8504.0, 1984.

Australian Wine and Brandy Corporation, *Annual Report*, Adelaide, 1983–4.

Australian Wine and Brandy Producers' Association, *The Australian Wine and Brandy Producing Industry*, Adelaide, 1983.

Benwell, W. S., *Journey to Wine in Victoria.*, (2nd ed.), Melbourne, 1975.

Brady, B., *Wines, Winemakers and Vignerons of the Southwest and Great Southern*, Perth, 1982.

Bradley, R., *Australian Wine Vintages* (3rd ed.), Melbourne, 1983.

Brien, C. J., Venables, W. N., James, A. T., and Mayo, O., 'An analysis of correlation matrices: equal correlations', *Biometrika*, 71, (1984) 545–54.

De Castella, F., 'Phylloxera-resistant vine stocks *vs*. considerations governing the choice of a stock,' *J. Agric. Victoria*, 34, (1936), 303–9.

Faith, N., *The Winemasters*, London, 1978.

Fornachon, J. C. M., *Bacterial Spoilage of Fortified Wines*, Adelaide, 1943.

Gaffney, D. O., 'Rainfall deficiency and evaporation in relation to drought in Australia', paper presented at 46th

REFERENCES

ANZAAS Congress, Canberra, 1975 (Available from Bureau of Meteorology, Melbourne.)

Galbraith, J. K., *A Life in Our Times*, Boston, 1980.

Gladstones, J. S., 'The climate and soils of South-western Australia in relation to vine growing', *J. Aust. Inst. Agric. Sci.*, 31, (1965), 275–88

— 'Temperature and wine grape quality in European vineyards', *Proc. III Tech. Conf. Aust. Wine Industry* (Albury, 9–11 August 1977), 1977.

Halliday, J., *Wines and Wineries of New South Wales*, Brisbane, 1980.

— *Wines and Wineries of South Australia*, Brisbane, 1981.

— *Wines and Wineries of Victoria*, Brisbane, 1982.

— *Wines and Wineries of Western Australia*, Brisbane, 1982.

— *Coonawarra*, Sydney, 1983.

Harslett, J. and Royle, M., *They Came to a Plateau: the Stanthorpe Saga*, Stanthorpe, 1973.

Heddle, E. M., *Story of a Vineyard: Château Tahbilk*, Melbourne, 1968.

Irvine, H. W. H., *Report on the Australian Wine Trade* compiled at the request of the Minister of Agriculture, Victoria, Robert S. Brain, Govt. Printer, Melbourne, 1890.

Johnson, H., *World Atlas of Wine*, London, 1982.

Kelly, A. C., *Winegrowing in Australia*, Adelaide, 1861.

Kent Berlow, R., 'The 'disloyal' grape: the agrarian crisis of late fourteenth-century Burgundy', *Agricultural History*, 56, (1982), 426–38.

Labys, W. C., 'An international comparison of price and income elasticities for wine consumption', *Aust. J. Agric. Econ.*, 20, (1976), 33–6.

Laffer, H. E., *The Wine Industry of Australia*, Adelaide, 1949.

Lake, M., *Hunter Wine*, Brisbane, 1964.

Livingstone-Learmonth, J., and Master, M. C. H., *The Wines of the Rhône*, (2nd ed.), London, 1983.

Mackay, G., *The History of Bendigo*, Bendigo, 1891.

Morrison, P., and Morrison, E. (eds.), *Charles Babbage and his Calculating Engines*, New York, 1961.

Pike, D., *Paradise of Dissent: South Australia 1829–57*, Melbourne, 1957.

Powell, A., *Faces in My Time*, Vol. 3 of *To Keep the Ball Rolling*, London, 1980.

Ramsden, E., 'James Busby, The Prophet of Australian

Viticulture', *Journal and Proceedings of the Royal Australian Historical Society*, 26, (1940), 361–86.

Rankine, B. C., Fornachon, J. C. M., and Bridson, D. A., 'Diacetyl in Australian dry red wines and its significance in wine quality', *Vitis*, 8, (1969), 129–34.

Rankine, B. C., Fornachon, J. C. M., Boehm, E. W., and Cellier, K. M., 'Influence of grape variety, climate and soil on grape composition and on the composition and quality of table wines', *Vitis*, 10, (1971) 33–50.

Schreier, P. 'Correlation of wine consumption with cultivar and site', Centenary Symposium (ed. B. C. Rankine), Roseworthy Agricultural College (1983), 63–95.

Shaw, T. G., *Wine, the Vine, and the Cellar*, London, 1863.

Simpson, R. F., Miller, G. C., and Orr, G. L., 'Oxidative pinking of white wines: recent observations', *Food Technology in Australia*, 34, (1982), 44–7.

Somers, T. C., and Evans, M. E., 'April Red – one year later', *Aust. Grape-grower and Winemaker*, 184, (1979), 2–4.

Starr, J., *Wines and Wineries of the Granite Belt*, Blackburn, 1982.

Sutcliffe, S., *André Simon's Wines of the World*, London, 1981.

Trollope, A., *Australia and New Zealand,* London, 1873.

Williams, C. H., and Raupach, M., 'Plant nutrients in Australian soils' in *Soils: an Australian viewpoint*, pp. 777–94. Melbourne, CSIRO/Academic Press, 1983.

Witcombe, R. K., 'Investing in wine grapes', Agbulletin AB1 (1980), Victorian Department of Agriculture.

Index

INDEX